Crime Files Series

General Editor: **Clive Bloom**

Since its invention in the nineteenth century, detective fiction has never been more popular. In novels, short stories, films, radio, television and now in computer games, private detectives and psychopaths, prim poisoners and overworked cops, tommy gun gangsters and cocaine criminals are the very stuff of modern imagination, and their creators one mainstay of popular consciousness. Crime Files is a ground-breaking series offering scholars, students and discerning readers a comprehensive set of guides to the world of crime and detective fiction. Every aspect of crime writing, detective fiction, gangster movie, true-crime exposé, police procedural and post-colonial investigation is explored through clear and informative texts offering comprehensive coverage and theoretical sophistication.

Published titles include:

Maurizio Ascari
A COUNTER-HISTORY OF CRIME FICTION
Supernatural, Gothic, Sensational

Hans Bertens and Theo D'haen
CONTEMPORARY AMERICAN CRIME FICTION

Anita Biressi
CRIME, FEAR AND THE LAW IN TRUE CRIME STORIES

Ed Christian (*editor*)
THE POST-COLONIAL DETECTIVE

Paul Cobley
THE AMERICAN THRILLER
Generic Innovation and Social Change in the 1970s

Christiana Gregoriou
DEVIANCE IN CONTEMPORARY CRIME FICTION

Lee Horsley
THE NOIR THRILLER

Merja Makinen
AGATHA CHRISTIE
Investigating Femininity

Fran Mason
AMERICAN GANGSTER CINEMA
From *Little Caesar* to *Pulp Fiction*

Linden Peach
MASQUERADE, CRIME AND FICTION
Criminal Deceptions

Alistair Rolls and Deborah Walker
FRENCH AND AMERICAN NOIR
Dark Crossings

Susan Rowland
FROM AGATHA CHRISTIE TO RUTH RENDELL
British Women Writers in Detective and Crime Fiction

Adrian Schober
POSSESSED CHILD NARRATIVES IN LITERATURE AND FILM
Contrary States

Heather Worthington
THE RISE OF THE DETECTIVE IN EARLY NINETEENTH-CENTURY POPULAR
FICTION

R.A. York
AGATHA CHRISTIE
Power and Illusion

Crime Files
Series Standing Order ISBN 978–0–333–71471–3 (hardback) 978–0–333–93064–9
(paperback)
(*outside North America only*)

You can receive future titles in this series as they are published by placing a standing order.
Please contact your bookseller or, in case of difficulty, write to us at the address below with
your name and address, the title of the series and the ISBN quoted above.

Customer Services Department, Macmillan Distribution Ltd, Houndmills, Basingstoke,
Hampshire RG21 6XS, England

Deviance in Contemporary Crime Fiction

Christiana Gregoriou
Lecturer in English Language, School of English, University of Leeds, UK

First published in hardback 2007
First published in paperback 2009 by
PALGRAVE MACMILLAN

Palgrave Macmillan in the UK is an imprint of Macmillan Publishers Limited, registered in England, company number 785998, of Houndmills, Basingstoke, Hampshire RG21 6XS.

Palgrave Macmillan in the US is a division of St Martin's Press LLC, 175 Fifth Avenue, New York, NY 10010.

Palgrave Macmillan is the global academic imprint of the above companies and has companies and representatives throughout the world.

Palgrave® and Macmillan® are registered trademarks in the United States, the United Kingdom, Europe and other countries

ISBN-13: 978–0–230–00339–2   hardback
ISBN-10: 0–230–00339–7   hardback
ISBN-13: 978-0-230-59463-0   paperback
ISBN-10: 0-230-59463-8   paperback

This book is printed on paper suitable for recycling and made from fully managed and sustained forest sources. Logging, pulping and manufacturing processes are expected to conform to the environmental regulations of the country of origin.

A catalogue record for this book is available from the British Library.

A catalogue record for this book is available from the Library of Congress.

10   9   8   7   6   5   4   3   2   1
18   17   16   15   14   13   12   11   10   09

Transferred to Digital Printing 2009

to mum and dad

Contents

Preface

> Like most people, Quinn knew almost nothing about crime.
> He had never murdered anyone, had never stolen anything,
> and he did not know anyone who had. He had never been
> inside a police station, had never met a private detective, had
> never spoken to a criminal. Whatever he knew about these
> things, he had learned from books, films, and newspapers. He
> did not, however, consider this to be a handicap. What inter-
> ested him about the stories he wrote was not their relation to
> the world but their relation to other stories. Even before he
> became William Wilson, Quinn had been a devoted reader of
> mystery novels. He knew that most of them were poorly
> written, that most could not stand up to even the vaguest sort
> of examination, but still, it was the form that appealed to him,
> and it was the rare, unspeakable bad mystery that he would
> refuse to read. Whereas his taste in other books was rigorous,
> demanding to the point of narrow-mindedness, with these
> books he showed almost no discrimination whatsoever. When
> he was in the right mood, he had little trouble reading ten or
> twelve of them in a row. It was a kind of hunger that took
> hold of him, a craving for a special food, and he would not
> stop until he had eaten his fill.
>
> Auster (1988: 7–8)

This excerpt, taken from 'City of Glass', a story from Paul Auster's *New
York Trilogy* (1988), expresses a view of detective literature that is
shared by many devoted crime readers, including myself. Auster's character Quinn is a writer as well as a reader of the genre, who finds
himself fascinated with the form to such an extent that there is little
crime literature which he would find unappealing. What emerges in
Auster's story is in fact an investigation into the art of story telling, as
well as an examination into the essence of language itself. Similarly,
this book is a study of the format of the genre and an exploration of
the language employed in selected extracts. Unlike Quinn, I additionally examine the form in relation to the world we live in, that is, in a
social context.

Detective stories have dominated paperback publishing since the twentieth-century revolution of the mass-market industry began. Though the term 'detective story' is long standing (as early as 1924, the term was 'the unprepossessing name by which this class of fiction is now universally known', Freeman, 1946: 7), in the USA the term 'mystery' is also used. I, however, favour the term *crime fiction* or *crime literature* in reference to the category, since I find that though the works I analyse certainly involve *detection*, it is quite often someone other than the detective doing the 'detecting'.

Christiana Gregoriou
December 2005

Acknowledgements

I take this opportunity to thank my PhD supervisor, Professor Peter Stockwell, for his professional guidance and advice while researching and writing an earlier version of this text as a doctoral thesis. His tremendous enthusiasm for stylistics and his thoroughness and insight will continue to influence me throughout my career as a stylistician and crime fiction analyst.

I would also like to thank my friends and colleagues for their encouragement over so many years.

Last but by no means least, I would like to thank my parents for their love and invaluable support. This book is dedicated to them.

1
Introduction: Narratology and Deviance

Aims, material and method

I aim to explore the *poetics of deviance* in the context of contemporary crime fiction. I use the term *poetics*, since it etymologically suggests a study concerned with the art or theory of 'making'. Though, as Wales (2001: 305) argues, the term since classical times has been linked with the art of *poetry*, its etymological definition suggests that it is concerned with the art of any genre, hence Aristotle's *Poetics* (1996), which discusses the art of drama and epic, but not specifically poetry.

The theme that connects my three types of analyses is that of *deviation*. Deviation is a term that means different things for different disciplines, and I want to explore the linguistic, generic and social manifestations of deviation in the genre. I take 'deviation' to refer to the difference between what we take to be normal or acceptable and that which is not. Although some writers (for example, Leech and Short, 1981) have tried to make a distinction between deviance and deviation (preferring *deviance* for divergence in frequency from a *norm*), I am using the terms synonymously.

In linguistics, deviance refers to special language usage, which in turn becomes prominent and stands out in some way (Leech and Short, 1981: 48). In terms of genre, deviance could be taken to refer to divergence from generic rules as to writing within a specific genre. Questions that arise include: How much variation or deviation is allowed in the context of a specific genre? How deviant does a crime novel need to be in order for it to develop into a new genre or subgenre of its own? Finally, in sociology (see, for example, Price, 1978), deviance refers to abnormality in behaviour, and in the context of the genre at hand, it is manifested in criminality. It is in fact rather

1

conventional to view criminals as deviant (see Foucault, 1979), but I challenge this social notion in the context of my analysis.

Since few linguists and stylisticians have been attracted to the genre (see, for example, Bönnemark, 1997; Emmott, 1999), the study provides new research in a previously under-researched area by analysing some of the linguistic features typical of the genre at hand. The study would additionally be of relevance to literary theorists working on reader response, as both our interests lie in the significance which *inferences* have to the overall interpretation of literary work. This book also has relevant applications in education, as it 'operationalises' the genre; educationalists could use linguistic information about this dynamic subgenre of popular narratives to develop techniques for teaching reading. Furthermore, it would be of interest to crime fiction and other genre analysts, as it investigates the contemporary crime fiction form and explores the flexibility of its generic boundaries. Finally, it has applications in criminology, since it aims to state that there is a specific set of criminal character types evident in the genre, which affects the way in which devoted readers view criminality overall.

I limit myself to three American novelists from the 2002 bestsellers chart: James Patterson, Michael Connelly, and Patricia Cornwell. I felt that these three writers' work fitted my definition of what constitutes a crime novel at its best; the genre that I have so far referred to as *crime fiction* is taken to only include 'detective' stories, the sort of stories that have to do with the detection of a criminal, who often happens to be a serial killer, not to mention that such novels are very often part of a series. Finally, despite the similarities that the chosen novels exhibit, they exhibit simultaneously a range of interesting differences, the main one of which is to do with the novelists' choice of 'detective'.

The protagonist of the James Patterson series is Alex Cross, a black homicide detective with a PhD in psychology, who lives and works in the ghettos of D.C. along with his grandmother and children. He is a good family man whose wife Maria was killed in a drive-by shooting, her killer never having been caught. He works for the force as a profiler, and as a liaison between the FBI and D.C. police.

Michael Connelly's protagonist, Hieronymus (Harry) Bosch, is a detective on the robbery and homicide table of the Hollywood branch of the L.A. police department. Since Bosch is infamous for not fitting in, for disobeying rules and regulations, he often comes across as a contemporary reincarnation of the classic private eye detective. It is hence argued that Connelly's police procedural could be recast as a series of private-eye novels.

Finally, the protagonist of the Patricia Cornwell series is Dr Kay Scarpetta, the chief Medical Examiner of the Commonwealth of Virginia. Scarpetta is a high-ranking professional (the novels are often read in terms of feminism; see, for instance Bertens and D'haen, 2001: 160–74) who makes use of recent advances in forensic science in her investigation into horrific murders.

James Patterson likes to read novels by Patricia Cornwell and Michael Connelly. Another interesting fact involves a survey carried out via the MichaelConnelly.com mailing list. Over 4,100 mailing list members responded to the survey, and according to the Results (published at http://www.michaelconnelly.com/Survey/survey.html, as on 9 November 2003), in answer to the question 'Excluding Michael Connelly, who are three of your favourite authors?', the top three authors mentioned were Robert Crais (whose Elvis Cole series is classified under contemporary private eye novels, much like Connelly's), James Patterson and Patricia Cornwell. Overall, I was pleasantly surprised to find that not only are readers of Connelly fond of the works of Patterson and Cornwell, but also that James Patterson himself enjoys reading the works of the other two.

When exploring *linguistic deviance*, I used Patterson as a case study since he employs deviant language when allowing readers access to the criminal's consciousness in a way that the other two authors do not. Even though works from Cornwell and Connelly are also analysed in the relevant chapter, since it is Patterson who uses language to evoke the criminal mind, the relevant section comes to focus on the figurative language used within the context of the Patterson criminals' conceptualisation of experiences.

When exploring *social deviance*, I used Connelly as a case study mostly due to the eccentricity of his protagonist. Since the section deals with definitions of normal and abnormal behaviour, an analysis of the Bosch series will help illustrate how such a distinction is not easy to make. One of the Bosch novels is analysed in depth, since in fact it questions whether the detective himself has turned into a serial killer. In discussing the types of criminal character evident in the genre, I draw on the work of all three: Connelly, Patterson, and Cornwell, as well as some other contemporary crime writers.

Finally, when exploring *generic deviance*, I used Cornwell as a case study. Her Dr Kay Scarpetta series stretches the boundaries of the genre itself, and that is why Cornwell has been specifically chosen for this type of analysis. It is in the same section that I look into the Kathy Reichs series featuring Dr Temperance Brennan, another female medical examiner, whose series shares similarities with the Cornwellian generic form. I also draw on comparative analyses of Paul Auster's 'City of Glass' (*The New York Trilogy*, 1988) and Philip Kerr's *A Philosophical Investigation* (1992) in the same chapter, since both works constitute deviations or variations of the crime writing form, and hence defamiliarise our perception of the genre.

Narratology and deviance

The structure of narratives

Narratives, like sentences, are codings of experience and constructions of reality. They can be said to have an internal structure similar to that of sentences, while the notion of 'well-formedness' is nearly as reasonable of stories as it is for sentences. Some, such as Fowler (1977: 24), have gone as far as to argue that sentences and stories share the same constructional principles and, seeing that the former – though brief – are no less complete narratively or conceptually than stories, simple sentences might be thought of as *mini narratives*.

Theorists and analysts have, at the same time, made it clear that there is some higher level of organisation taking place in stories, one that does not take place in unconnected strings of sentences. As Rumelhart (1975: 213) has suggested, the structure of stories is ordinarily more than pairwise relationships among sentences. He instead argues that strings of sentences combine into psychological wholes, and further points out that connected discourse such as that of narratives differs from an unrelated string of sentences in that it is possible to pick out what is important in connected discourse and summarise it without seriously altering the meaning of the discourse. Rumelhart (1975: 226) claims that the same is not true of strings of unrelated sentences. Such strings lack structure and do not make meaningful wholes; they cannot be summarised at all.

Literary texts such as narratives are 'commonly regarded as objects, things, artefacts, having a similar objective status to the organic and inorganic entities which fill our world' (Fowler, 1977: 26). According to Fowler, it is due to this 'abstract' status of the literary work that we seem to be in need of a 'model' to represent its features to ourselves, to think about its elements in terms of some other, and yet relevant object which we know better or can conceive of more directly. If, for instance, literature is to be seen as an imitation, or rather a representation of the world, then its parts need to correspond to the various major elements which the human body recognises in its intuitive engagement with the world. Theorists such as Culler (1975: 189), have argued that narratives may well serve as 'the model by which society conceives of itself, the discourse in and through which it articulates the world', for the basic convention governing such literary forms (and which also governs those which set out to violate it) is our expectation that the narrative is to produce a world.

Additionally there can be said to be a need for the narrator to master the world, so as to tell a civilised company of listeners about a series of events which are to be named and composed. Hence, the text is to be ordered as the *discourse* of an explicit or implicit narrator who tells us about events in a world. It is for this reason that analysts have consistently persisted in making a distinction between *plot* and *discourse* (see, for instance, Simpson and Montgomery, 1995: 141). In short, *plot* is the crude storyline material which the writer moulds into an artistic narrative design, the *discourse*. The Russian Formalists (notably Shklovsky, 1925) introduced the alternative pair of terms, *fabula* and *sjužet*, in the 1920s. Similarly to 'plot and discourse', fabula refers to the logical ordering possible of the events, whereas sjužet describes the actual sequence of events as narrated: deep versus surface structure, so to speak. In simple narratives, fabula and sjužet will normally coincide. These terms were in turn aligned with the French terms *histoire* and *discours* of Benveniste (1966), but because the latter term is itself ambiguous, the term *récit* is sometimes used to render *sjužet* (Wales, 2001: 301).

It is in Chapter 2 that I introduce the argument that, in the course of a crime novel, the criminal produces the sjužet, whereas the detective the fabula. Since the fabula refers to the mere chronology of narrative events, it is attributed to the detective's pole of what is normally a chronologically-ordered investigation. Also, it is the detective who comes to reconstruct events so as to bring us back to the very beginning of the story. Since the sjužet is the story as shaped and edited by the teller, it is hence attributed to the criminal, who in turn embodies the literary pole of the story.

However, as Culler has pointed out, for a sequence to count as plot, one must be able to isolate not just the actions which contribute to a thematic modification. As Culler (1975: 213) himself put it, '[t]hose aspects of the movement from the initial situation to the final situation which help to produce a contrast between a problem and its resolution are the components of the plot'. Every narrative may, therefore, be said to integrate a succession of events of human interest oriented toward a goal. It is on the same trail of thought that Brémond's (1966:

62–3) classification of 'narrative cycle' lies, according to which narrative events can be classified into two categories of elementary sequences: amelioration and degradation, referring correspondingly to states that either favour or oppose a human project. At the beginning of a narrative, either a deficient or a satisfactory state exists. The narrative goes through at least one cycle, ending either with a satisfactory state or a state of deficiency, while the maintenance of the possibly acquired state of prosperity depends on the observation of certain conditions or rules. Culler (1975: 212) seems to follow this line of thought, as he seems to agree that it is in fact problems or enigmas that lead to a structuring of the text; 'only when a problem is maintained does it become a structuring force, making the reader organise the text in relation to it and read sequences in the light of the question which he is attempting to answer'.

Specifically, in the reading of a crime novel the initial satisfactory state is interrupted by a state of deficiency whereby an event of murder takes place. Such narratives go through at least one cycle, where the state of prosperity is reinstated by the resolution, whereby the murderer is discovered and brought to justice. Hence it is the enigma of 'who did it?' that forms a structuring force. The readers are invited, therefore, to organise the text in the light of this question, so that they are eventually able to answer it by the time they reach the end of the novel.

Moreover, what needs to be pointed out is that overall narratives are produced so as to accomplish certain communicative aims or, as Polanyi (1985: 21) puts it, to 'make a point, to transmit a message [...], often to bring about some sort of moral evaluation or implied critical judgement about the world'. And it is at this point that the narrative function that has come to be referred to as *evaluation* becomes clear. This device allows the story recipients to build up a model of the relevant information in the text which matches the teller's intention. In other words, the burden, of making the relevance of the telling clear, lies upon evaluation.

This narrative device forms part of a widely employed analytical model developed by Labov (1972) in his study of the Black English Vernacular (BEV) narrative form. Labov was prompted to attempt a structural description of his BEV informants' oral narratives of personal experience, since, despite their cultural differences, the narratives shared great structural similarities. As Labov and his collaborator Waletzky (Labov and Waletzky, 1967) claim to be primarily concerned with the characteristics of the narrative itself rather than with the syntax and semantics of English below the sentence level, their work is simultaneously made applicable to written narratives' analysis, not to mention narratives produced in languages other than English. At the same time, their analysis was claimed to be *functional* in that it distinguished two functions of narrative: the *referential* and the *evaluative*.

Labov defines *narrative* as

> [o]ne method of recapitulating past experience by matching a verbal sequence of clauses to the sequence of events which (it is inferred) actually occurred [...] With[in] this conception of narrative, we can define a *minimal narrative* as a sequence of two clauses which are *temporarily ordered*: that is, a change in their order will result in a change in the temporal sequence of the original semantic interpretation.
>
> Labov (1972: 359–60)

He defined narrative clauses as those with a simple preterite verb or, in some styles, a verb in the simple present, and suggested that a fully-formed narrative is made up of the following sections;

1. Abstract.
2. Orientation.
3. Complicating action.
4. Evaluation.
5. Result or resolution.
6. Coda.

Labov (1972: 363)

Even though many storytellers dispense with one or more of these ingredients, according to this model, a well-formed narrative would not. In addition, each of these categories could overlap with anything from a single sentence to a stretch of several clauses.

Toolan (2001: 143) suggested that the Labovian model is a structural one; it is based on the perception of a bordered set of recurrent patterns and, setting aside what they take to be local differences, it is a model in the pursuit of deeper structural narrative similarities. This, in turn, suggests that the attraction of these principles lies in their clarity, replicability and their search for a basic pattern, from which more complex narratives might be derived (Toolan, 2001: 145).

This model has received widespread application within stylistics even though it was originally developed from 'social' stories told in casual conversation, and also elicited from black youths in New York City and hence most of the illustrative examples are consequently in BEV (Simpson, 1988: 7). In other words, it is intriguing that a spoken-discourse model generated for stories in a non-standard English variety could receive widespread application to written discourse in predominantly Standard English. Even though Labov's work on oral narratives may be one of the few bodies of data-based research dealing with aesthetically structured discourse, this discourse is not, by anybody's definition, literature. Pratt (1977) was one among those who applied the model with caution to literary written texts having made a number of adjustments mostly in as far as those narrative aspects dealing with the *abstract, orientation*, and *coda* sections are concerned.

More specifically, Pratt (1977: 60) suggested that the abstract of a novel may well be its title in that it is always taken by readers to be an important and relevant clue as to what the author considers to be the main point or theme of the narrative. Titles further function as invitations to people to commit themselves to the 'narrative audience' role, and also serve as devices for referring to works, much like abstracts do for natural narratives. Pratt (1977: 53) suggests that it is common for the orientation to be set apart by a paragraph or a space in fiction, or even to be made an independent textual unit such as a prologue, an opening chapter, or a preface. In any case, Pratt adds that the orientation of novels can vary widely in length as well as scope. Finally, Pratt (1977: 56) argues that novels do not need codas to signal the end of narratives 'since the end of the text visibly and palpably signals the end of the story'. Nevertheless, novels often have elaborate codas that, much like those of natural narratives, explain, revise, and evaluate the story's outcome, informing us of the ultimate consequences of the narrative (for an application of the refined model onto short written stories translated from Greek for example, see Gregoriou, 2002a).

Crime novels certainly lend themselves to Labovian analysis. To begin with, abstracts, like codas, constitute the margins or frames of crime narratives, abstracts being introductory concepts and codas being end ones. The abstracts of crime novels may well be their titles, these often specifying the nature of the story to be told, as well as the generic category that it may fall into. For instance, Cornwell's *Body of Evidence* (1991) and *Cruel and Unusual* (1993) certainly indicate, as titles, that they are to deal with brutal murders and the investigation into the identity of the relevant perpetrators. They further give some indication as to the nature of the investigation to be undertaken, here from the medical examiner's viewpoint, as opposed to that of a detective. In addition, the reader-orientating function of the abstract may also be realised in the presentation of authors and their works, the awards they have received, as well as in the account of their lives.

The openings of novels themselves additionally often function as reader-orientating devices, as these can often be taken to be declarations of what will follow:

> Nothing ever starts where we think it does. So of course this doesn't begin with the vicious and cowardly murder of an FBI agent and good friend of mine named Batsey Cavalliere. I only thought it did. My mistake, and a really big and painful one.
>
> Patterson (2001: 3)

In the case of this James Patterson novel, *Violets Are Blue* (2001), the opening offers orientating information, in that it describes the circumstances under which the narrative events will take place, while it additionally leads readers right into the middle of the story itself (in an *'in medias res'* type of way). Also note that it is through negation ('this doesn't begin') and presupposition (a murder has indeed occurred) that we are told of the circumstances, rather than directly.

As previously noted, the natural position of the orientation is as a preliminary before the complicating action starts, but it can also be presented later, or be scattered throughout a whole work of fiction. In crime series that focus on one or more particular characters, the readers are expected to know certain information. In any case, the action is usually summarised and brought up to date before the story proper begins:

> As we drove up in front of the Sojourner Truth School, I saw Christine Johnson welcoming kids and their parents as they arrived, reminding everyone that this was a community with good, caring people. She was certainly one of them.
>
> I remembered the first day we met. It was the previous fall and the circumstances couldn't have been any worse for either of us.
>
> We had been thrown together – *smashed* together someone said to me once – at the homicide scene of a sweet baby girl named Shanelle Green. Christine was the principal of the school that Shanelle attended, and where I was now delivering my own kids. Jannie was new to the Truth School this semester. Damon was a grizzled veteran, a fourth grader.
>
> Patterson (1997: 14)

In one of the opening chapters from this James Patterson novel, *Cat and Mouse* (1997), the personal life of Alex Cross, the detective at hand, is brought up to date even though his children and new girlfriend are well-known characters from previous novels in the series.

A great deal of the complicating action of crime novels is rendered directly (in the form of descriptive prose) while in other cases it is rendered in the form of dialogues. Often in dialogue or narration, a seemingly unnecessary summary is additionally given, since the reader is already aware of all the relevant facts that relate to the story line:

> An hour later I lay in bed, trying to sort and evaluate what I knew.
> Fact: My mysterious foot did not belong to Daniel Wahnetah. Possibility: The foot came from a corpse at the courtyard house. The ground contained volatile fatty acids. Something had decomposed there. Possibility: The foot came from Air TransSouth 228. Biohazard containers and other body parts had been recovered near the wreckage.
>
> Reichs (2002: 251)

In as far as evaluation is concerned, it often takes place in discussions among police officers, or in the detective's own thoughts:

> Primrose lying in a body bag.
> Why, dear God?
> Was she carefully chosen, researched, stalked, then overpowered as part of an elaborate plan? Or was she selected by chance? Some psycho's sick impulse. The first blue Honda. The fourth woman to exit the mall. The next black. Was death part of a plan, or did things go badly wrong, spinning out of control to one irreversible moment?
>
> Reichs (2002: 253)

In this extract cited from Kathy Reichs's *Fatal Voyage* (2002), the protagonist Dr Brennan attempts to reason with herself, engaging in a fake dialogue with her own thoughts, so as to account for the reasons underlying the death of her colleague. Not only are these evaluative extracts used to emphasise the relative importance of some narrative units compared to others, but also to represent time-outs from the bare bones of the storyline, bringing out suspense by suspending the progress of the action.

The problem-resolution structuring is evident in all crime novels where, as mentioned, the commission of a murder is followed by the discovery of the murderer. In such novels, the resolution often takes the form of direct speech, whereby the detective discloses the identity of the perpetrator. In classic detective writing, this often takes place once the detective assembles all suspects and recounts the story from beginning to end, allowing the perpetrator to often give him/herself away (as in Agatha Christie's *The Murder of Roger Ackroyd*, 1924). It is additionally not uncommon to have evaluations particularly prevalent in the result/resolution sections of crime novels.

As far as codas are concerned, these often take the form of reflection from the viewpoint of the detective, while the readers are told what happened to the main characters after the story's result.

> Bosch left then, not turning around when the adjutant called after him for his name. He slipped through the double doors and headed down to the elevator. He felt good. He didn't know if anything would come of the illegal tapes he had given the police chief, but he felt that all decks were cleared. His show with the box earlier with Chastain would ensure that the word got back to Fitzgerald that this was exclusively Bosch's play. Billets and Rider should be safe from recriminations by the OCID chief. He could come after Bosch if he wanted, but Bosch felt safe now. Fitzgerald had nothing on him anymore. No one did.
>
> Connelly (1997b: 432)

Whereas there are novels where the account of answers to remaining questions is given directly, there are also novels where such accounts are hinted at, while it is not uncommon for a whole evaluative section to be set apart from the rest of the text in a special chapter or paragraph, in either the form of narration or dialogue. Finally, secondary themes, such as romance, can also be resolved in codas. In the same novel as above, Michael Connelly's *Trunk Music* (1997b), the final chapter is descriptive of a romantic scene between the detective Bosch and his estranged wife Eleanor, with whom he has been unexpectedly reunited.

To sum up this section's discussion, what a narrative analyst needs to focus on is necessarily the structure underlying the stories themselves. The analyst, however, needs to additionally consider the process by which prominence is assigned in the telling.

Crime fiction as genre and as popular literature

In the context of literary theory there have existed, and still exist a variety of definitions of the term *genre*. By the term is generally meant a class, kind, type or family of literature, while genres are distinguished according to the type of plot, theme, characters, narrator(s) and intended audience, not to mention structure, technique, devices, style, and so on.

In linguistics, however, genre is usually seen as a network of expectations or codes, or a set of communicative events. According to this discipline, how a work of literature should be read is in fact indicated by its genre, which can also be seen as constituting a set of codes that give information about the reality the text purports to represent (Jauss, 1985: 620). These genres have been referred to as 'horizons of expectation' for readers and as 'models of writing' for authors (Todorov, 1990: 18), in that readers have expectations about texts, and authors write according to genre rules in order to satisfy or adhere to these expectations, if not surpass them. Bönnemark (1997: 8) describes this relationship between writers and readers as a 'contract', which is a metaphor that might help clarify the concept of genre in itself, while it is obvious that there is no way in which parties can be forced to honour the obligations of this 'contract'. In other words, though there are issues of responsibility when it comes to writing or reading under a certain genre, these rules can and indeed are often broken; besides, literary innovation has always balanced conformity.

Genre is sometimes pitted against the notion of *register*, though indeed some linguists have abandoned the latter term altogether. Register or 'functional language variation' (Swales, 1990: 40), is often seen as a contextual category correlating groupings of linguistic features with recurrent situational features, and is a category typically analysed in terms of three variables labelled *field* (indicating the type of activity in which the discourse operates), *tenor* (handles the status and role relations of the participants), and *mode* (concerned with the channel of communication, prototypically speech or writing) (see Halliday, 1985).

There is a major difficulty in distinguishing the uses of the two terms, but if a distinction between genre and register *can* be made, Wales (2001: 178) suggests that it is best to follow McCarthy and Carter (1994), who see genre at a 'higher level' than register; any group of texts which show similarity of register, or similarity to do with linguistic choices, can be said to belong to the same genre. Wales also suggests that another model is to see genre at a 'deeper' level, with register the 'surface' manifestation of genre.

Overall, the difficulty in establishing the difference between the two terms seems to derive from the fact that register is a central and well-established concept in linguistics, while genre is a recent appendage found to be necessary as a result of important studies of text structure (Swales, 1990: 41). In this study, genre is associated with complete works or texts (in accordance with Couture, 1986), whereas register is considered to be associated solely with linguistic choices. The rules and constraints of the genre of crime fiction are analysed in Chapter 2.

Fiction is differentiated from non-fiction in that the first genre *pretends* to be about real events, and the latter in fact *claims* to be so. As Wales (2001: 150) put it, fiction is more likely to be thought of as a genre, constituted of imaginative or imaginary prose narratives, chiefly novels, but also short stories: in other words, the essence of literature. What Wales also recognises, however, is that fictional literature is not all fiction (some novels may refer to 'real' events or non-fictitious characters, such as Truman Capote's *In Cold Blood: A True Account of a Multiple Murder and its Consequences*, 1966); not all literature is fiction (there is poetry and drama as well as the novel); nor is all literature fictional (we may study versions of the Bible as literature). Conversely, she adds, not all fiction is literature (fictional or imaginative discourse can be found in jokes, TV and radio advertising, and so on).

According to Priestman (1990: 181), crime, or detective fiction, has been submitted to 'ghettoisation' from 'serious' fiction. That is, the genre under analysis has been classified under the guise of *popular fiction*, which is defined and set apart from other types of fiction according to various criteria, such as the following offered by Boëthius (1995) and translated by Bönnemark (1997: 13):

1. its audience, as popular literature is supposed to be read by the masses,
2. the conditions of its production and distribution, as popular fiction is supposed to be geared to mass publication and distribution outside the ordinary channels of the book market,
3. its aims, which are supposed to be primarily entertainment and relaxation,
4. a particular type of reading; a reading of *plaisir* in contrast to a reading of *jouissance*,
5. its simplicity, of language as well of structure,

6. its internal norms, as popular literature is inherently inferior, either aesthetically and/or morally, and
7. external norms (according to the sociology of taste, in Boëthius's terms), as popular literature is defined as having a large audience, and as being considered inferior by critics according to moral and/or aesthetic norms.

These criteria appear to be of two main types: those that pertain to internal textual factors (see criterion 5), and those that pertain to external factors of production and distribution (see criterion 7), while the large number of criteria offered make one's job of distinguishing popular literature from non-popular literature quite difficult.

Pepper (2000) agrees that the question of what actually constitutes something as 'popular', indeed how one should judge whether something is popular or not, is not at all clear. He argues for the need to distinguish between different types of popular culture and different ways of using it. He claims that crime writers 'inevitably steer their work into the realm of the "unpopular popular", and in doing so suggest that the appeal of certain kinds of popular culture relates to its utopian *and* distopian impulses' (Pepper, 2000: 17).

Bönnemark (1997: 13), on the other hand, draws on the distinction between *category literature* and *genre fiction* to resolve the problem. She defines 'category literature' as a prototype around which other less easily situated works situate themselves, as a literature that conforms to a particular format and answers to particular needs of the reader. It is written in a simple manner with little realism, psychological characterisation, complication and originality, is produced in long series at a low price, and is sold as other consumer goods. It is read by and large by a heterogeneous public, remains unreviewed by critics, its authors are often anonymous and low-paid, and aims primarily to please and entertain. She concludes that the prototypical detective (or crime) story does not belong to category literature, although some detective works do. She contrasts this category to the partly identical category of 'genre fiction', discussed by Talbot (1995: 36–40), a 'non-literature', subdivided into marketing categories (for example, science fiction, fantasy, romance, and so on), and defined in terms of particular narrative formulas, character and situation types, and target audience expectations. Bonnemark concludes that as detective fiction is formulaic, and in many ways adheres to reader expectations, it can be called a kind of 'genre fiction'. This distinction, however, seems rather unhelpful and the terms, as defined, appear not only vague, but also quite similar.

In as far as the external factors pertaining to popular fiction are concerned, she argues that

> [m]ost factors of production and distribution used to distinguish popular fiction from other fiction are not relevant to detective fiction: there are detective works that can be categorised as popular fiction and produced and sold under mass circumstances whereas other works are produced and sold as serious literature.
>
> Bönnemark (1997: 15)

Crime fiction's large readership constitutes the genre as 'popular' in a particular sense of the term. Some works, such as those of Poe and Chandler, however, have moved into the canon of classic literature.

Bönnemark adds, nevertheless, that even though popular fiction of this sort in general fulfils important needs of the readers (seen, for instance, as a possible escape from reality, where readers who feel unjustly treated by society find compensation, an outlet for their aggressions and protests, as well as a confirmation of their own ideals and evaluations), it is also seen as inviting a rather passive reading, in that it seduces or manipulates the readers in a reading lacking in actual analysis of the events and characters, or any such engagement with the material.

In as far as the internal factors pertaining to popular fiction are concerned, Bönnemark discusses issues of plot and schematisation. She argues that the formulaic nature of crime writing places the genre into popular fiction; it is the lack of originality in the characteristics of the generic plot that constitutes the genre as 'popular'. This seems to be in accordance with Todorov (1973: 6), who claims that only literary works that are original get a place in literary history, whereas other works pass automatically into another category, viz. 'popular' or 'mass' literature.

Since, however, I later argue (Chapter 5) that crime writing in fact often deviates from genre requirements, such an argument seems invalid. Regardless of the formulaic nature of crime fiction, works assigned under this generic category do in fact depart from the necessary conventions. Would this departure classify such works as 'non-popular'?

Another internal or textual factor pertaining to popular fiction is the issue of simplicity. Popular works are said to be characterised by simplistic language use, many clichés, trivial description, and lack of informativeness. Nash's (1990) investigation into the nature of popular fiction has been criticised by Talbot (1995: 40) for having introduced 'a cline of quality (with "pop fiction" at one end and "classics" at the other), but the treatment is to reinforce with a vengeance the mainstream genre distinction and the prejudices associated with it'. Other scholars have also used similar qualitative criteria to distinguish between literature, here seen as more of an art form (to be compared with music, painting and sculpture), and popular texts. Besides, literature is often discussed in terms of aesthetic value or effect (poetic texts are admired for their formal 'beauty', arising from their structural patterning, expressive and connotative qualities of meaning, and their imagery), whereas popular fiction is often characterised as aesthetically inferior to literature. The question of 'literariness' – though developed in distinguishing literature from non-literature – is therefore also of relevance here, in discussing whether crime fiction is a popular form or not.

Foregrounding, 'the "throwing into relief" of the linguistic sign against the background of the norms of ordinary language' (Wales, 2001: 157) is one of the effects often claimed to contribute to literature's aesthetic characterisation. Foregrounding is achieved by a variety of means, which have largely been grouped under two main types: *deviation* and *parallelism*. Whereas deviations are violations of linguistic norms, parallelism refers to unexpected repetition of such norms.

The early Russian Formalists saw literary language as a set of deviations from a norm, a kind of 'linguistic violence', while the idea that poetry specifically violates the norms of everyday language was much propounded by the Prague School (see, for instance, Mukařovský, 1970). Literature is, within such contexts, seen as a 'special' kind of language, in contrast to the 'ordinary' language we commonly use – though admittedly to spot a deviation implies being able to identify the norm from which it swerves. As Carter and Nash put it (1990: 31), their main theoretical position was that literary language was deviant language and, in accordance with this deviation theory, 'literariness or poeticality inheres in the degrees to which language use departs or deviates from expected configurations and normal patterns of language, and thus defamiliarises the reader'. In other words, language use in literature is said to differ because it makes strange, or disturbs our routinised normal view of things and thus generates new or renewed perceptions.

Another influential Formalist definition is associated with Roman Jakobson (1960), who articulated a theory of poetic language which stressed its *self-referentiality*. In his account, literariness results when language draws attention to its own status and as a result there is a focus on the message for its own sake (see Carter and Nash, 1990: 32). This definition, in accordance with that of the Russian Formalists, again assumes a distinction between that language which is poetic and that which is not. As Carter and Nash add, not only do Jakobson's criteria as to the nature of literary discourse work better in respect of poetry than prose, but he supplies no clear criteria for determining degrees of poeticality in his examples. In addition, he stresses too much the production of effects, at the expense of the process, the recognition and reception of such effects.

As Carter and Nash (1990: 18) add, however, a main point to be made is that features of language use more normally associated with literary contexts are found in what are conventionally thought of as non-literary contexts, and therefore the term *literariness* is preferred to any term which suggests an absolute distinction between literary and non-literary. They instead suggest that literary language should be seen as a continuum, a cline, with some language uses being marked as more literary than others. The claim could be stretched to popular versus strictly literary contexts, in that writing classified as 'popular' isn't necessarily any less 'literary' than that which is classified under a strictly literary category. Therefore, complexity of language, as well as 'literariness' (attributing aesthetic value), cannot be considered important factors in defining crime writing as 'popular' or not. Since Carter and Nash (1990: 35) further argue that one crucial determinant in a text's literariness is whether the reader *chooses* to read the text in a literary way (as a literary text, as it were), then the extent to which crime writing is considered under the guise of popular literature or not should additionally be a matter of reader approach. There is a whole tradition of empirical reader-response analysis (see, for instance, Ingarden, 1973a, 1973b; Iser, 1974, 1978), but what is worth noting at this point is that though my analysis of crime fiction is readerly, it in fact primarily draws from the theory of stylistics, sociology and narratology (that is, it is a triangular approach) rather than psychology.

Finally here, I study *best-selling* fiction. Bloom (2002: 6), in theory, defines bestsellers as those works 'of fiction sold in the most units (books in a given price range) to the most people over a set period of time', though he does admit that 'units' are difficult to define, as is 'a set period of time'. McCracken (1998: 20) refers to bestsellers as the 'most familiar kind of popular fiction', as that sold in large numbers in supermarkets, train stations and motorway department stores, while adding that the term 'bestseller' usually means high sales in the short term rather than enduring popularity. He also notes that the world of bestsellers is more than economics alone; it instead involves a complex combination of cultural and political processes, a 'total system', imposing norms on a passive populace. He hence argues that popular culture cannot be understood in terms of individual texts alone – 'those texts must be read and interpreted in relation to the totality of production, distribution and consumption that organises the conditions of their reception' (McCracken, 1998: 24–5). As Bloom (1996: 35) also notes, newspapers, fiction and cinema have enjoyed a symbiotic relationship since the First World War while, during the 1950s, publishers also came to realise the power of television promotion, alongside book buying and library borrowing. The nature of this interconnected world of industry, politics and culture hence, need to be kept in mind.

Deviance

So far, I briefly defined deviance (as mentioned, a term used synonymously to deviation) in linguistic, social and generic contexts. I aim to illustrate that in addition to meaning different things for different disciplines, deviance remains difficult to define in the context of any one discipline as well. In this section, I introduce the models and theoretical frameworks relevant to the study of deviance, under the guise of the three different disciplines, before proceeding to apply the models to novels from the genre at hand, correspondingly in Chapters 3, 4 and 5 (for a brief reference to these types of analyses, see Gregoriou, 2003b).

Linguistic deviance

Even though stylistic analysis is often framed as a validation of reader intuition, the sort of insight that such an investigation can provide goes a lot further than that. Stylistics was, initially, born of a reaction to the subjectivity and imprecision of literary studies and, in short, attempted to put criticism on a scientific basis (see Short, 1982). That is, whereas the literary meaning of any one extract seems to derive from presumed assumptions to do with readership and offers no operable principles of analysis, stylistics offers *linguistic* operable principles and hence possesses a kind of objectivity that literary criticism seems to lack. Practical stylistics is, in other words, a process of literary text analysis, the basic principle of which is that without '*analytic* knowledge of the rules and conventions of normal linguistic communication' we cannot adequately validate the readers' intuitive interpretations (Carter, 1991: 5). Fish (1980: 28) similarly suggested that what the method does is 'slow down the reading process' so that events one does not notice in normal time 'are brought before our analytical attentions'.

Short (1982: 61) has argued that the method's advantages are accuracy and clarity of presentation, along with that general characteristic of literary critical analysis of showing that superficially unconnected and previously unseen points can all be related in a particular overall analysis. He, however, also argued that we had better used linguistic stylistic analysis as a means of supporting a literary or interpretative thesis, and further added that the former analysis is likely to be of service to literary criticism if it follows its general aims and strategies. It is for this reason that stylistic analysis is often used to support initial impressions in various extracts' readings. Even though this might point to such analyses being those of *specific readings* and not analyses of *texts*, what needs to be kept in mind is that this is a method of analysis that takes into full account the reader as an actively mediating presence, and hence it is able to describe the reader's responses with some precision.

Though the procedures of stylistics do maintain certain defects (such as the absence of any constraint on the way in which one moves from description to interpretation, with the result that any interpretation one puts forward is arbitrary: Fish, 1980: 73), what needs to be emphasised is that it is a method that remains faithful to its principles as it is a process that talks about experience and focuses on effects (see Short, 1996: 349).

The stylistic models I have chosen to use in this book include the type of narration chosen, the viewpoint and mind style conveyed, and the figurative language employed. All these models are essential in one's analysis of the notion of *linguistic deviance*, as further discussed throughout Chapter 3.

A primary distinction to be made is that between first- and third-person narrators. The choice of a first-person narrator – where the 'I' is also a primary character in the story – is called *homodiegetic* narration (Genette, 1980). This is a type of narration that often 'convert[s] the reader to views he would not normally hold for the duration of the story' (Leech and Short, 1981: 265). If the narrator is not a character in the fictional world and hence reference to characters in this world involves the use of third-person pronouns, the sort of narration adopted is called *heterodiegetic* third-person narration (Genette, 1980). Such a narration further implies the merging of the author and the narrator though, as Short (1996: 258) argues, there is no *necessary* reason for this to be the case. It is in Chapter 3 that I draw on this distinction, when investigating the language of extracts from crime novels, in either the form of first- or third-person narration. Though most crime novels (for example, James Patterson's Alex Cross series) make use of third-person narration when addressing the criminal consciousness, the first-person narration is often preferred when addressing the detective's consciousness.

Short adds that the lack of a straightforward identity relation between a third-person narrator and the author requires us to interpose another layer of discourse structure between the author-reader and narrator-narratee levels, which would involve an *implied author* and an *implied reader*. Whereas the notion of implied author refers to that author implied by our understanding of the text, an implied reader is that reader which we have to become so as to read and react sensitively to the text or, as Leech and Short (1981: 259) put it, 'a hypothetical personage who shares with the author not just background knowledge but also a set of presuppositions, sympathies and standards of what is pleasant and unpleasant, good and bad, right and wrong'. Such a *mock* (Booth, 1961) or *implied reader* is therefore ostensibly guided toward particular judgements of characters and events. In the case of the reading of a crime series, the implied reader is that who shares background information as to the characters on which the series is based, as well as some awareness as to the generic nature of the series at hand. Expectations of this sort would guide the reader in making predictable judgements and reacting aptly to the information presented.

A further distinction that needs to be made is that between the *internal* and *external* narrative events, the former being those mediated through the subjective viewpoint of a particular character's consciousness, and the latter being those described *outside* the consciousness of any participating character (Simpson, 1993: 39). In the case where readers get information which they would not ordinarily have access to, namely, the thoughts and feelings of the characters, the relevant narrators are additionally described as *omniscient*, because they take on absolute knowledge and control of the narration of the events. Such narrations involve readers in a personal relationship with characters, manipulate sympathies, and cause bias. This is yet again another distinction I draw on in Chapter 3, when analysing the language of crime fiction extracts taken in either third-person internal or third-person external narration. The choice of one of these types of narration over another will prove to influence the reader's reaction and judgement over the events described.

The particular angle or perspective from which *fictional* worlds are presented, or the so-called *point of view*, 'concerns all features of orientation', including 'the position taken up by the speaker or author, that of the consciousness depicted by the text, and that implied for the reader or addressee' (Fowler, 1986: 9). By focusing on the stylistic choices that signify particular and distinctive outlooks of the world (see Short, 1996: 286), one can gain insight as to the nature of the character-character and the character-narrator relationships, as well as come to an understanding of how it is that the author manipulates the readers' sympathy toward the characters. The different viewpoint types are worth defining here, as the analysis will later come to focus on those extracts that allow access to the criminal viewpoint, whilst elaborating on the nature of that viewpoint.

Groups of indicators can be linked together interpretatively, namely in terms of *spatio-temporal, psychological* and *ideological viewpoint* (see Simpson, 1993: 11). Spatio-temporal viewpoint 'refers to the impression which a reader gains of events moving rapidly or slowly, in a continuous chain or isolated segments' (Fowler, 1986: 127). It is the viewing position – such as in the visual arts – which the readers feel themselves to occupy, the position from which their chain of perceptions seems to move. Psychological or perceptual viewpoint refers to the way in which narrative events are mediated through the consciousness of the 'teller' of the story. Finally, ideological viewpoint, or worldview, refers to the set of values, or belief system, communicated by the language of the text and shared by people from similar backgrounds to the speaker. In this case, viewpoint expresses 'a generalised mind-set or outlook on the world that a person, often as a representative of a *group* of people, might have' (Short, 1996: 227).

It is in Chapter 3 that I draw parallels between ideological viewpoint and the notion of *mind style*, developed by Fowler (1977: 76), to refer to 'cumulatively, consistent structural options, agreeing in cutting the presented world to one pattern or another', giving rise to 'an impression of a world-view'. Since mind style is a realisation of narrative viewpoint that *deviates* from a commonsense version of reality, it is a necessary notion to consider in an analysis of extracts allowing access to the criminal consciousness. It is where the fiction writer, though not compelled to take on a single character's viewpoint, voluntarily 'limits' his omniscience to those things which belong to a criminal's world view, that the notion needs to be considered. This limitation is often referred to as a form of *focalisation*, a term originating from the work of Genette (1980), and which Bal (1985: 100) adopted to refer to 'the relations between the elements presented and the vision through which they are presented'.

Stylisticians are additionally interested in the choices which authors have available to represent character speech and thought, and how these choices affect meaning and viewpoint. I do not wish to describe the speech and thought presentation categories in detail here, but will introduce that category referred to as *free indirect discourse,* which will prove relevant to my analysis in Chapter 3. Whereas *direct* presentations claim to contain the actual words and grammatical structures which the character used in the original utterance (whether speech or thought 'utterance'), *indirect* presentations refer to the propositional content of that utterance, but in the words of the narrator. *Free indirect* presentations, on the other hand, represent a 'semantic halfway house' (Short, 1994: 186) between the faithfulness claims of direct and indirect presentations and it is hence difficult, if not impossible, to work out whether the words and structures represented are those of the narrator or the character. It is for this reason that Short argues that the semantic indeterminacy opens up myriad possibilities for the manipulation of point of view. This mixing or merging of narratorial indirectness and characterological directness through *Free Indirect Discourse* (FID, in some of the stylistic literature, is used to refer to instances of both *free indirect speech* and *free indirect thought,* but I use it as synonymous to the latter term) has been endorsed as a powerful mode of representing characters in an (allegedly) authentic-cum-realist way. The effect achieved through the use of such a presentation is one whereby the readers feel that they are getting a more vivid and immediate representation of the character's thoughts as they happen, producing a sense of *irony* and *empathy* at the same time.

Another distinction that needs to be made, which I later claim is necessary for the construction of character mind styles in fiction, is that between *literal* and *figurative* language. Such a distinction would assist in clarifying the linguistic construction of the criminal consciousness in the genre at hand, especially in relation to those extracts focalised upon the criminals. The criminal viewpoint is established through their characteristic language choices, hence how they metaphorically configure the world, such as is the case for the James Patterson series, will prove to be a large part of this.

Figurative meaning, in semantics, describes 'a very common type of extension of meaning for a word (resulting in polysemy or multiple meaning), i.e. by metaphoric transfer of senses' (Wales, 2001: 151). *Dead metaphors* derive once the figurative meaning of a word becomes so common that the original, literal meaning is superseded. Such metaphors are also referred to as *faded* or *fossilised* (Saeed, 1998: 16), since they fade over time and become part of normal literal language: their metaphorical quality is no longer apparent to users. In fact, the English language consists of hundreds of words of classical origin in 'figurative' senses that we nowadays assume to be literal. It is the use of such dead metaphors in extracts allowing access to the criminal consciousness that I investigate, among others, in Chapter 3. Specifically, Patterson will prove to employ such apparent metaphors in their literal senses, so as to achieve specific effects.

Whereas seventeenth- and eighteenth-century scholars of the like of Thomas Sprat classified the figurative word meanings as 'deviations' from the 'true' meanings of words, deconstructionists would go as far as to deny any clear-cut distinction between literal and figurative word meaning (Wales, 2001: 152). Going further than deconstructionists, cognitive linguists such as Lakoff and Johnson (1980) and Gibbs (1994) would argue 'not only for the fundamental importance of figurative "language", ubiquitous and non-deviant, but also of what they term *figuration*, for human thought' (Wales, 2001: 152). In other words, cognitive linguists see figurative language as an integral part of human categorisation, a basic way of organising our thoughts about the world. Unlike scholars in favour of the *literal language theory*, whereby metaphors and other non-literal uses of language require a different processing strategy than literal language, researchers such as Gibbs and Lakoff would argue that figurative language is not something extra, or different from, ordinary literal language.

Metaphor, according to the former, is seen as a departure from literal language, detected as anomalous by the receiver, who then has to employ some strategies to construct the producer's intended meaning. According to the latter, however, metaphor does not require a special form of interpretation from listeners or readers. It is a cognitive linguistic approach that I adopt in this study, since the use of figurative expressions in Patterson's criminal-focalised extracts will provide insight into the way in which the relevant characters organise their view of the world, and additionally offer some justification as to the crimes committed.

Metaphor has traditionally been viewed as the most important form of **figurative** language use, and is usually seen as reaching its most sophisticated forms in literary or poetic language (Saeed, 1998: 302). When words are used in *metaphoric* senses, one field or domain of reference is mapped onto or carried over another on the basis of some perceived similarity between the two fields (Wales, 2001: 250). The starting point or described concept is often called the *target* domain, while the comparison concept or the analogy is called the *source* domain. In Richards's (1936) terminology, the former is called the *tenor* and the latter, the *vehicle*.

Since most metaphors are patently false, that is, refer to impossible statements as to the nature of the world, they appear to flout the Gricean maxim of quality (see Grice, 1975). It is the motivation behind the analogies made and the particular features which bind the two domains together that are of interest to stylisticians, while the indeterminacy or ambiguity in determining both the connection and the motivation behind it that makes metaphor a powerful source of multiple meaning. In addition, metaphor, in its expression of the familiar by the unfamiliar, is a good example of *defamiliarisation*; metaphor reconceptualises experience. Finally, metaphors that work in even more extended ways across whole sections of text or indeed across novels are referred to as *sustained* metaphors or *megametaphors* (see Werth, 1999). In Chapter 3, I investigate the sustained metaphors employed in criminal-focalised extracts so as to arrive at the motivations behind the analogies made, and explain the connections established.

Metonymy describes a referential entity where a speaker refers to an entity by naming something associated with it. We can refer, for instance, to a book or books by the author's name and say sentences like '*Patterson is on the top shelf*'. As Wales (2001: 252) puts it, in semiotic terms, metonymy is an indexical sign in that there is a directly or logically contiguous relationship between the substituted word and its referent. Also, with metonymy, truth is maintained; there is no flouting of the 'quality' maxim. Moreover, whereas in the case of metonymy the meanings associated are in the same domain, with metaphor there is transfer of field of reference. Saeed (1998: 78) recognises some resemblance between metonymy and the semantic part-whole relation of *meronymy*, but indicates that whereas metonymy is a process used by speakers as part of their practice of referring, meronymy describes a classification scheme evidenced in the vocabulary.

Since the work of Jakobson (1956) on language disorders, and on the structural dichotomy between metaphor and metonymy and their formal similarities and differences, the two figures have often been discussed as a binary pair (Wales, 2001: 252). However, in the context of deconstruction theory as well as in cognitive linguistics, the opposition between metonymy and metaphor is erased, purely on the basis that many common metaphors indeed have a metonymic basis. Nevertheless, in the context of my linguistic analysis in Chapter 3, such metonymies are treated as separate to metaphors. The choice of metonymic expressions in the criminal-focalised extracts will again provide insight into the characters' state of mind and psychological state.

In the context of linguistics, *idiom* is used to refer to strings of words or phrases that are idiomatic or idiosyncratic, in that they are socially language-specific and in that their meaning is not easily determined from the meanings of their constitutive parts. Much like phrasal verbs, idioms are strings of words which correspond to a single semantic unit. Since idioms are instances of expressions where the individual words have ceased to have independent meaning, these are also a type of language fossilisation, a process under which they become fixed. Furthermore, idioms are commonly metaphorical, and whereas some are strictly lexical, others have grammatical peculiarities.

As to their usage, Wales (2001: 198) argues that idioms are associated with informal rather than formal settings (lexical idioms are associated with the vividness of *colloquial*, everyday speech), though it is hard to imagine any kind of discourse without some idioms occurring. Finally, Wales argues that idioms represent the poetic diction of everyday language, much like *proverbial phrases*, *clichés*, *similes* and *slang*. Slang is popularly used as an equivalent to jargon, but has a wide circulation in its more general sense and its association with social groups such as adolescents and dialect speakers; as Turner (1973) notes, it lacks the finer cognitive distinctions that usually motivates technical jargon.

It is in Chapter 3 that I analyse the idioms employed in the criminal-focalised extracts, and yet focus on those adopted idioms that are used literally, so as to achieve particular special effects. Though idioms are strings of words which have ceased to have independent meanings, the idiomatic expressions that Patterson employs in such extracts will prove to have been unidiomatised.

Social deviance

In fiction, the language of the criminal mind becomes noticeable not only because of the extent to which it differs or deviates from the language of, say, the detecting mind. It *becomes* deviant due to the fact that it is attached to individuals who readers *take* to be deviant and abnormal. *Abnormals* (that is, criminals) are expected to conceptualise the world *abnormally* and, in real-life, criminals' labelling as such may even contribute to their course of actions and behaviour. Readers tend to tolerate, for instance, the detective's social abnormalities only because these are attached to individuals we take to be *normal*. Therefore, in discussing deviance, it is necessary to consider the social manifestations of the term.

One of the concepts that are central to my analysis of the social deviance of contemporary crime fiction (in Chapter 4) is that of the Carnivalesque, a term in literary criticism popularised through the writing of the Russian theorist Mikhail Bakhtin (1984b) on Rabelais (for the controversy surrounding the authorship of texts published under the names V.N. Voloshinov, P.N. Medvedev and I. Kanaëv that might actually be attributable to Bakhtin himself, see Clark and Holquist, 1984: 146–67; Todorov, 1984: 3–13; Rzhevsky, 1994; Morson, 1991: 1072).

Bakhtin was responsible for shifting attention from the abstract system of *langue* to the concrete utterances of individuals in particular social contexts: Language was to be seen as inherently 'dialogic', in that it could be grasped only in terms of its inevitable orientation towards another. As Eagleton puts it,

> [t]he sign was to be seen less as a fixed unit (like a signal) than as an active component of speech, modified and transformed in meaning by the variable social tones, valuations and connotations it condensed within itself in specific social conditions. Since such valuations and connotations were constantly shifting, since the 'linguistic community' was in fact a *heterogeneous* society composed of many conflicting interests, the sign for Bakhtin was less a neutral element in a given structure than a focus of struggle and contradiction. It was not simply a matter of asking 'what the sign meant', but of investigating its varied history, as conflicting social groups, classes, individuals and discourses sought to appropriate and imbue it with their own meanings.
>
> Eagleton (1996: 101–2)

In short, Bakhtin insisted that there was no language which was not caught up in definite social relationships, which were in turn part of broader political, ideological and economic systems. His work has remote relations with *Speech-Act theory*, which began in the work of J.L. Austin (1962), a theory that is concerned with the linguistic acts made while speaking, and which have interpersonal purpose and pragmatic effect (Austin took note of the fact that not all of our language actually describes reality, and that some is 'performative').

Based on Bakhtin's idea that every utterance has some kind of dialogic relationship with other utterances which have preceded it, *intertextuality* refers to the way in which a text may invoke other texts through the use of particular words, phrases or ideas, so the reader or listener's knowledge of that other text comes into play in their interpretation of what the current author is saying. Consequently, even within a single text there can be a continual 'dialogue' between the text given and other texts that exist outside it, whether literary or nonliterary: either within the same period of composition, or in previous centuries (Wales, 2001: 220). In fact, in accordance to this theory, no text is 'free' of other texts or truly original.

Within this matrix of dialogic relationships, struggles for power between texts and between speakers take place, in the context of different kinds of institutions and different kinds of economic relationships. Bakhtin's theory (1981: 270–5) consists of a process of ongoing struggle between centralising and decentralising tendencies, within language between centripetal and centrifugal forces. Centripetal forces pull inwards towards a standard language, an authoritative canon and political and structural centralisation, while centrifugal forces push outwards towards variation, resistance and disunification. Taylor (1995: 17) suggests that whereas centripetal forces perpetuate the myth of a unitary language and thus contribute to the process of social and historical cohesion, centrifugal forces lay bare the full range and diversity of speech types.

Bakhtin's carnival(esque) is a term popularised 'to signal any demotic heteroglossic or "multi-voiced" counter-culture in comic or exuberant opposition to a hegemonic official culture: a kind of subversive anticulture, often with its own anti-language' (Wales, 2001: 48). Bakhtin (1984a: 217–18) uses the term 'carnivalesque' to refer not only to carnival in its narrow sense (the specific festivals and feast days celebrated over the course of the year), but also to the whole range of popular, festive practices that developed during the Middle Ages. It is where the whole structure of society is, for a time, inverted, turned inside out, subject to ridicule.

According to his theory, carnivalesque imagery offers an alternative to official imagery, but by suspending and/or inverting social hierarchies carnival provides an alternative construction of social relations (Taylor, 1995: 20). Since carnival provides a dialogic response to the official structures of fear, intimidation and prohibition (Bakhtin views the legalisation of carnival not as a static state of affairs but as an ongoing process of negotiation), it can be said to be similar to his concept of heteroglossia (a term referring to the 'internal differentia-tion or stratification of language', Wales, 2001: 186–7); there are ongoing struggles in carnival, just like there are ongoing struggles at the level of language between centripetal and centrifugal forces.

Carnivalesque practices were imbued with images of the *grotesque body*, images of '[e]xaggeration, hyberbolism [... and] excessiveness' (Bakhtin, 1984a: 303). The grotesque body, which dominated carnival-esque imagery, simultaneously represented birth and death, feasting and defecation, and therefore represented an alternative to the symbol-ism and ideologism of officialdom. Such imagery celebrated the freedoms permitted during the period of festivities while, at another level, it contributed to the alternative construction of reality provided by carnival as a whole (Taylor, 1995: 21). Finally, grotesque imagery signified an 'alternative to the fear inspired by official imagery' (Taylor, 1995: 21); whereas official imagery traded on the cosmic threats of potential catastrophe, famine, drought, floods and disease to introduce a sense of fear (Bakhtin, 1984b: 335), grotesque imagery 'overcame this sense of fear by assimilating humans with the cosmic elements' (Taylor, 1995: 21).

The idea of carnival has proved to be one of the most productive critical themes in cultural theory in recent years, for approaching all kinds of social and material interactions and behaviours (see, for example, Fiske, 1987, 1989a, 1989b for applications of carnival to wrestling, game shows, MTV, and so on). In addition, Bakhtin's *Rabelais and His World* provides us with a ground-breaking analysis of the relationship between popular culture and literary forms.

It is my argument, in Chapter 4, that the reading of crime fiction can be thought of as a manifestation of the notion of carnival in itself. Much like the notion of carnival, crime novels provide a site where pleasures (such as the enjoyment of crime) can be exploited to the full, and where the enjoyment of such pleasures carries with it both a celeb-ratory and a critical potential. While the reading of such novels celeb-rates the access to proscribed forms of pleasure, at the same time it enacts a critique of the structures which officially restricted such plea-sures. The same argument can in fact be made of pornography; porn is a genre that is concerned with the body, profanes and degrades, insults political and religious authorities, as well as provides escape from social controls, and therefore may also be considered as a manifestation of the carnivalesque. Additionally it is indeed the case that both porn and crime fiction tend to eventually confirm social hierarchies rather than invert them; male dominance over women is reasserted in porn (see, for instance, Dworkin, 1981) much like the detective's eventual supremacy over the criminal is reasserted in crime fiction.

One of the arguments that could be raised against these analogies is to do with *function*. If crime fiction and pornography are perceived as carnivalesque practices, then would such material be classified as cathartic – in that it deflects readers and viewers from killing and raping others – or does it in fact give readers and viewers the incentive to perform such acts? In other words, does such material safely discharge aggressive tendencies much as carnival discharges social tensions, or does it – for at least some people – inflame and incite such tendencies? In response to such a question, I would argue that discussing such a 'cause and effect' relationship between such material and the actual actions of murder and rape is neither necessary nor helpful. The cause is not 'in' such texts but in fact in the interaction between text and reader, for which the reader must bear responsibility; there can be no direct cause and effect relationship because the text is mediated by human consciousness, hence what one does with one's interaction with such material need necessarily be one's own responsibility (see Cameron and Frazer (1992), for a paper on pornography that tries to provide a corrective by getting beyond crude causal views). In other words, whilst not resolving the issue, my book is concerned with discussing mainly the reader's experience in their interaction with carnivalesque material, rather than referring to the nature of the fictional worlds portrayed in the crime novels.

Another point of concern relates to the overall usefulness of Bakhtin's model of the carnivalesque. Humphrey (2000: 166) suggested that though comparisons with historically-remote forms of culture can be illuminating, when engaged with this way of working, we can lose the sense of where a contemporary practice has developed from, and hence overlook the specific social and economic conditions that shaped its formation. In the context of this study, however, I draw on the *ideas* of carnival in both synchronic and diachronic terms, as opposed to discussing contemporary popular culture in conjunction with the relevant medieval festival. It is also my argument that whereas social deviance had, in the course of medieval carnivals, been more of an issue of time (it is recorded as a 'once a year' type of event), it is nowadays manifested as an issue of space and/or place. Perfect reincarnations of the carnival are evident, for instance, in Disneyland, in the visiting of certain art galleries, as well as in the reading of certain genres. In other words, carnivalesque practices are no longer a holiday, and contemporary manifestations of the notion are much more accessible than they had once been, not to mention evident in widely different shapes and forms.

When concentrating on the social deviance of the genre at hand, it is also necessary to consider the types of abnormal behaviour evident. I therefore bring in the work of Carl Jung on the notion of *archetypes* in order later to arrive at a classification of the type of criminals evident in the genre. 'Archetype', in the context of literary criticism, is particularly associated with the work of Northrop Frye (1957) who identified recurrent symbols of themes in literature. Wales (2001: 29) notes that archetypal criticism of this kind is additionally indebted to the work of anthropologist Sir James Frazer at the turn of the twentieth century, and to the psychiatrist Carl Gustav Jung (particularly the latter's theory of the 'collective unconscious').

Since archetypes are here used to refer to patterns of character behaviour, they can additionally be characterised as character-type *schemata*, hence parallels will later be drawn between the Jungian theory of archetypes and *schema theory*. The general term 'schema theory' covers a range of work, from early psychological experiments by Bartlett (1932) to recent cognitive psychology. Central to the schematisation of the theory is the work of Roger Schank (Schank and Abelson, 1977; Schank, 1982a, 1982b, 1984, 1986), while associated works that proceed along very similar lines includes Minsky (1975, 1986), Tannen (1984), Fillmore (1985), Sanford and Garrod (1981), Rumelhart (1975, 1980, 1984), Rumelhart and Norman (1978), Thorndyke (1977) and Thorndyke and Yekovich (1980). Finally, the framework has itself been set out clearly in Semino, 1997: 119–233; Culpeper, 2001: 63–86, 263–86, and Stockwell, 2002: 75–89. As Stockwell puts it,

> [e]ssentially, the context that someone needs to make sense of individual experiences, events, parts of situations or elements of language is stored in background memory as an associative network of knowledge. In the course of experiencing an event or making sense of a situation, a *schema* is dynamically produced, which can be modelled as a sort of script based on similar situations encountered previously. New experiences and new incoming information are understood by matching them to existing schematic knowledge.
>
> Stockwell (2003: 255)

Though Stockwell argues that there is a wealth of empirical evidence that suggests such a mechanism may be in operation, he adds that it is schema theory itself that has gone on to provide analytical detail to account for the workings of the process. Since the individual experiences that a reader brings to the reading can also be seen as a schema or set of schemas, then one's familiarity with the reading of crime fiction may be argued to involve a set of expectations as to certain character schemata. And it is the nature of the archetypal criminal schemata that I investigate in the Social Deviance section of this study.

Generic deviance

The character roles are part and parcel of the generic conventions that govern contemporary crime fiction, or any one genre for that matter. Therefore, in addition to considering the (criminal) character types that characterise the genre at hand, I find it necessary to analyse the wider generic conventions that govern it; hence social deviance is analysable alongside generic deviance.

So far I have defined *genre* both in the context of literary theory and linguistics, while the notion was pitted against *register* or *functional language variation*. It is in Chapter 5 that I consider *genre* in the context of folklore as well as literary studies, and define the notions of *genre evolution* and *generic convention*, both of which are vital in my analysis of contemporary crime fiction's generic deviance. I argue that generic 'rules' were not always slavishly followed, hence genres present a more dynamic and flexible aspect with, for instance, one genre developing out of another (for example, as will later be shown, how the *forensic* or *medical examiner*'s genre evolved out of the *detective* or *crime fiction* genre).

In this section, I offer some background on three concepts that are central to my discussion of generic deviance in Chapter 5: Wittgenstein's *Family Resemblance* theory, *prototype* and *defamiliarisation*.

Wittgenstein's (1953) *Family Resemblance* theory implies that members of a particular family share resemblances rather than defining characteristics, and that a family can be easily recognised, although all characteristics are not exhibited by any single individual member. In other words, novels that are classified under the same genre (for example, crime fiction) do not share any single characteristic, but are instead related to each other in a number of ways; they share family resemblances. Hence 'Wittgenstein's discussion of family resemblances and subsequent comment have given rise to a "prototype" or cluster category designed to account for our capacity to recognise instances of categories' (Swales, 1990: 51).

Because of problems with the traditional approach of describing concepts using definitions, several more sophisticated theories of concepts have been proposed. One influential proposal is due to Eleanor Rosch and her co-workers (see Rosch, 1973, 1975; Rosch and Mervis, 1975; Rosch et al., 1976), who have suggested the notion of *prototypes*. According to Saeed (1998: 37), 'this is a model of concepts which views them as structured so that there are central or typical members of a category such as BIRD and FURNITURE, but then a shading off into less typical or peripheral members' (for instance, 'chair' is a more central member of the category FURNITURE than 'lamp').

In extension, the extent to which a certain novel will be considered under a certain genre will depend on its similarity with typical members of the generic category. For instance, if one considers an Agatha Christie detective novel such as *The Murder of Roger Ackroyd* (1924) as prototypical of crime literature, then the extent to which they classify other novels under the same generic category will depend on their similarities with the former novel.

A final notion to be defined here is that of *defamiliarisation* (also *de-automatisation*), used by the Russian Formalists and Prague School linguistics in discussions of literary (especially poetic), and non-literary language. As mentioned earlier, the notion has been raised in relation to the so-called automatising tendencies of everyday communication and its subsequent overfamiliarity. According to the theory, poetry by contrast de-automatises language itself while literary language from all genres, as Wales (2001: 94) puts it, not only highlights or *foregrounds*, but also alienates or creates estrangement (*ostranenie*), forcing readers to look afresh at what has become familiarised (see Shklovsky, 1965).

However, what critics acknowledge, is that what is novel or strange can itself become automatised; 'Literary language through the ages reveals successive reactions, revolutions, against equally successive tendencies to conventionalisation' (Wales, 2001: 94). Furthermore, defamiliarisation is a notion that Cook (1994) describes as literature's *schema-refreshing* property. A notion that forms part of *Schema Theory*, schema-refreshment refers to the disruption of our conventional ways of viewing the world. Cook stresses that schema-refreshment is reader-dependent and, similarly, it is in fact difficult to see how the concept of defamiliarisation can exclude the reader and refer to a quality of text rather than to a quality of discourse.

Ironically, this central weakness in the theory is suggested by the word itself. (These points are as true of the Russian word 'ostranenie' as they are of its English translation.) Though a neologism, the word 'defamiliarisation' may be regarded as a nominalization of a verb. This verb could be transitive and always predicate an object, with an optional adjunct 'for x'. The text defamiliarises something for someone. This 'something' is the world (though in a sense which includes texts and language) and the 'someone' must be the reader.

Cook (1990: 241–2)

He concludes that defamiliarisation is equally reader-dependent: a relationship between a reader and an object of perception, even if that object of perception is another text or the language itself.

In the context of genre theory, defamiliarisation contributes to the disrupting or challenging of conventional forms and therefore makes readers aware of the nature of the genre in the first place. By defamiliarising genre, the existence of the generic conventions that govern its past is reasserted, the genre becomes 'perceptible'.

Bringing it all together: review of the tripartite model

I have so far offered some historical background to the theoretical frameworks employed in this study. I drew on important distinctions when defining terminology, and further established a number of connections among the models used and others.

Overall, I assert that there are clear links between the three types of deviance to be investigated in the context of crime literature. The social and generic deviance manifested in such novels may help explain why certain linguistic choices are treated as deviant. Similarly, deviant language presents readers with a generic innovation therefore additionally constituting generic deviance. Finally, extracts taken from abnormal characters' viewpoints are expected to have deviant linguistic structuring. Auster's 'City of Glass', a story forming part of *The New York Trilogy* (1988), proves to be a case in point. In the narrative, the character of Peter Stillman Junior engages in a lengthy dialogue with Daniel Quinn, whom he believes to be a private detective, where he tells the story of his life. Peter was an isolated child, subjected to almost total sensory deprivation from birth until the age of 12. Though he was able in adulthood to learn fairly successfully the language of which he was deprived in childhood, his speech is deviant particularly because of the way in which he conveys information:

> 'No questions, please,' the young man said at last. 'Yes. No. Thank you.' He paused for a moment. 'I am Peter Stillman. I say this of my

own free will. Yes. That is not my real name. No. Of course my mind is not all it should be. But nothing can be done about that. No. About that. No, no. Not anymore.

'You sit there and think: who is this person talking to me? What are these words coming from his mouth? I will tell you. Or else I will not tell you. Yes and no. My mind is not all it should be. I say this of my own free will. But I will try. Yes and no. I will try to tell you, even if my mind makes it hard. Thank you.

Auster (1988: 15–16)

Even though the language employed here is not grammatically deviant, it lacks background; Peter cannot rely on the 'givens' which underlie most linguistic communication. He violates a whole range of communicative rules (asserts necessary truths and presuppositions, and often lapses into tautologies which are totally uninformative), and fails to comply with the apparent purpose of the exchange within the detective story's narrative (for a detailed analysis of this story see Chapman and Routledge, 1999). It is this linguistic deviance that constitutes the character as an abnormal, while the employment of such a deviance further violates the generic conventions that underlie the nature of the novel itself; the extract at hand hence manifests all three types of deviance: linguistic, social and generic.

Outline of remaining contents

In Chapter 2, '*Contemporary Crime Fiction: Constraints and Development*', the genre is described according to general ideas presented in handbooks and articles, while its history is rendered in brief. I address the rules, regularities and constraints of the genre, discuss the attraction that it has been claimed to maintain, and finally draw on issues to do with the genre's characters and realism.

In Chapter 3, '*Linguistic Deviance: The Stylistics of Criminal Justification*', I draw on two studies of the language of extracts portraying the criminal consciousness. The first draws on the notion of *mind style* as a vital medium for one to get from the stylistic analysis of such extracts to the moral justification of crimes. The second addresses the nature of the criminal mind in Patterson and investigates the figurative language employed in such extracts.

In Chapter 4, '*Social Deviance in Contemporary Crime Fiction*', I examine the rule-breaking of the social perspective of abnormality, with a focus on Connelly's Bosch series. I discuss crime fiction as *carnival*, and finally analyse the genre's three criminal *archetypes*, giving various examples from the genre as illustrations of each one.

In Chapter 5, *'Generic Deviance in Contemporary Crime Fiction'*, I revisit the definition of the genre at hand using *family resemblance* theory, *prototypes*, and *defamiliarisation*. Though various crime fiction analysts' definitions of the genre are offered in Chapter 2, here I attempt to define the genre at hand on the basis of these three theoretical frameworks. I also analyse novels that dismember the conventions of the crime fiction genre, and question whether the Cornwellian form constitutes a *subgenre* of crime fiction or an altogether new genre.

2
Contemporary Crime Fiction: Constraints and Development

Introduction

Much has been written about crime fiction, and treatments of the subject vary greatly. Whereas, for instance, some writers view such material as no more than entertaining, crime fiction has been elsewhere treated more seriously. Theorists, critics and analysts have described both the history of the genre and changing attitudes to it (Ball, 1976; Winks, 1980; Roth, 1995; Messent, 1997; Knight, 1980, 2004; Scaggs, 2005; Horsley, 2005 and so on). According to Knight (1980: 1), less evaluative approaches have tried to establish why crime fiction is so compelling; psychoanalysts found the basis of the form's patterns in the psychic anxieties of writers and readers, while another type of analysis has seen the social attitudes and the pressures of the modern environment as the basic drive in crime fiction. Overall, though the development of the genre was traced by literary critics, 'culturally' attuned critics, psychoanalysts and sociologists, little *linguistic* work has been undertaken in the area. It is in Chapter 3 that I aim to apply analytical stylistic frameworks to crime fiction extracts, and hence put forward the argument that the discipline of linguistic stylistics has a great deal of insight to offer as to the genre's form, preferred structures, and effects.

This section aims to form a literary review of many of those who have been attracted to crime fiction, in one way or another. As Winks (1980: 208) suggests, 'nothing which has been created can be adequately or accurately criticised without an understanding of the special purpose of its creation'. Therefore, in order to interpret the detective story, we must first understand why detective stories are written, in what tradition and for what audience.

Crime fiction: origins and development

Theorists disagree as to the genre's origins and, as Porter puts it, historians of detective literature may be differentiated according to whether they take the *long* or the *short* view of their subject:

> Those taking the long view claim that the detective is as old as Oedipus and serendipity or at least eighteenth-century China. Those maintaining the short view assume that detective fiction did not appear before the nineteenth century and the creation of the new police in Paris and London, that its inventor, in the 1840s, was Edgar Allan Poe, and that it reached its golden age in the opening decades of the twentieth century with the non-violent problem novel.
>
> Porter (1981: 11)

Porter suggests that clearly a case may be made for both views that chiefly depends upon the definition adopted, but the view preferred will also be conditioned by the way one *evaluates* the representation of crime in literature. In other words, in order to decide which was the first crime novel we need to define the genre, as well as to consider briefly its relationship with the much larger and more vague category of crime literature.

In this book, the definition I adopt of the crime fiction genre is that of a novel that combines two forms of suspense: the desire to know 'whodunit' along with that suspense derived by the fear that whoever it was might repeat his/her crime. In other words, it is that *short* view of historians of detective literature that I adopt when attempting to define its nature, that is, its constraints, rules, and formulaic regularities.

Rankin (2000: 3) argues that the 'golden age' of crime fiction is supposed to be in the 1920s and 1930s, when the traditional English whodunit was at its height, with practitioners such as Agatha Christie (1890–1976) giving it style and substance. He goes on to add that, in the States, Raymond Chandler and Dashiell Hammett reacted against this 'cosy' school; Chandler in particular felt it his duty to take crime writing back onto the 'mean streets', by making it 'urban and relevant to its time and place'.

Bönnemark (1997: 54) suggests that the peak of British detective fiction was reached in the period between the two world wars, and, during this Golden Age, the 'literacy' of the detective story was improved, it became more plausible, and it placed more emphasis on character instead of only mechanical plot (see Haycraft, 1972: 121).

The most important writers of the Golden Age have been called the Big Five and Haycraft (1972: 125) suggests that they were H.C. Bailey, Freeman Wills Crofts, R. Austin Freeman, Dorothy Sayers and Agatha Christie. Other authors have also been suggested, viz. Ellery Queen, S.S. Van Dine, John Dickson Carr, Michael Innes, and Nicholas Blake (Symons, 1994: 147).

Whereas in Britain, detective fiction has been said to develop towards a deeper characterisation of protagonists – approaching mainstream fiction – in America, the genre has taken a rather different turn. A whole new subgenre of detective fiction has developed in the USA, viz. the feminist hard-boiled novel, with authors such as Sue Grafton, with her private investigator Kinsey Millmore, Sara Paretsky with V.I. Warshawski, and Laurie R. King with Kate Martinelli.

Bönnemark (1997: 57) argues that many literary genres go through a development from a humble beginning to a peak, 'a Golden Age', then into a period characterised both by levelling off and greater variety, before the genre ceases to exist. She adds that often humorous varieties develop too, for instance, where elements of the formulaic story are left out and rules are overtly violated. This is the case with detective fiction in that ironic varieties developed in the USA, with Dashiell Hammett and Raymond Chandler as its two main representatives, while the many contemporary humorous writers of detective fiction include Colin Watson and Dan Kavanagh.

Parodies, entertaining imitations which borrow the style and technique of the originating genre, have also developed. These 'can be regarded as a trustworthy indication of the existence of a genre: where there are parodies, the constraints of a particular genre are so well known that they create humour if exaggerated' (Bönnemark, 1997: 57). There are also pastiches (Symons, 1981: 136), which are difficult to distinguish from parodies in that such forms' borrowings are also for satirical or humorous purposes. As the name of the form suggests, however, pastiche is additionally characteristically a 'pasting together', a patchwork of *different* borrowed styles. Examples of such pastiches are the works set in Britain written by the American author Elizabeth George, and all the many pastiches on the Sherlock Holmes stories, such as *The Last Sherlock Holmes Story* by Michael Dibdin (1989), and *The Beekeeper's Apprentice* by Laurie R. King (1996).

The American hard-boiled school has also given rise to such parodies and pastiches. It has been the object of literary experiments, such as Paul Auster's *The New York Trilogy* (see Chapter 5 for an analysis of one of the stories in the trilogy), while there also exists a contemporary subgenre of detective fiction which, according to Bonnemark (1997: 57), has been used for deconstructive and meta-fictional purposes, an 'anti-detective fiction' by Jorge Luis Borges, Alain Robbe-Grillet, and others. Bönnemark, finally, suggests that in such contemporary versions of the genre, there are novels with alternative endings, where the question of the murderer is left open. Such experiments, however, have been conducted before, including Berkeley Cox's *The Poisoned Chocolates Case* from 1929, a detective story with six separate solutions, and Noyes Hart's *Bellamy Trial* from 1927, rendered as a day-by-day account of a murder trial, built on a real case (correspondingly referred to in Haycraft, 1972: 146 and 1972: 163).

Rules, regularities and constraints

Defining the crime fiction genre

Roth (1995: xi) suggested that '[a]nyone who writes about mystery and detective fiction inherits a history of subdivisions that are expected to have a prescriptive force'. According to Symons (1973),

> [i]t has been said already that crime fiction is a hybrid, and that too much categorization is confusing rather than helpful, but within the hybrid form detective stories and crime novels are of a different strain from spy stories and thrillers. The lines of demarcation are vague, but everybody recognises their existence.
>
> Symons (1973: 230)

Symons seems to base his argument on an assumed shared scale of values for all readers of literary texts which I would be inclined to disagree with. It is, in other words, unlikely that all readers of crime novels come to value such texts in the same manner. Whereas some, for instance, appreciate the formulaic nature of such texts, others value most those crime novels that depart from the formula's restricting regularities.

However, his claim as to the complicated categorisation of the so-called *crime fiction* genre does seem rather valid. Those who have been attracted to the genre have, in other words, come to face a variety of classifications, most of which have been limiting and confusing rather than helpful, while the definitions adopted were often of a rather overlapping nature. As a result, they have all come to acknowledge different sets of general categories of detective fiction, often failing to both clearly define the differences that keep one category distinct from others, and to explain how their chosen categorisation relates to that of others.

In attempting to define the *detective thriller*, Priestman (1998: 5) refers to it as a hybrid form between the *detective whodunnit* and the *thriller* whereby the *whodunnit* is that which is primarily concerned with unravelling past events which either involve a crime or seem to do so, and the *thriller* is that in which the action is primarily in the present tense of the narrative. According to this classification, the placement of the *detective thriller* in between the other two divides Priestman's interest between solving a past mystery and following a present action in which the protagonists confront a dangerous conspiracy alone, or step outside the law, or both (Priestman, 1998: 2). Later on, however, Priestman came to argue in favour of the 'interpermeability of genres' (1998: 50), that is, the fluidity of the barriers supposedly separating one popular genre from another.

Roth, on the other hand, acknowledged three general categories of detective fiction – the analytic, the hard-boiled, and the spy thriller (1995: xii) – and yet pointed out that, in making this categorisation, his critical task was 'one of *adjustment* rather than that of an institutional inscription of differences'. According to the same source,

> [f]or almost a century, another group of popular culture critics who do *not* like detective fiction have dismissed all internal demarcations and insisted that detective and mystery fiction in all its generic permutations, in fact, amounts to one extended repetition.
>
> Roth (1995: xii)

Roth, however, not only fails to name this group of so-called 'popular cultural critics', but further seems to insinuate that it is only those who *dislike* the genre that are able to see how one subgenre often blends with another, and thus how difficult it is to ascertain the differences keeping one distinct from another.

Bönnemark (1997: 59–60) attempted to distinguish the characteristic features of detective fiction, and set out the differences between that and suspense fiction. For instance she, among other things, claimed that detective stories primarily mystify and demystify, while suspense stories primarily create and release suspense. As Haycraft (1972: 81), however, argues, many stories are difficult to categorise and some do in fact situate themselves on the border between detective and suspense fiction.

In this study, the genre that I have so far referred to as *crime fiction* is taken to include detective stories, and not spy narratives or mysteries. The sort of stories I will be looking at, that is, are to do with the detection of (most usually) a murderer, regardless of whether it is a police officer, a private detective, or someone else doing the detecting. Furthermore, the sort of definition I adopt for *crime fiction* narratives rather coincides with that definition Priestman adopted when defining the *detective thriller*: a past event of murder gets to be resolved, and yet a present action of events is followed. The two terms, *detective* and *crime fiction* from now on will be used interchangeably.

Rules and constraints

During the Golden Age of detective fiction, several authors published more or less humorous rules on how to write detective stories (Bönnemark, 1997: 46). A good example is given by Knox, who offered 'Ten Rules for a Good Detective Story':

1. The criminal must be someone mentioned in the early part of the story, but must not be anyone whose thoughts the reader has been allowed to follow.
2. All supernatural or preternatural agencies are ruled out as a matter of course.
3. Not more than one secret room or passage is allowable.
4. No hitherto undiscovered poisons may be used, nor any appliance which will need a long scientific explanation at the end.
5. No Chinaman must figure in the story.
6. No accident must ever help the detective, nor must he ever have an unaccountable intuition which proves to be right.
7. The detective must not himself commit the crime.
8. The detective must not light on any clues which are not instantly produced for the inspection of the reader.
9. The stupid friend of the detective, the Watson, must not conceal any thoughts which pass through his mind; his intelligence must be slightly, but very slightly, below that of the average reader.
10. Twin brothers, and doubles, generally, must not appear unless we have been duly prepared for them.

Knox (1929: 1739)

Though these rules are intended to be rather humorous, they, in fact, can be said to be genuine prohibitions, or rules of an exclusive nature. That is, in the 1920s, only those stories that adhered to these so-called rules would qualify as 'good' detective stories; they represent a summary of the generic features of detective stories, in the form that these were produced during that period of time.

Other sets of rules have been put forth by Van Dine (1946), which, though fundamentally the same as Knox's, clearly make a distinction between obligatory and optional elements, and, according to Bönnemark (1997: 46), stress the necessity for concentration, in that there must not be several detectives. As Van Dine (1946: 192) puts it, there must also be no 'literary dallying with side-issues, no subtly worked-out character analyses, no "atmospheric preoccupations".'

More recently, Ball (1976: 67) argued that a mystery novel must accord with the following fewer rules; (a) every clue discovered by the detective has to be made available to the reader, (b) early introduction of the murderer, (c) the crime must be significant, (d) there must be detection, and (e) the number of suspects must be known and the murderer must be among them. What, however, Ball failed to mention, is whether all these so-called rules are prescriptive, descriptive, core, comprehensive, inclusive or exclusive ones. He, for instance, failed to explain whether the rules he outlined are ones that a novel need adhering to in order to be defined as a detective novel (*exclusive rules*), or whether a novel adhering to a collection of these would still qualify (*inclusive rules*).

To take things to some other extent, according to Roth (1995: xi), '[c]lassic detective fiction differs from other fiction in at least one way: it challenges us to read it faster than the words appear on the page'. What he seems to suggest, in this rather poetic manner, is that detective literature offers books that prompt readers to read them faster than all other literary genres. Roth, however, does not offer an adequate basis for this claim, since readers of other literary genres might find their preferred genres equally stimulating. The challenge, Roth continues, is covered by a rule that supposedly governs the analytic or puzzle-solving branch of the crime fiction genre, the principle which we know as the 'Fair-Play Rule' (see Sayers, 1947a: 225). According to Roth (1995: xi), this rule – that the reader must have as much information relevant to the solution of the crime as the detective – 'is played out according to a fantastic scenario by which various triumphant readers solve the mystery as they read page 64, 91, or 113, respectively, at which point the rest of the book becomes redundant to them'. He, however, does confess that he does not believe that detective fiction works this way, as this implies a highly gratifying and diminished reading – and a work not worth reading in itself.

Mandel (1984: 16), on the other hand, defines this so-called fair-play rule as a 'battle of wits', simultaneously unfolding at two levels:

between the great detective and the criminal, and between the author and the reader. According to Mandel,

> [i]n both battles, the mystery is the identity of the culprit, to which the detective and reader alike are to be led by a systematic examination of the clues. But while the story's hero always succeeds, the reader ought not succeed in outwitting the author. Otherwise the psychological need to which the detective story is supposed to respond is not assuaged: there is no tension, suspense, surprising solution or catharsis.
>
> Mandel (1984: 16)

In other words, Mandel argues that the detective story need to achieve the reader's surprise when the murderer's identity is revealed, and with no violation of the 'fair-play' rule, meaning without cheap tricks such as the withholding of clues. And that is the case, since he claims that 'to surprise without cheating is to manifest genuine mastery of the genre' (1984: 16). Mandel himself, however, further on admits that reading such stories is – in fact – not fair play, but 'fake play under the guise of fair play' (1984: 48). Classical detective writing, he asserts, is more of 'a game with loaded dice', since the winner is predetermined by the author and, like the hunted fox, neither the criminal ever wins, nor the reader ever outwits the author.

In any case, the rules presented above have certainly been violated, for example, by the novels belonging to the 'Had-I-But-Known' school, so named by Nash (1954), for instance whereby the authors consistently conceal clues from the reader. What, however, one need to keep in mind is that all rules of art were made to be broken (Steeves, 1946: 518), and, as a matter of fact, the flowering of the most successful period of detective fiction, the Golden Age, developed as a revolt against the rules presented above (Bönnemark, 1997: 47).

Bönnemark (1997: 48) proceeded to outline certain *content* constraints to the genre, which are to do with the *theme, plot, characters* and *setting* of detective novels. In short, she argues that murder is the crime that is usually investigated by the genre at hand, and that it is two stories that are told – that of the crime and that of its investigation. She adds that *thinking* as opposed to *action* is the main type of subject, and insofar as characters are concerned, there need be a detective, a victim, and a perpetrator, and yet it is most usually the detective or 'commentator' (Dr Watson type) who focalises events. Finally, Bönnemark claims that though there are no constraints on the setting of detective stories, certain settings are preferred (for instance, the British puzzle story is often set in an isolated place such as a locked room or a lonely house).

Having said that, it would be fair to say that the crime fiction genre has shown a never-ending capacity to reinvent itself; crime fiction's rules and constraints have come to change with the times. The genre, in its present form, no longer adheres to the rules or generic features of the prototypical detective novel that started it all. The so-called rules that were on offer at the time, and most of which were exclusive rather than inclusive, were violated to such an extent that it is, nowadays, no longer possible to come up with a set of features that all contemporary crime novels adhere to. There is, however, a set of formulaic regularities that crime novels may be said to feature.

Formulaic regularities

According to Ball (1976: 71), the disciplines that govern the mystery are actually the rules 'masquerading incognito' which structure the whole art of fiction, and, 'truly revealed, these Rules form the complete training ground in the art of communicating through story-telling'. In other words, Ball suggests that crime literature is a microcosm of the narrative form, and the mystery (a term he seems to use to refer to detective novels) makes a good training ground for the novel, since it is of a higher rank compared to that of a novel:

> A good mystery writer can write a better novel than a good novelist can write a mystery. This is because the mystery writer has had to develop the disciplines of the novel form to a far higher degree than is required of the straight novelist. The mystery is a craft within a craft and all that pertains to the art of the mystery pertains to the art of the novel.
>
> Ball (1976: 74)

What Ball is suggesting here is that such mystery (that is, detective) novels are superior to novels overall because the disciplines one need follow to write a mystery are somewhat of a higher rank to those of a novel. Not only does he, however, fail to explain what he means by 'the disciplines of the novel form', but he additionally fails to justify his argument as to why these are 'better' than those rules a mystery novel need accord to (as outlined in the previous section).

Porter (1981: 87) seems to somewhat agree with Ball when arguing that almost all novels demand a form of 'retrospective repatterning' as a reader advances through a text constructing and reconstructing hypotheses concerning a work's meanings, and yet 'nowhere does it occur with such formulaic regularity as in a detective story'. In fact, the concept that Porter refers to as 'retrospective patterning' seems to be similar to what Emmott (1999: 225) refers to as *frame repairing* in her study of narrative comprehension and *frame theory*. Emmott uses the term *frame repair* to refer to instances where a reader becomes aware that they have misread the text either through lack of attention or because the text itself is potentially ambiguous. Similarly, Porter's use of 'retrospective repatterning' seems to refer to this sort of repairing that readers engage in when the hypotheses they formed as to the work's meanings come to be challenged. And, Porter adds, it is that desire of the reader to know which of these hypotheses is the right one, that is stipulated by the author so that it functions as a 'structuring force'. Emmott's (1999) theory of narrative comprehension provides an analytical framework that would assist one's attempts to describe how this repatterning or repairing takes place. Indeed, Emmott does draw on detective fiction extracts herself to stress that this function does in fact appear with extreme formulaic regularity in this genre specifically.

Rather than a craft within a craft, others argue that detective fiction is a genre that is not only distinct from novelistic works but, even more so, is *anti-novelistic* or *anti-literary*;

> the aim of the narration is no longer the character's development into autonomy, or a change from the initial situation, or the presentation of plot as a conflict and an evolutionary spiral, image of a developing world that it is difficult to draw to a close.
>
> Moretti (1983: 137)

Moretti here seems to presuppose that there is such a thing as a universal aim of narration, which is to do with a change from some initial situation, presentation of plot as conflict, character development, and so on. I would tend to disagree with this point, as all sorts of narration cannot be said to share the same identical aims at a generalised level.

Moretti goes on to argue that, on the contrary to his so-called 'aim of narration', the objective of detective fiction is to *return to the beginning*, as the individual initiates the narration not because he lives – but because he *dies*. He goes on to add that detective fiction's ending is its end indeed: its solution in the true sense, and further states that, in the terms of the Russian Formalists, it is the criminal that produces the *sjužet* whereas the detective the *fabula* (Moretti, 1983: 146). Whereas the former term, attributed to the criminal, refers to the story as shaped and edited by the storyteller, the latter, attributed to the detective, refers to the story as a mere chronology of events. Since it is the detective who reinstates the relationship between the clues and their meaning, Moretti further argues that the criminal embodies the literary pole, and the detective the scientific.

On a similar note, Todorov (1977: 44–5) opposed the *story of the crime* to the *story of the investigation*: the first ends as the actual book begins; the second element is largely what we read. Between the beginning and the end of the narration – between the absence and the presence of the *fabula* – Moretti argues that there is no 'voyage', only a long *wait*, and therefore 'detective fiction declares narration a mere deviation'; since the fabula narrated by the detective in his reconstruction of the facts brings us back to the beginning, Moretti claims that 'it abolishes narration'. The validity of this point, however, would depend on what it is that he means by 'narration' and 'story', terms which he inadequately defines. Oates (1995: 38) seems to be arguing on the same line, when claiming that 'in this genre, more than in any other, anticipation is all, revelation, virtually nothing'. Similarly, Moretti (1983: 147) claims that 'detective fiction's scientific loftiness *needs* literary "deviation", even if it is only to destroy it: a solution without a mystery, a *fabula* without a *sjužet*, would be of no interest'. Moretti (1983: 149) further suggests that in detective fiction, reading is no longer an investment or intellectual effort: it is a waste, and 'giving into appearances'; it is only *distance* and *delay* with regard to the *revealed solution*. In other words, Moretti does not seem to regard lyrical description or any amount of problem solving as valuable or 'readerly'. According to his position, people only read for information, which seems to me a misguided argument to make. Not everybody reads for information, and hence the puzzle-solving element of detective stories need not be discarded as insignificant. Moretti argues that detective fiction is 'useless', but further adds that though reading one such novel 'doesn't help you in life', it does have meaning, one that is 'hidden', 'acts behind the reader's back', and 'has become uncontrollable' (Moretti, 1983: 155).

Overall, there has been a critical mass of commentary that relished the cultural inferiority of detective fiction, in that writers reported all sorts of bad things about it; for example, according to Roth (1995: 8–9), some (such as Jameson, 1970: 647) argued that it was 'formulaic', by which they meant mechanical, or it was 'conventional', by which they meant inert or dead. According to Roth, detective fiction was also said to be abjectly repetitive in that it consisted of the same few stories written over and over, therefore adhering to the same regularities, or somewhat constituting variations of the same pattern.

To use Porter's terms (1981: 245), one can argue that whereas much of the serious fiction of our time, often by means of a more or less explicit parody of the detective genre, has been committed to the task of 'defamiliarisation', the detective story has pursued the goal of 'perceptual re-familiarisation' (though, as will be pointed out in Chapter 5, many detective novels indeed *defamiliarise*). In other words, the crime novel, whether English or American, can be identified as an essentially conservative form. Eco made the following suggestion:

> We might compare a novel by Fleming to a game of football, in which we know beforehand the place, the number and the personalities of the players, the rules of the game, the fact that everything will take place within the area of the great pitch...[Actually,] it would be more accurate to compare these books to a game of basketball played by the Harlem Globe Trotters... We know with absolute confidence that they will win: the pleasure lies in watching the trained virtuosity with which the Globe Trotters defer the final moment, with what ingenious deviations they reconfirm the foregone conclusion, with what trickeries they make rings round their opponents.
>
> Eco (1966: 58)

The point that Eco seems to be making through these analogies is that the detective novel is a story we are more or less happy to reread, and yet the deviations, ingenious or otherwise that he refers to, are the conventions in variant forms. One, however, need keep in mind that it is this formulaic property of such popular literary types that actually constitutes them. As Porter (1981: 99) suggests, 'formulaic popular literature is so readable because the limited number of story types it contains is already familiar to the average reader'. Even more so, he argues that both detective novels and folk fairy tales confirm that the reading of fiction invariantly has something of the character of a rereading.

> The most readable novel is, in fact, not only one which derives from a familiar model but also one we have previously read. Consequently, it is no accident if, with the possible exception of children, readers of detective novels show a higher degree of loyalty

to certain authors than any other class of readers. Such fans return as often as possible to their Christies, their Simenons, or their Freelings, and they do so in order to encounter more of the same.

Porter (1981: 99)

And yet an important point to make at this juncture is the fact that this sort of 'loyalty' Porter assigns towards certain authors of popular literature is not necessarily limited to crime fiction. Readers of other literary (science and romance fiction) or even non-literary forms (cookery, self-help books and so on) can be said to also share this sort of loyalty to preferred authors.

In any case, Porter goes on to argue that if reading detective novels is always a rereading,

> it is a rereading in which a limited number of structural constants are combined with an indefinite number of decorative variables in order to make the familiar view. As in the equally formulaic minor genre of joke telling, the audience's pleasure depends both on being familiar with the structure of the whole and on not knowing the specific outcome. The final solution of a crime, like a punch line of a joke, is recognized as the predictable formal term whose actual content is appreciated most when it comes as a surprise.

Porter (1981: 99)

Porter here draws on yet another analogy, that of crime fiction and jokes. He claims that both genres work under the constraint that there is a certain formula to be followed, one which need consist of a set of structural constants, in combination with a so-called 'indefinite number of decorative variables'. Not only does Porter, however, fail to define the nature of these decorative variables, but he seems to imply that these are as simplistic as those encountered in the minor genre of joke-telling. In any case indeed, it appears that both genres feature surprise at the very end, one that is definitive of the genres, a so-called 'predictable formal term', and yet the nature of which we are not to have access to until the very end of the story.

What sort of an attraction does crime literature hold for its readers?

As Messent (2000: 124) puts it, one needs to keep in mind that any answer to the question of '*How do we explain the attraction crime litera-*

ture holds for its readers?' is going to be speculative and tentative, given the problems in identifying the different 'readerly' communities, as well as the different social and historical circumstances in which such texts have been produced and received. For this reason, the content of the whole of this section needs to be seen as exploratory and provisional, as not all crime literature is consumed by the same reader, or within some constant historical and social situation.

One needs, for instance, to take into account the different 'readerly' communities that especially the early 1920s novels have been exposed to. The effect that the earliest detective novels had on their early readers is quite different from the effect on the readers in the course of the intervening time. In other words, since the historical and social contexts within which these texts were primarily displayed have changed immensely, so also have their effects, one may argue, upon their audience. Now I will turn to consider crime fiction as 'pleasure' and as 'an addiction'.

Crime fiction reading as pleasure

As Messent (2000: 124) puts it, 'pleasure and desire offer a helpful prompt for thinking about contemporary crime fiction and exploring the nature of its appeal'. In a way, by investigating the sort of pleasure that comes with this form of entertainment, one will be able to appreciate how readers interact with such novels, how they understand and are moved by them.

Many, such as Porter (1981), Mandel (1984) and Ball (1976), have asserted that novels such as detective stories constitute a literature of 'escape and relaxation'. According to Porter (1981: 3), 'escape' is taken, of course, to suggest 'a flight from something frightening', and 'relaxation' 'an unwinding after a protracted period of unpleasurable effort or work'. However, since he suggests that people do not escape into literature under compulsion, out of an urge for self-improvement, or with the hope of acquiring useful information (all reasons why people undertake certain kinds of reading), one needs to consider how a popular literary genre caters to reader pleasure.

In order to identify the reasons why many people are attracted to detective novel reading, one needs to take a closer look at the properties that the genre exhibits. The various narrative devices of many detective novels that Porter examined have the primary function of preventing premature disclosure in the interest of suspense, and therefore he suggests that there is a need for a direct link between the pleasure derived from a book and the suspense it produces. According to

Porter (1981: 50), '[o]nly a story that embodies an appropriate quantity of resistance in its telling is experienced as satisfactory; the longest kept secrets are the ones we most desire to know'. Porter, however, fails to give any explanation as to what he means when referring to a 'satisfactory' story, or what it takes for a reader's desire to be gratified.

He further argues that what emerges most clearly from an analysis of detective fiction is that the art of such narratives is one of *withholding* as well as of *giving* information and, in this connection, reading narrative fiction can be seen to involve a form of participation that is rather different from that of looking at a painting or listening to music.

When referring specifically to the genre of detective fiction, moreover, Porter (1981: 219) suggests that 'it may be regarded as a pleasure machine in part because of the predictability with which it engages our fear and then goes on to exorcise it with such finality'. Knight (1980: 115) seems to be also fascinated by the idea of readers taking pleasure out of being in fear and then released, when arguing that the Freudian reading of crime fiction shows killing to be the authentic wish and fear of the reader; 'The threat of sudden death is euphemised like that of guilt, and the protected reader can contemplate the fear of receiving or of causing such a crucial disturbance to individual life.' In other words, what Knight seems to suggest is that detective fiction is read as much for the uncertainties provoked by the unknown (or the still-to-be-revealed) as for the security given by the conclusion.

This idea is further supported by Steward (1997) when arguing that crime writing engages quite opposite emotions, feeding on a popular *fear* of crime as a threat to the reader's own security; the desire for transgressive excitement and the need for safety are therefore ambivalently weighed against each other. Besides, as Ball suggested (1976: 206), the writer's role is to lead the reader through a mythos of life and death, violence and redemption, and yet without putting the reader through hurt or distress.

Porter (1981: 102), moreover, is careful to point out that the idea of what he refers to as 'a given level of tolerance to fear' suggests that 'the reason why fans of detective fiction return again and again to a favourite author is that they are certain to find in his works the dosage of fear they know they can enjoy'. He further adds that pleasure is based on the experience of contrast, constructing his argument on the understanding that pleasure is not pleasure without the prior experience of pain. Overall however, all these claims, based on the Freudian reading of the genre, again, have no scientific evidence, not to mention any analytical framework underpinning them (see

Chapter 4 for another explanation as to readers' fascination with crime and violence).

Crime fiction reading as an addiction

As Auden once argued, the reading of detective stories is very much like one's addiction to tobacco or alcohol.

> The symptoms of this are: firstly, the intensity of the craving – if I have any work to do, I must be careful not to get hold of a detective story for once I begin one, I cannot work or sleep till I have finished it. Secondly, its specificity – the story must conform to certain formulas [...] And, thirdly, its immediacy, I forget the story as soon as I have finished it, and have no wish to read it again. If, as sometimes happens, I start reading one and find after a few pages that I have read it before, I cannot go on.
>
> Auden (1974: 400)

According to Roth (1995: 17), to take Auden at his word would account for many of the features of such reading, including 'the compulsion to read, the demand for similarity, the disappointment and, afterward, shame'. The claims both Roth and Auden put forward somewhat function to justify the basis for this 'crime fiction is a drug' metaphor. On the same note, Stern also metaphorically notes that the readers 'take their daily dose of murder with the frenzied enthusiasm of a drug addict' (1974: 531–2), while Blake (1946: 398) answered his own question of, 'Why do we read detective stories?' – '[b]ecause the drug addict (and nearly every detection writer is an omnivorous reader of crime fiction) always wants to introduce other people to the habit.'

Many arguments can be offered to counter the 'crime fiction is a drug' metaphor, one of which is the fact that such fiction is not the only popular genre that has featured the sort of 'addictiveness' described here. Readers of romance (see Radway, 1987: 87) or science fiction stories, like crime fiction, can also be said to experience similar 'cravings' such as 'the compulsion to read' and 'the demand for similarity'. Needless to say, another argument against the metaphor is that no addictive or potentially hazardous chemical drug is involved in the reading of a crime novel. Unlike common drugs, crime reading does not restrict human freedom in a destructive way. Mandel (1984: 70–1) seems to have made a better use of the same metaphor when claiming that crime fiction is a 'psychological drug' that simply 'distracts from the intolerable drudgery of daily life'.

Rankin offers an even better explanation for the attraction that the genre holds for its readers. He suggests that crime writing simply has the power to seduce, giving the reader a 'vicarious thrill'. Rankin (2000: 7) suggests that the detective story simply makes it possible to experience without danger all the passion, excitement and desirousness which must be suppressed in a humanitarian ordering of society. Crime writing, in other words, rather than an addiction, or a form of writing that is supposedly read aggressively or shamelessly, is something readers go to out of interest as to *the darker side of human nature* (see Chapter 4, on the carnival of crime fiction).

In any case, and as Roth (1995: 1) suggests, the special pleasure generated by crime writing, whether addictive or not, has produced a substantial literature of apologetics, available for reading alongside detective fiction itself.

Crime fiction and the notion of realism

The genre as a mirror to society

According to Bönnemark (1997: 164), as detective stories are supposed to present facts in such a way so that the reader him/herself can reach the correct solution, the story need be rendered in a manner that makes it *seem* factual and reliable. It is, therefore necessary for such texts to be *realistic*, meaning that they need purport to 'the illusion of life', or claim to be real. As Furst (1992: 4) argues, the concept of *realism* is both complex and sophisticated, and recently, 'the call for life was amended to the prescript of verisimilitude, plausibility, life-likeness'. *Verisimilitude* is a term that plays down the notion of actual truth. Contrary to realism as illusionism, verisimilitude adds an 'air of reality', an 'impression of life' (science fiction, for instance, is verisimilar, but it does not pretend to be realistic). *Naturalism* is, on the other hand, where texts try to get as close to the truth as possible, for instance, by incorporating normal non-fluency in characters' speech. Finally, *plausibility* refers to that 'reasonable' property of texts. Whether true or not, a plausible text *could* be so.

Haut (1999: 2) suggested that contemporary crime writers 'created a genre whose predominant artifice is its apparent lack of artifice; consequently, the line separating fiction and reality has become increasingly blurred'. Readers have, therefore, been given a vivid conviction of fact, 'the sort of conviction that used to lead people to address letters to Sherlock Holmes Esq., 221 Baker Street, begging him to investigate their problems' (Sayers, 1947b: 10). What, however, these claims fail to indicate is that, however close crime fiction brings us to authentic crime cases, it is only the psychologically imbalanced that would go to the extent of mistaking crime literature for 'the real thing'. That is, all readers would, in their good minds, recognise the existence of the line separating fiction and reality, no matter how increasingly blurred this line is claimed to have become.

Bönnemark (1997: 74) suggests that detective fiction often aims at creating an *illusion* of reality, and this illusion is accepted as such by readers. The fact that the influence of real crime and real investigations on detective fiction is slight can be seen as evidence of this: 'Most detective stories give a **verisimilar** picture of detective work, police procedurals usually more so than other detective stories, although even they show romanticised versions of routine investigations' (Bönnemark, 1997: 74). Bönnemark seems to take for granted that there is indeed a slight influence of real crime and real investigations on detective fiction, without however giving any evidence to support her claim. She further argues that police procedurals are a lot closer to routine investigations than detective stories, and yet their reflection of reality is still flawed. Similarly, Oates (1995: 34) points out that it is only police detective mysteries that would qualify as 'realistic' variants of the genre 'for private detectives are rarely involved in authentic crime cases, and would have no access, in contemporary times, to the findings of forensic experts'. In other words, Oates also claims that authentic crime situations are only realistically portrayed in police procedurals, though what she fails to mention is that even within this so-called 'realistic' genre variant, authentic routine investigations can be misrepresented.

Haycraft (1972: 228–9) has also argued that real crimes and detection have sometimes been used as an inspiration for detective stories, but further noted that characters, style, dialogue, and setting have been transformed so as to fit the fictional format. That is, even though the sense of reality appears to be one that is essential to the detective novel, certain adjustments to how the real event was like, or might have been like, need be made since the detective genre has a certain format it needs to fit into.

Furthermore, Haut (1999: 2–3) argues that in the mid-late 1970s, such novels obsessed with *verisimilitude* could be said to have required one to reappraise the genre's relationship to the culture. In other words, having claimed that 'to examine a culture one need only examine its crimes', Haut suggests that, as a popular and often lucrative genre, contemporary crime fiction has come to address the social contradictions and conditions of a decaying society. It is along the same lines that crime fiction, as Reginald Hill believes (cited in Cooper, 2000: 9), can be said to hold a mirror to society, while leaving it for the reader to work out whether the spots, fractures and distortions it shows are in the society or the mirror.

Finally, what needs to be mentioned is the depiction of the Law in detective stories. The existence of this genre, perhaps more than any other, depends on the knowledge that everything will be 'made right in the end', and this necessity for narrative closure is identified with the existence of the Law. Such narratives adopt an ideological division between the legal and the illegal that at close inspection appears to be paradoxical. The law – being an issue directly in the investigation any detective undertakes – is never put on trial, even when the form itself reveals corruption not only among leading citizens and public officials, but in the face of the detective him/herself. And that is the case since no matter how many individual crimes are solved, in the larger social scheme of things nothing changes, and corruption indeed prevails.

Challenging the masculinity, whiteness and straightness of the genre

According to Messent (1997: 1), hard-boiled detective fiction in America has been filtered through a white, heterosexual, and male perspective. It is along the same lines that Roth (1995: xiv, 113) claims that 'in detective fiction gender is genre and genre is male' with women only figuring to 'flesh out male desire and shadow male sexual fear'. In other words, hard-boiled detective fiction has been characterised as a genre whose most distinctive narrative codes, conventions and characterisations have traditionally been structured around a white male heterosexual subject's consciousness. It has, that is, been accused of being a strictly 'masculine genre' (Nickerson, 1997: 750–1), one might argue, of the white heterosexual type. It is on the same ground that Oates (1995: 34) argues in favour of the idea that the mystery-detective novel is for men what the romance is for women.

However, since the detective genre is symptomatic of the experience of modernity, several subgenres featuring female, ethnically diverse and homosexual detectives, and, in quite a few cases, ones featuring two or all three of these have developed. In a way, such novels featuring anything other than white, male, heterosexual detectives could be described as parodies since, by adopting the formula but changing this one significant element, authors can be said to undercut their protagonists so as to reinforce a social standard of female, gay or racial inequality.

With regards to the surveying of feminist crime fiction in particular, Munt has argued that a differentiation must be made between two types:

(a) those models which are consciously satiric, employing a heroine who undermines her own transcendence (diverse writers include Barbara Wilson, Sarah Dreher, Mary Wings, Sara Schulman, and Gillian Sloro), and (b) those novels which operate primarily within the romance mode, such as in the sub-genre of lesbian pulp, which deploy a mystery element primarily to frustrate the love interest (writers include Vicky P. McDonnell, Claire McNab, Zenobia N. Vole, Marion Foster).

Munt (1994: 196)

Munt goes on to argue that there is some overlap, but, in principle, within the romance framework everyone is promised happiness ever after, and within the satire nothing really seems to change. Munt (1994: 207), finally, points out that, despite its apparent 'unsuitability for women, crime fiction clearly can manifest feminine novelistic forms and feminist political agendas'. Bertens and D'haen (2001: 12) further add that in the context of the second Golden Age of crime writing that we are currently witnessing, 'female crime writing stands out because of its power, its breadth, its innovation, and even its irreverence, no matter if that irreverence at times takes the form of a somewhat childish mischievousness'. Whatever the case may be, the detective novel has come to be a generic house with many different rooms (Messent, 1997: 18). Besides, as Pepper suggests (2000: 167), crime novelists have come to exploit the form's formulaic regularities and, more specifically, the crucial question of character, so as to problematise their audience and have them simply question why it is that 'good' detectives have, up to recent decades, all been white, male and straight.

From private eye novel to police procedural

To another extent, the crime novel has developed from *private eye novel* to the genre that has come to be referred to as the *police procedural*. In the former, the private eye detective has to break or bend the law himself in order to reassert a world of equality and justice, such a reassertion often being incidental and temporary. However, the latter so-called *police procedural* genre, Priestman (1998: 29–30) argues, is one that 'usually expresses almost as much interest in the way a team of professionals, with various problems of their own, work together as in the solutions of crime'. Not only does Priestman claim that the crimes presented in procedurals tend to be multiple rather than single – for the investigators, several major investigations are on the go concurrently –, but also the adopted 'win some, lose some' formula this enables does in fact allow a welcome new level of realism into the genre (Priestman, 1998: 30). In other words, since police procedurals feature cases that are not always solved, they maintain a better illusion (*realism*) or impression (*verisimilitude*) of reality than private eye novels. In addition, Taylor suggests that the police procedural seems to be supplanting the private eye novel as 'realistic' crime fiction:

> While the latter relies on a model of rule-bending individualism, the former puts its extra emphasis precisely on procedure and *collective* agency. A fantasy of extra-systemic freedom and authenticity gives way to a more problematic vision of individual detectives operating through systemic procedures.
>
> Taylor (1997: 27–8)

Taylor suggests that it is the police procedural's emphasis on collective agency that constitutes the genre as more realistic than the old-fashioned private eye detective novel, which was originally based on individuals breaking the rules of the system and failing to follow police procedure. Also, as Bertens and D'haen (2001: 3) add, 'in much 1990s crime fiction the protagonist, if male, no longer is a professional private investigator, but rather someone who drifts into "detecting" almost by accident and often against the grain'; such investigators only start out in the detecting business once they have fallen on hard times.

Pepper (2000: 169) suggests, however, that tensions are produced by the uneasy conflation of individual agency and institutional authority, and there are clear crossovers between the two generic variants. For instance, as Taylor (1997: 12) argues, 'the police procedural, *despite* the bureaucratic machinery it engages, is not necessarily any more sceptical about individual agency and the power of the I/eye of the detective'.

According to Taylor (1997: 27–8), another difference that the police procedural has when compared with the private eye novel is that, rather than unearthing the truth (that is, revealing the secret of a crime and bringing the criminal under the law), cops get involved in hypothetical story-telling and tentative interpretation so as to prevent subsequent crimes: '[C]ops piece together stories that are in process and driven by continuously shifting imperatives, in the hope that their story is accurate enough to allow a prediction of what the next – and maybe crucial – narrative move will be.'

Finally, there comes the issue of *serial killing*, another feature that, though typical of the police procedural, is certainly not a defining aspect of the private eye novel. As Bertens and D'haen (2001: 8) point out, this late 1980s and 1990s fascination with serial killers was undoubtedly sparked off by a number of notorious real-life instances. According to Haut (1999: 206), the most extreme crime – multiple murder – is now thought of as an increasingly fashionable form of social art; '[c]ompeting against reality, crime fiction, while reflecting the era, has come to seek ever-greater horrors and facsimiles'.

To another extent, Swales argues that seriality has come to be *inseparable* from the excitement of the detective story:

> At the simplest level, it imparts the urgency of the chase: the murderer has to be caught before he can kill again. Hence the retrospective force of the analysis of past events acquires an urgent, forward-directed thrust. At more complex levels, seriality engenders a sense of pattern while withholding the explanation of that pattern. What seems random to the quotidian mind probably has coherence for the pathological mind.
>
> Swales (2000: xiii)

What Swales is saying is that seriality has become fashionable not only because it brings an urgency to the chasing of the murderer at hand, but also in that it brings out the issue of there being a pattern, one whose justification remains withheld up until the story's end.

From there on, Swales (2000: xiii) argues, '[f]amiliar motivations for murder – greed, ambition and jealousy – no longer prove adequate to account for the incalculable repetitive form', hence '[r]eason is, in every sense brought to its limits – and to its knees – by the force of unregenerate, frequently sexual, obsession'. In other words, Swales claims that the sexual charge that seems to lie behind much recent detective story writing has come to make it no longer possible for the detectives to rely on traditional motivations for murder leading them to the murderers. The investigators come to deal with criminal minds with no reason, ones who are psychologically imbalanced and sexually obsessed, and therefore ones who are more difficult to trace than the old-fashioned criminals of the genre.

Nevertheless, there are a number of contemporary private eye series in the crime fiction market, such as Robert Crais's Elvis Cole series (2001). In the series, Elvis Cole, a good old-fashioned private eye, is hired to find missing people (such as husbands, ex-wives and children), and goods (such as a stolen valuable thirteenth-century Japanese manuscript), only to stumble across dirty family secrets, the Mob, and dirty cash, not to mention a world of drugs, sex and murder. Cole regularly beats his opponents into submission (he keeps in form by practising hatha yoga, tai chi, and tae kwon do), regularly leaves dead bodies in his wake, and is saved at least once in each of the novels in the series by his reliably loyal partner Joe Pike, an ex-marine and ex-LAPD officer who owns a gun shop in Culver City.

Not only, however, do series of this kind fail to preoccupy themselves with murder cases (murder is, in any case, a matter for the police and medical examiners, and not private eye detectives), but they feature a number of humorous situations and a strong element of sarcasm, making them appear to be forms of parody (as previously defined, parodies are kinds of amusing imitations which borrow the style and technique of a text, in this case, old-fashioned private eye novels). Bertens and D'haen (2001: 4) also agree that though Crais's private investigator comes across as absolutely credible and simultaneously conveys a reasonably optimistic message, Crais in fact succeeds in ironising his classic hard-boiled predecessors.

Character in detective fiction

In detective fiction, there is a specific set of roles that a character would have to fit into, and this set, according to Cawelti (1976), includes that of the perpetrator, that of the victim, that of the detective and that of the bystander. According to Bönnemark (1997: 79), though one character for each one of these roles would be adequate in defining the crime fiction genre as such, there quite usually are several detectives, victims, as well as perpetrators. As various people, such as Wright (1946: 40), have claimed, the victim is usually the least important role in a detective story, the perpetrator has a more prominent place, but the main protagonist is the detective. As my subsequent analysis will, however, point out, this hierarchy has come to be challenged with the genre's evolution.

The detective as the criminal's double

To begin with, the detectives most often appear to sacrifice their individuality and personal life to their work, and they do so in their attempts to 'understand' the criminals; by thinking in a similar mode as the latter, the former believe that they can predict their next moves. It is on this basis that ffrench (2000: 227) argues that there is a parallel between *psychoanalysis* and the detective novel:

> Psychoanalysis seems to have become a hidden or acknowledged subtext for the detective, who is now not so much in search of the truth of the crime he or she is investigating, as in search of the truth or trauma of a past, often his or her own past.
>
> ffrench (2000: 225)

Therefore, ffrench continues, the detective, like the analyst, must engage in transference with the criminal or the patient, must identify with the criminal in order to trace the path back to the original trauma, and hence 'the criminal becomes the double of the detective'.

To this extent, the detectives are seen as somewhat taking up the role of *artists* in that, like poets, they surrender themselves wholly to the work to be done (see Moretti, 1983: 142–3), whatever the sacrifice may be. It might be for this reason that the detective figures are often presented to exude a kind of tragic aura; they appear to suffer via this association they share with those who are criminal minded. As Swales (2000: xv) argues, 'it is perhaps not too fanciful to claim that the detective may be the last tragic protagonist still available to our culture'; the hero or heroine of tragedy, now in the face of the detective, not only suffers, but 'that suffering produces knowledge, perhaps even insight'. Swales, finally, goes on to suggest that '[i]n the person of the detective, the insight coexists with a will to action; the detective understands the puzzle and is instrumental in bringing the perpetrators to justice'.

Overall, this notion of equating the detective with the criminal is by now commonplace:

> In fact, the literary figure of the detective typically was and continues to be an extraordinary, marginal figure who frequently bears a closer resemblance to the criminal he pursues than to the police officers with whom he supposedly collaborates.
>
> Black (1991: 43)

That is, the detective comes to understand the criminal to such an extent, that not only does he become his double so that he is enabled to predict his next move, but also ends up resembling him in character even more than he resembles his own fellow officers.

Writers focusing on the murderer

In Symon's (1994) study of detective fiction *Bloody Murder*, he argued that what detective fiction lacks as literature is *character*. In effect, and as Roth (1995: 4) suggested, since only two characters are central to the plot of the genre, the remedy is rather simple: since the detective failed to pay off in literary currency, writers had to invest in the murderer: 'Refocus the form on the criminal, and the potential for growth would be as various as in the novel itself'. 'The groundwork', Roth claims, 'was already there because every work of detective fiction contained, however implicitly, the story of a murderer and his or her crime; a story of psychological depth and intensity lay buried in the form'.

Roth (1995: 4) goes on to suggest that the real crime in detective fiction was in fact the narrative suppression of the criminal who, as O' Faolain (1935: 243) put it, is the only true principal, the 'one *free* agent, the one person not circumscribed by the necessity of having to catch someone'.

One way in which this was accomplished was by giving the criminal a voice of his/her own, and somewhat allowing readers access to his/her consciousness. This, in effect, gave rise to the notion of the glamorous or sympathetic criminal in twentieth-century fiction, a figure that, according to Priestman (1998: 39), forcefully emerged as a primary object of reader identification. What Priestman suggests is that novels focusing on the murderer in this manner intend to shock the reader into accepting that there are people for whom cruelty, in both its physical and psychological sense, is a normal way of life. A further issue that arises here, as well as in occasions where criminals remain unpunished by getting away with their crimes, is whether indeed readers care about the human cost of murder, or simply enjoy the vicarious thrill of identifying with the police. In other words, the technique employed in criminal-centred contemporary crime novels brings out a range of social judgements issues.

Finally, this focusing on the murderer gave rise to a distinction between those crimes placed in the world of social cause and effect, and those consigned to the category of *pure evil*. It is, however, the latter type of criminal violence that readers find to be of most interest: that which is *monstrous*, dependent on the purely personal motivation and disturbed psychological condition of the single criminal figure (see Chapter 3; on the linguistic construction of mind style, and the 'Stylistics of Justification' continuum). In detective fiction, disequilibrium and disruption figure literally as physical violence which, as Neale (1981: 7) argues, 'marks the process of the elements disrupted and [...]

constitutes the means by which order is finally (re)established'. And it is the monstrous criminal figure, and the disorder it initiates and concretises, that often disrupts the social order of things by initiating 'a series of acts of murder and destruction which can only end when it itself is either destroyed or becomes normalised' (Neale, 1981: 8).

The future of crime fiction

Haut (1999: 225) suggested that the future of crime fiction will depend on its ability to plunder other genres, and its willingness to feed off various cinematic devices. He goes on to argue that the future of such fiction is also dependent on the perpetuation of crime – 'the aesthetics of the genre are such that without the need to commit crimes, there would be no need for cultural investigation'. Hence he suggests that fortunately for the genre and its development, one cannot, at this point, foresee a society free of crime, nor one in which hierarchy has become irrelevant.

Indicative of changing times, contemporary crime fiction features a new type of crime, a corporate and anonymous one, which would in turn affect the style and content of future *noir* fiction. Despite this, Haut (1999: 225) claims that, addressing themselves to crime committed in the pursuit of revenge, power and wealth, crime writers 'won't forsake the genre's time-honoured strictures and tendency to leave traces of its history'. Similarly, Haut adds, the genre cannot help but critique the culture since that, after all, is its function: So long as crime and corruption exist, the genre will remain an integral part of the cultural narrative.

The rest of my book directly explores the three types of deviation the genre exploits; Chapter 3 considers linguistic deviation (in constructing the mind style of criminals, in particular), Chapter 4 the social deviation (in defining the nature of criminal behaviour), and Chapter 5 the generic deviation (in challenging the boundaries of the crime fiction genre).

3
Linguistic Deviance: The Stylistics of Criminal Justification

Introduction

This chapter consists of two studies that explore the stylistic forms involved in the production of contemporary crime novels and it aims to contribute to both the discipline of literary criticism and that of cognitive stylistics.

The first study focuses on the portrayal of the criminal mind as figured in contemporary works by James Patterson, Michael Connelly, and Patricia Cornwell, and directly addresses the issue of how this mind comes to be morally situated (for an earlier version, see Gregoriou, 2003a). These three have been chosen not only because they are best-selling authors, but also to illustrate three different criminal types. Extracts are taken from Patterson's *Cat And Mouse* (1997), Connelly's *The Poet* (1996), and Cornwell's *Southern Cross* (1998). Whereas Patterson's portrayed criminal is a serial killer, Connelly's is a paedophile and Cornwell's a thief.

In addition, whereas the first two excerpts allow access to the criminal's consciousness respectively in the form of third-person internal and first-person narration, the third excerpt is in the form of a third-person external narration, and hence the selection would cover various forms of the criminal portrayal in the field. Though the excerpt from the Cornwell novel is not one from her best-known series (featuring Chief Medical Examiner Kay Scarpetta) and is not an excerpt from the criminal's viewpoint, it does however implicitly deal with the matter at hand: the issue of how the criminal's actions are evaluated and justified. Altogether, the selection will allow me to contrast the different criminals in an attempt to provide answers to the question, 'Are contemporary crime fiction criminals presented as having been *born evil* or are their actions justified, for instance by means of their childhood traumatic experiences?'

The second study is a more specific investigation into the criminal mind as portrayed in two contemporary works by James Patterson, *Along Came a Spider* (1993) and *Cat and Mouse* (1997), both of which are part of the author's celebrated series featuring detective/psychologist Alex Cross (also explored in Gregoriou, 2002b). The criminal under analysis is Gary Soneji, a psychopathic serial killer who figures in both novels. *Cat and Mouse* (1997) further features Mr Smith, an equally dangerous madman terrorising Europe, and his criminal mind is also portrayed through extracts that allow access to his viewpoint, and which will also be analysed. The extracts portraying the two criminals' viewpoints are analysed linguistically, in an attempt to establish the way in which their actions are morally, socially and stylistically situated.

The stylistics of justification in contemporary crime fiction

As mentioned in Chapter 2, contemporary crime writers have come to refocus the genre on the criminal, and one way in which this was accomplished was by giving the criminal a voice of his/her own and allowing readers access to his/her consciousness. It is this focus on the criminal that gives rise to the distinction between those crimes placed in the world of social 'cause and effect' and those consigned to the category of *pure evil*.

Contextualising the crime fiction extracts

One of the criminals under analysis in this chapter is Gary Soneji, a psychopathic serial killer who recurrently figures in a James Patterson series featuring detective/psychologist Alex Cross. Cross makes his fourth appearance in Patterson's *Cat and Mouse* (1997), which also marks the return of the villain Soneji from *Along Came a Spider* (1993). Soneji goes on a murder spree at train stations in Washington and New York, but his ultimate goal is killing Alex Cross. In the extract under analysis, Gary Soneji's evil mind appears to be as twisted as ever, as he somehow gains access to the detective's cellar to go through his family's personal belongings and 'fuel his hatred.' The killer is back to wreak vengeance on the detective and his family while the latter is on the trail of an equally dangerous madman terrorising Europe, Mr Smith.

> He was inside the Cross house!
> *He was in the cellar: The cellar was a clue for those who collected them. The cellar was worth a thousand words. A thousand forensic pictures, too.*

It was important to everything that would happen in the very near future. The Cross murders.

There were no large windows, but Soneji decided not to take any chances by turning on the lights. He used a Maglite flashlight. Just to look around, to learn a few more things about Cross and his family, to fuel his hatred, if that was possible.

The cellar was cleanly swept, as he had expected it would be. Cross's tools were haphazardly arranged on a pegged Masonite board. A stained Georgetown ballcap was hung on a hook. Soneji put it on his own head. He couldn't resist.

He ran his hands over folded laundry laid out on a long wooden table. He felt close to the doomed family now. He despised them more than ever. He felt around the hammocks of the old woman's bra. He touched the boy's small Jockey underwear. He felt like a total creep, and he loved it.

Soneji picked up a small red reindeer sweater. It would fit Cross's little girl, Jannie. He held it to his face and tried to smell the girl. He anticipated Jannie's murder and only wished that Cross would get to see it, too.

He saw a pair of Everlast gloves and black Pony shoes tied around a hook next to a weathered old punching bag. They belonged to Cross's son, Damon, who must be nine years old now. Gary Soneji thought he would punch out the boy's heart.

Finally, he turned off the flashlight and sat alone in the dark. Once upon a time, he had been a famous kidnapper and murderer. It was going to happen again. He was coming back with a vengeance that would blow everybody's mind.

He folded his hands in his lap and sighed. He had spun his web perfectly.

Alex Cross would soon be dead, and so would everyone he loved.

Patterson (1997: 4)

The second criminal under analysis is the Eidolon, featuring in Michael Connelly's *The Poet* (1996), the author's first non-series book that broke into the bestseller lists. Though the novel is a pulse-pounding mystery about a serial killer, Gladden, it is the Eidolon and his criminal role as a paedophile that is the focus of the extract's analysis. In *The Poet*, an embittered journalist investigating the death of his police officer brother is stalked by a twisted aficionado of internet child porn and betrayed at every turn by the officials he thought would help him. It is the Eidolon's paedophilia that is portrayed in the extract, which is a script Gladden comes across at a website from and for paedophiles.

> Gladden looked at the words on the screen. They were beautiful, as if written by the unseen hand of God. So right. So knowledgeable. He read them again.
>
> They know about me now and I am ready. I await them. I am prepared to take my place in the pantheon of faces. I feel as I did as a child when I waited for the closet door to be opened so that I could receive him. The line of light at the bottom. My beacon. I watched the light and the shadows each of his footfalls made. Then I knew he was there and that I would have his love. The apple of his eye.
>
> We are what they make us and yet they turn from us. We are cast off. We become nomads in the world of the moan. My rejection is my pain and motivation. I carry with me the vengeance of all the children. I am the Eidolon. I am called the predator, the one to watch for in your midst. I am the cucoloris, the blur of light and dark. My story is not one of deprivation and abuse. I welcomed the touch. I can admit it. Can you? I wanted, craved, welcomed the touch. It was only the rejection – when my bones grew too large – that cut me so deeply and forced on me the life of a wanderer. I am the cast off. And the children must stay forever young.
>
> Connelly (1996: 299)

The third and final criminal I investigate is Smoke, featured in Patricia Cornwell's *Southern Cross* (1998). This teenager is the head of a gang referred to as The Pikes, who seem to be responsible for a series of robberies taking place in Virginia. The fast-moving adventure follows the work of the police department in its attempts to eradicate the teenage gangs and prevent the robberies from cash dispensers. Multiple points of view add change of pace to the narrative, in the course of which southern personalities make up the fabric of the interwoven storylines. The extract under analysis is the narrative's first reference to Smoke and is the only extract out of the three analysed that is not taken from the criminal's viewpoint.

> Smoke was a special needs child. This had become apparent in second grade when he had stolen his teacher's wallet, punched a female classmate, carried a revolver to school, set several cats on fire and smashed up the principal's station wagon with a pipe.

Since those early misguided days in his hometown of Durham, North Carolina, Smoke had been written up fifty-two times for assault, cheating, plagiarism, extortion, harassment, gambling, truancy, dishonesty, larceny, disruptive dress, indecent literature and bus misconduct.

He had been arrested six times for crimes ranging from sexual assault to murder, and had been on probation, on supervised probation with special conditions, in an Alternative to Detention Program, in detention, in a wilderness camp therapeutic program, in a community guidance clinic where he received psychological evaluation and in an anger-coping group.

Unlike most juveniles who are delinquent, Smoke had parents who showed up for all of his court appearances. They visited him in detention. They paid for attorneys and dismissed one right after another when Smoke complained and found fault. Smoke's parents enrolled him in four different private schools and blamed each one when it didn't work out.

It was clear to Smoke's father, a hardworking banker, that his son was unusually bright and misunderstood. Smoke's mother was devoted to Smoke and always took his side. She never believed he was guilty. Both parents believed their son had been set up because the police were corrupt, didn't like Smoke and wanted to clear cases. Both parents wrote scathing letters to the district attorney, the mayor, the attorney general, the governor and a U.S. senator when Smoke was finally locked up in C.A. Dillon Training School in Butner.

Of course, Smoke didn't stay there long because when he turned sixteen, he was no longer a minor according to North Carolina law and was released. His juvenile record was expunged. His fingertips and mug shots were destroyed. He had no past. His parents thought it wise to relocate to a city where the police, whose memories were not expunged, would not know Smoke or harass him any more. So it was that Smoke moved to Richmond, Virginia, where this morning he was feeling especially in a good mood to cause trouble.

Cornwell (1998: 17)

It is not until later in the chapter that readers are allowed access to the criminal's consciousness as he cruises the streets of the city looking for other teenagers to recruit into his gang. It is for this reason that this extract is only to be analysed in terms of the type of narration chosen and the scale of interference that narration allows. Since we do not get access to this character's consciousness, we cannot analyse his individual mind style.

Stylistic analysis of the extracts

Type of narration

To begin with, the narration portraying Soneji's consciousness seems to be of the 'internal' type, meaning that it is mediated through the subjective viewpoint of this particular character's consciousness (Simpson, 1993: 39). In other words, the narrator is presented here as *omniscient*, controlling the narration of events and displaying 'privileged access to the thoughts and feelings of the characters in a way that an ordinary external observer [would] not' (Fowler, 1986: 127).

Furthermore, this type of narration is one that produces a personal relationship with the reader as well as sympathy, both of which inevitably bias the reader in favour of the character. Despite this effect, the fact that what is represented is a criminal slipping in and out of fantasies of murdering little children will presumably produce some sort of tension for readers. On one hand, the omniscient narration has readers sympathising with the character, and yet on the other we might feel that we should not do so, on account of the content of the thoughts and fantasies Soneji is engaging in. In effect, we get a strong impression that this animal-like criminal has no remorse for the crimes he has committed, and since the only justification he gives for his actions is that of getting vengeance over the detective, we are invited to believe that he was *born evil*.

The type of narration employed in the Eidolon's written message is rather different. Though the narration is still that of the *internal* type, allowing readers access to the paedophile's consciousness, it nevertheless is homodiegetic, as presented in the first-person. Such a narration is instead *expected* to be *limited* (the characters don't know all the facts) as opposed to omniscient (Short, 1996: 257), as well as being flawed and opinionated. Here, the narrator describes a character's (Gladden's) reading/response to a text written by another character (the Eidolon), in the first person. In effect, the analysed passage above is a quotation. The voice the Eidolon adopts is additionally rather biblical in that it draws on language to be found in religious material ('beacon', 'pantheon', 'Eidolon') with even Gladden marking it as such: 'as if written by the unseen hand of God'.

This piece nevertheless can also be argued to produce tension amongst readers, mostly due to the fact that the text is written for other paedophiles to read, and uses the second person: 'My story is not one of deprivation and abuse. I welcomed the touch. I can admit it. Can you?' This level of personal involvement with paedophilia is likely to make most readers uncomfortable in that it presupposes not only that the readers are paedophiles themselves, but also that they are unable to admit to the fact that they enjoyed the abuse, here referred to as 'love': 'Then I knew he was there and that I would have his love'. Further tension is created by the use of the inclusive 'we' and 'us' in 'We are what they make us and yet they turn from us. We are cast off. We become nomads in the world of the moan'. Here, it also seems to be the case that 'we' and 'they' are used to refer to the same group of people, the paedophiles. It gives the impression that, not unlike vampires, paedophiles abuse children who grow up to become paedophiles themselves. It is for this reason that readers might get the impression that the Eidolon was *made evil* when abused as a child and therefore it is his traumatic childhood experience that is to be blamed for his current paedophilia.

One can however argue that since the reader of the novel is not the intended audience of the character's website (which is written for fellow paedophiles), and the reader is in fact aware of this at the time, the excerpt additionally provides insight into Gladden's consciousness. His reaction to the words on the screen ('They were beautiful, as if written by the unseen hand of God. So right. So knowledgeable') therefore gives the impression that Gladden shares the same positioning as the Eidolon. Both paedophiles are presumed to have been through similar experiences, and hence both are thought of as having been *made evil*.

In contrast to the narration of these two extracts, the one that displays the character of Smoke is of the *external* type, in that events are described outside the consciousness of any participating character (Simpson, 1993: 39). Here, the third-person narration adopted relates to events and describes people from a position outside Smoke's consciousness, while the fact that the narrator declines to report any of the character's psychological processes adds an intuitively objective, neutral, and impersonal impression to the theme.

The type of impersonal third-person narration employed here is additionally interesting in that it draws on the sort of register one would expect from a social worker, a probation officer, or a psychologist as the jargon 'special needs child', 'misguided days', and 'juveniles who are delinquent' reflects. However, this formal, distant, and apparently objective register is often interrupted by casual conversational jargon such as 'had been written up', 'smashed', and 'showed up', which adds a strong sense of irony to the claims made. Additional irony is produced by the fact that while the narrator uses a format suggesting that Smoke shares little if any responsibility for the crimes he committed, the actual content of the extract gives a rather different story. His early crimes and punishments are provided in lists, while some responsibility is indirectly assigned to the youth's parents who appear to have been over-supportive and extremely suspicious of the police. It is this duality of the narrator's voice that makes the extract appear to be so ironic. On one hand, the format and the grammatical and lexical choices (from the field of social work) suggest that the narrator is giving Smoke the benefit of the doubt. On the other hand, the actual content of the piece, the informal register creeping in, and the narrator's assertiveness leave no doubt as to his guilt.

Interesting forms are also in use when we get shifts to the parents' viewpoints, such as in reference to the mother who 'never believed he was guilty', where it is the fact that we get a negation of the expectation that he was indeed guilty, which raises the expectation in the first place. A similar impression is achieved when we are given access to the father's viewpoint: 'It was clear to Smoke's father, a hardworking banker, that his son was unusually bright and misunderstood'. Here, the subordination of the claim for the son's intelligence and individuality adds an additional ironic layer to the claim itself. We are strongly asked to believe ('It was clear') that the teenager was misunderstood even though we are given a rather large list of crimes, one that he is highly unlikely to have been set up for by the police.

Even further, the extract is suffused with words that are linked to criminality and the semantic field of *finding fault*, and yet these come to be attached to either the boy's attorneys, the schools the boy attended, or the police, but never to the boy himself: 'when Smoke complained and found fault', 'enrolled him in four different schools and blamed each one when it didn't work out', 'Both parents believed their son had been set up because the police were corrupt', 'would not know Smoke or harass him any more'. In effect, we are given the impression that though Smoke and his parents were indeed in search of someone to blame for the situation the boy constantly found himself in, they never looked to the boy for fault. Overall, the blind trust the parents maintain as to the boy's innocence is reinforced in more ways than one, making it even clearer how likely it is it that he was indeed guilty.

Finally, irony is further diffused over the last paragraph, where the readers are told that once the juvenile turned sixteen, his record and therefore his past was expunged. In contrast to the long subordinated sentences of the previous paragraphs, we are given a series of three short sentences: 'His juvenile record was expunged. His fingertips and mug shots destroyed. He had no past', which may be argued to suggest that the cause of actions was unfair. The last sentence ('He had no past') especially conveys irony in that it states an impossible state of affairs: everybody has a past, and yet Smoke got away with his because of his age. A loophole in the American legal system is revealed, and, therefore, some responsibility as to the course of criminal action that Smoke is to engage in later on is indirectly assigned to the system itself.

It is not until the final sentence of the extract that we are allowed access to Smoke's actual consciousness: 'he was feeling especially in a good mood to cause trouble'. Here, the fact that Smoke was the type of teenager who would be in a mood for trouble, something so far only implied, is now confirmed. The overall impression we are given about Smoke is that of a spoiled child who was both *born and made evil*; though it was rather early on in life that he displayed criminal behaviour, it is also the parents' over-sympathising that may have led him to become the criminal he is at this point in the narrative. In addition, the system appears to also be at blame, in that by deleting his records it allowed him to make a new start in an even more criminal new life.

Criminal mind style and viewpoint

Roger Fowler (1977) coined the term *mind style* to describe the phenomenon in which the language of a text projects a characteristic world view, a particular way of perceiving and making sense of the world.

> A mind style may analyse a character's mental life more or less radically; may be concerned with relatively superficial or relatively fundamental aspects of the mind; may seek to dramatize the order and structure of conscious thoughts, or just present the topics on which a character reflects, or displays preoccupations, prejudices, perspectives and values which strongly bias a character's world-view but of which s/he may be unaware.
>
> Fowler (1977: 103)

Fowler uses the term to refer to any distinctive linguistic presentation of an individual mental self and, according to Semino and Swindlehurst

(1996: 145), introduced this notion of *mind style* as an alternative to *ideological point of view* or *point of view on the ideological plane*. According to the same source, ideological viewpoint refers specifically to the attitudes, beliefs, values, and judgements shared by people with similar social, cultural, and political backgrounds.

Since then, however, the notions of *ideological viewpoint* and *mind style* seem to have taken on separate definitions, and studies have tended to deal exclusively with either one (on ideological viewpoint see, for example, Simpson, 1993) or the other (on mind style see Leech and Short, 1981; Bockting, 1994; Semino and Swindlehurst, 1996). The definition I adopt for the term *mind style* is the following one, which Bockting offers: 'Mind style is concerned with the construction and expression in language of the conceptualisation of reality in a particular mind' (1994: 159). This definition, Semino and Swindlehurst (1996: 144) argue, rests on two central assumptions. 'The first assumption is that what we call "reality" is the result of perceptual and cognitive processes that may vary in part from person to person', and the second assumption is 'that language is a central part of the process by which we make sense of the world around us; thus the texts we produce reflect our particular way of conceptualising reality'. Such a definition of *mind style* appears to be rather distinct from that of *ideological viewpoint*; whereas the latter term is now taken to capture the evaluative and socially shared aspects of world views, *mind style* captures their cognitive and more idiosyncratic aspects.

Since I take this latter sense of the term *mind style* to refer to the way in which a particular reality is perceived and conceptualised in cognitive terms, it may now be related to the mental abilities and tendencies of an individual, traits that may be completely personal and idiosyncratic, or ones that may be shared, for example by people with similar cognitive habits or disorders. It is for this reason that I borrow this sense of the term in reference to the criminal persona and mind. Even though I would not go to the extent of marking criminality as a mental disorder, it can surely be taken to be an idiosyncratic tendency certain people are prone to, regardless of whether they are *born with it* or whether they have come to adopt it later on in life. Criminality could be perceived as some rather special mental tendency, one that may be idiosyncratic, or one that is shared among other criminals with similar tendencies.

The range of linguistic phenomena portraying such a distinctive presentation of an individual's mental self includes primarily choices of transitivity (Leech and Short, 1981: 189), where semantic matters like agency and responsibility are indicated, and metaphorical patterns (see Semino and Swindlehurst, 1996). In addition, choices of register and lexis, the figure of metonymy, as well as certain instances of speech and thought presentation can prove to be important aspects of mind style. Rather distinct linguistic patterns can be seen in my three extracts, leading towards the construction of quite distinct mind styles.

Firstly, with regards to register, the extract portraying Soneji's viewpoint marks the criminal as a persona that is intelligent and careful, in that he takes precautions in his trespassing of the Cross household. Despite this fact, the narration contains elements that portray a rather childlike viewpoint. The anticipation and excitement marking out every single one of Soneji's actions in the cellar seem more appropriate for a child rather than a serial killer: 'A stained Georgetown ballcap was hung on a hook. Soneji put it in his head. He couldn't resist'. In addition, the structure of the passage is simple, full of coordinated clauses, while constructions such as 'Once upon a time, he had been a famous kidnapper and murderer' are there to mark out the fact that, though a criminal, his viewpoint often blends with that of a child at play.

Additionally he seems to be in control of his actions as well as his thoughts, in that his free indirect thought processes represent not only clues to the cause of his past criminal actions, but also clues to the nature of those that are to come next. For instance, '*The cellar was a clue to those who collected them. The cellar was worth a thousand words. A thousand forensic pictures, too*' is marked out as a clue regarding the sort of death he anticipates for the family. The fact that this passage is in italics further signals its prominence from the remaining text.

The word *feel* is used both literally (to mark out physical perceptions) – 'He felt around the hammocks of the old woman's bra' – and in a non-tactile sense (to mark out emotions and mental sensations): 'He felt close to the doomed family now', 'He felt like a total creep, and he loved it'. The use of the verb *feel* in its various senses brings out sinister qualities to the criminal persona.

The extract further contains metaphors that are literalised such as 'He was coming back with a vengeance that would blow everybody's mind'. The narrator plays around with the 'blowing someone's mind' metaphor that he uses as a clue, as the criminal indeed intends to set off on a murder spree at a train station and blow people's heads off. More remarkably, this narration includes a few instances of metonymy, such as 'Soneji picked up a small reindeer sweater [...] He held it to his face and tried to smell the girl'. Even though the criminal appears to smell the sweater, in his mind it is the girl that he smells. It is also worth pointing out that the original referent is phonologically as well as graphologically associated with 'sweat', therefore bringing out the impression that the criminal attempts to smell the girl's sweat.

Overall, even though there is nothing in Gary Soneji's actions to cause terror or fear directly, the nature of his thought processes as well as the way he uses metaphors literally and as clues could make readers feel uncomfortable with such an access to the disturbed individual's mental consciousness. Sentences such as 'He had spun his web perfectly' are used to mark out the killer as an individual who is so disturbed that he even sees himself as a spider looking out for victims to catch in his web. Even though this metaphor is rather conventional, it is used to such a great extent (note especially the title of a previous novel in the series – *Along Came a Spider*) that it may be said to be a 'sustained metaphor' (see Werth, 1999), meaning one that provides a sustained frame of reference as well as a means of thematic coherence.

The narrator however distances himself from the criminal's position by repeatedly stating that it is Soneji's thoughts that are represented, and therefore naming him where a personal pronoun would be more normal: 'but Soneji decided not to take any chances', 'Soneji put it on his head', 'Soneji picked up a small reindeer sweater', 'Gary Soneji thought he would punch out the boy's heart'. The narrator avoids repeatedly using the pronoun *he* to signal that the thoughts are strictly the responsibility of the killer, while the criminal's full name is given in the last instance to distance the narrator even further from the killer's disturbing fantasies.

The Eidolon's mind style on the other hand portrays rather different linguistic forms. The structure 'My story is not one of deprivation and abuse' negates the expectation that he regards his abuse as such, and therefore raises it in the first place. In other words, this structure confirms the fact that he is aware of people in general viewing stories such as his as ones of abuse. Even though the paedophile makes reference to vengeance, he does so in the context of being vengeful towards his abusers not for carrying out the abuse in the first place, but for rejecting him once he became too old for their tastes. That is, though he does admit to feeling motivated and in pain, he claims that it was because the abuse eventually had to come to an end. In his mind, the paedophile appears to be of the belief that he keeps the children young by abusing them and sees it as his duty to carry on abusing them, which in turn helps them maintain their youth: 'And the children must stay forever young'. In addition, it is worth pointing out that this belief is reinforced by the fact that this last statement is one of the few in this extract that is given an impersonal and rather generalised tone. Rather than claim that he is the one who is to help children stay forever young, he uses this impersonal tone to take no responsibility for this claim and yet imply that he would be involved in the process of keeping them young.

The extract portraying the Eidolon is extremely personal, though there appears to be a short shift from the 'I' of the first paragraph ('I await them. I am prepared to take my place [...] I feel as I did as a child [...] I could receive him [...] I watched the light [...] I knew that he was there and that I would have his love') to the 'we' of the beginning of the second paragraph ('We are what they make us [...] We are cast off. We become nomads [...]'), only to switch back to the first person singular later on ('I carry with me the vengeance [...] I am called the predator [...] I am the cucoloris'). This transition indicates the paedophile's belief that his view of paedophilia is one shared among other paedophiles surfing the net. (At this point, it is also worth pointing out that the name the criminal adopts – *Eidolon* – comes from Greek, and means *idol* or *image*. By choosing such a name for himself, the paedophile is portrayed as a mental representation of others who share his state of mind and views on paedophilia.) It also reinforces his belief that these others need feel not only that they are not on their own in their search for young victims, but also that they are right to do so.

There appear also to be verbless clauses such as 'The line of light at the bottom', 'My beacon', and 'The apple of his eye', which have connotations of inactivity and repress the agency function. This choice of structuring has the connotation of 'reduction in the strength of the will in those human characters to whom this style is applied' (Fowler, 1977: 111). In other words, it adds to the impressions that those carrying out the abuse had little or no choice in the matter and that they ought not be blamed for it. Moreover in the extract feelings, states, and responses tend to be given in a non-judgmental tone through the process of nominalisation: 'the moan', 'my rejection', 'my pain and motivation', 'the touch.' This pattern allows emotions and qualities to be presented as '*possessions* which can be discarded, passed from person to person, traded, manipulated, etc.: non-inherent, not demanding commitment' (Fowler, 1977: 112). In other words, these feelings and emotions appear to be taken for granted, are passed on from the abuser to the abused, and simultane-ously take responsibility away from those who experience them and act upon them.

The extract is at the same time full of metaphors ('The apple of his eye', 'nomads in the world of the moan') as well as some literal, identificational, or predicative constructions ('I am the predator', 'my rejection is my pain and motivation'). The author (who, in the analysed extract, is the Eidolon whose writing is being *quoted* by Gladden), however, appears to elaborate on and combine conventional and unconventional metaphors with certain literal, identificational, or predicative constructions to project a distinctive mind style. It has also been suggested that personifying metaphors are often used 'to project a world view that attributes a potentially threatening animacy to nature' (Semino and Swindlehurst, 1996: 148). When discussing a similar occurrence in the mind style of Lambert Strether in *The Ambassadors*, Fowler argues:

> It is as if his feelings are disconnected from his own psyche; as if his perceptions assail him from the outside, beyond his control; as if he relates to others and himself only through intermediaries; and it seems that he pictures others as suffering the same divided self.
>
> Fowler (1977: 112)

A similar effect seems to be achieved in the Eidolon's extract. Even though it is not inanimate objects but the feelings and emotions of the paedophile that come to be animated here, the effect achieved is still just as strong. The man who experiences the emotional states becomes merely a potential onlooker of the states themselves that are animated by movement, motive, and awareness. The feelings are the ones that overtake the paedophile, acting on his behalf, and taking responsibility of those actions away from him who performs them.

The study's conclusions

Overall, there appear to be certain correlations between the stylistic forms chosen and the way in which the criminal mind is morally situated and rationalised.

In the case of Soneji, the third person narration is of the internal type and correlates with the impression of a criminal who was born as such. No justifications for his actions are provided and no excuses given. The literalising of the everyday metaphors add to an image of an *animal-like* criminal who is not only proud of the crimes he has committed in the past, but willing to commit many more in the future. The criminal consciousness portrayed often blends with that of a child at play, while the use of the various senses of *feel* combined with metaphors and metonymies add *sinister* qualities to the disturbed persona. These are used as narrative clues not only to the nature of his past crimes, but also to the nature of those to come. Overall, strong tensions are created in the use of stylistic forms that convey sympathy with the consciousness portrayed, with a content of fantasies that draw on anything but sympathy.

The Eidolon's first-person internal narration instead correlates with the impression of a criminal who was *made*: it is his traumatic childhood experience that is to blame for the abuse he currently carries out. The paedophile holds the belief that, much like the myth of vampires, he was made into the abuser he now is by the abuse(s) he himself suffered when he was a child. Though he admits to feeling vengeful and in pain, he claims that it was only because the abuse ended and not because it took place. The form of the language adopted causes tension in that it comes to presuppose not only that the readers are paedophiles themselves, but also that they are in denial as to having enjoyed the abuse. The extract is further suffused with first-person pronouns adding a strong personal impression to the theme, while the occurrence of verbless clauses carries connotations of inactivity and the repression of agency.

Moreover, the recurring metaphorical expressions, identificational constructions, and process of nominalisation project a mind that views its feelings as disconnected from its own psyche. The feelings and emotions are presented as animate entities, taking the responsibility of the crimes away from the criminal who experiences them and acts upon them.

The overall impression we get of Smoke is that of a spoilt child who was both *born* and *made* evil. Though Smoke's consciousness does not get portrayed through the Cornwell extract (with the exception of the last sentence), the third-person external narration adopted has strong ironic effects and deals however implicitly with issues of responsibility. The extract draws on a social worker's jargon, which gives the theme a rather objective tone, and yet the everyday expressions encountered, the grammar, as well as the content portray a narrator that is anything but objective. Interesting forms are in use when we get momentary shifts to the parents' viewpoint, where expectations are negated and strong implications are drawn upon. Responsibility for the crimes carried out therefore gets implicitly assigned not only to the juvenile himself, but also to the parents' blind trust, and the system's loopholes.

Overall, though these correlations have been made, I do not mean to argue that each of these three types of narration would correlate with each of these justifications for the crimes directly or necessarily. It is not the case that all first-person narrations allow access to criminals who were *made*, or that third-person internal narrations would correlate with criminals who were *born*, or that third-person external narrations would bring out the impression of ones who were both *born* and *made*. The content of each excerpt would certainly contribute to the effect just as much as the type/tone of narration would. But it does seem to be the case that the positioning of the criminal on the cline of the moral justifications of crime would depend upon the nature of the narration chosen, the extent to which the reader is allowed access to the criminal's consciousness, and the way in which that consciousness is portrayed. And all these are aspects of what I shall refer to as *criminal mind style*.

This study has several implications as to the notion of *mind style* in general. Even though the notion was originally coined as an alternative to that of *ideological viewpoint*, the definition I adopt for the term in this study is rather different. I instead use the term to refer to the way in which a particular reality is perceived and conceptualised, and hence it may relate to the idiosyncratic tendencies of individuals. Therefore, the term now has an interesting application in reference to the criminal persona and mind. Though primarily the range of linguistic phenomena portraying such a distinctive presentation of an individual's mental self includes metaphorical patterns, transitivity, and lexical choices, other linguistic choices have also proved to be relevant. Certain instances of thought presentation, the grammatical process of nominalisation, the deletion of agency, the figure of metonymy, as well as the type and tone of narration can all contribute to the construction of the *criminal mind*. It is the use of patterns involving these aspects of the language of such extracts that need be further explored, as these not only reveal the poetic structure of the criminal mind but also the ways in which it comes to be morally situated.

In the context of the next section, I concentrate on a larger variety of excerpts that portray the criminal consciousness, namely extracts from the Patterson series, and examine the extent to which the *figurative* language of such excerpts can specifically mirror the way in which authors realise the notion of *criminality*. Overall, I aim to prove that since the constraints of how we speak and write are not imposed by the limits of language but by the ways we actually think of our everyday experiences (Gibbs, 1994: 8), it follows that the way that the criminal mind is linguistically portrayed is closely tied to the way the criminals are believed to conceptualise their lives and actions.

A further investigation into the portrayal of the criminal mind in Patterson

Contextualising the criminally-focalised extracts

James Patterson is one of the world's top-selling fiction writers today. *Along Came A Spider* (1993) is his first of five books in the series featuring detective/ psychologist Alex Cross, and is temporally followed by *Kiss the Girls* (1995), *Jack and Jill* (1996), *Cat and Mouse* (1997) and *Pop Goes the Weasel* (1999).

In the first thriller featuring the Washington DC detective and psychologist, Cross must track down a serial killer who has kidnapped the daughter of a famous Hollywood actress and the son of the secretary of the treasury. That killer is the previously analysed Gary Soneji, a docile mathematics teacher at a private school for socially privileged children. When one of the children is found dead in a river, badly beaten, all hope is lost for the other child. A ransom is demanded and paid in full but the money disappears and is never found. The murderer/kidnapper is eventually found and arrested but in addition to there being no sign of the money, the kidnapper claims to have no recollection of asking for the money. He appears to have a split personality.

Soneji escapes police custody only to return in the fourth novel in the series, *Cat and Mouse* (1997). It is here that Soneji goes on a murder spree at train stations, with the ultimate aim of killing Alex Cross and his family, which consists of his two young children, Jannie and Damon, and his grandmother (referred to as Nana) who has raised him from a child. Meanwhile, FBI agent and profiler Thomas Pierce is tracking Mr. Smith, a brutal serial killer, across Europe. As the body count rises, both Alex and Pierce continue their pursuits, and as their cases become intertwined, the question becomes 'who is chasing whom'.

Both novels have all the elements readers have become accustomed to in an Alex Cross thriller – mystery, action, suspense, references to current pop culture, and *alternating points of view*, while Patterson's trademark of two-and-three-page-chapters is also retained.

The poetics of the criminal mind

As Gibbs (1994: 5) argues, recent advances in philosophy, psychology, cognitive linguistics and anthropology show that not only is much of our language metaphorically structured but so is much of our cognition; 'People conceptualise their experiences in figurative terms via metaphor, metonymy, irony, oxymoron and so on, and these principles underlie the way we think, reason, and imagine'. There is, he argues, considerable evidence for the inextricable link between the figurative nature of everyday thought and the ordinary use of language. There is now much research (Lakoff and Johnson, 1980; Turner and Fauconnier, 1995) 'showing that our linguistic system, even that responsible for what we often conceive of as literal language, is inextricably related to the rest of our physical and cognitive system' (Gibbs, 1994: 5).

Since language is not independent of the mind but reflects our perceptual and conceptual understanding of experience, then it may be argued that when novelists employ *deviant* linguistic structures to portray the criminal mind, they are in fact allowing readers access to the criminal's conceptualisation of reality. And one may even argue that there lies the key to demystifying criminal behaviour. Criminality, here seen as a tendency that certain people are prone to, is often mystified; it is thought of as unconventional, antisocial, unusual, unexpected and unpredictable. One could argue that crime writers attempt to demystify it; by offering us the poetics of the criminal mind, we are allowed access to the criminal's world or reality, where their crimes are justified and accounted for. Hence, we are, to a certain extent, being put in a position where we understand the criminals, share their conceptual viewpoint and are even forced to sympathise with their behaviour and course of actions.

Since criminal behaviour is itself unusual and unconventional, it can be argued to be somewhat demystified via *linguistic deviation*, a term most commonly used to refer to divergence from the norms of everyday language. Leaving aside for the moment the problem of determining the norm, Leech and Short (1981: 48) define *deviance* as 'a purely statistical notion: as the difference between the normal frequency of a feature, and its frequency in the text or corpus'. Prominence is the related psychological notion, whereby some linguistic features stand out in some way through the effect of foregrounding.

The term *figurative language* is used here to refer to that language which is not to be taken literally. Though the term is frequently used to simply mean *metaphorical language*, here *metaphor* is seen as a very important or basic aspect of figurative language. Leech (1969) considers *metaphor*, and also *synecdoche* and *metonymy* under this heading. Cognitive linguists, such as Gibbs (1994) regard *slang metaphors*, *hyperbole* or *exaggeration, simile, idioms, proverbs,* and *irony* as aspects of figurative language in addition to the ones that Leech considers. In this study, I take up Gibbs's definition, and consider most of these features in connection to the portrayal of the criminal mind.

Extended metaphorical mappings

According to Lakoff and Johnson (1980), in metaphor, there are two conceptual domains, and one is understood in terms of the other (for example, LOVE is understood as a kind of nutrient in 'I'm drunk with love', 'He's sustained by love', 'I'm starved for your affection' and so on). Creative individuals will often provide unique artistic instantiations of conceptual metaphors that partially structure our experiences. In the Patterson novels, there seem to be a number of such metaphors, which are 'sustained' (see Werth, 1999) or 'extended' (see Nowottny, 1962), that is, work on even more extended ways across the whole of both novels and give rise to related metaphors, as well. Werth (1999: 323) refers to such sustained metaphorical undercurrents as *megametaphors.*

The first noticeable metaphor in the two novels of the Patterson series is the KILLERS ARE SPIDERS metaphor. Sentences such as 'He had spun his web perfectly' (1997: 5), 'Mr Smith had to bend low to talk into Derek Cabott's ear, to be more intimate with his prey' (1997: 7), 'He had been *Mr Soneji – the Spider Man*' (1997: 26), and 'Then Soneji was lost in his thoughts. His memories were his cocoon' (1997: 30) are used to mark out the killer as an individual who, as previously noted, sees himself as a spider looking out for victims to catch in his web. The conventional and yet 'sustained' KILLERS ARE SPIDERS metaphor is elaborated across the novels; the criminal's planning of the crimes is thought of as the web, victims are viewed as prey, and the criminal's thoughts and memories are his cocoon, the protective silky thread to be found around insects.

This metaphor is very closely connected to the larger KILLERS ARE ANIMALS / INSECTS TO BE FED metaphor, which further underlies the two novels under analysis. Examples from the first novel in the series include '[H]e moved closer and closer to his first moment of real glory, his first kill' (1993: 3), 'Here comes Mr Fox' (1993: 5), 'He watched the blubbery blob the way a lizard watches an insect – just before mealtime' (1993: 100), 'As he walked outside to the car, he felt like an animal, suddenly on the loose' (1993: 157), all of which present the criminal as an animal/insect out in search of food. The combination of similes and metaphors somewhat justify the killings as necessities; the killer is presented to kill out of need for survival, just like an animal/ insect kills to feed. Note especially the title of the second novel under analysis, *Cat and Mouse* (1997) which, as noted, raises the question of 'who is chasing whom'; though it is Cross who is once again in pursuit of Soneji, Soneji's attempts at killing Cross offer the impression that it is Soneji who is metaphorically conceived of as the hunter (cat), and Cross the hunted (mouse). Similar occurrences of the same metaphorical mapping are further evident in this novel, as well, for example, 'The Cross house was twenty paces away and the proximity and sight of it made Gary Soneji's skin prickle' (1997: 3), and 'Cats were such little ghouls. Cats were like him' (1997: 49). According to this mapping, the killer is conceived of as the hunter on the loose, the (potential) victim as the hunted – the (potential) kill under observation, the killing as the feeding, and the anticipation of the crime as the physical reaction the animals get to the killing; the growing of a small sharp point on the animal's skin ('prickle').

Another *megametaphor* that is evident in both novels in the series is that of CRIMINAL BEHAVIOUR IS PLAY-ACTING or CRIMINALS ARE ACTORS. There are many good examples of the use of this metaphor in the first novel in the series; 'He thought of his nickname at the school. Mr Smith! What a lovely, lovely bit of play-acting he'd done. Real Academy Award stuff' (1993: 49), 'And that performance was a classic. De Niro himself had to be a psychopath in real life' (1993: 49), 'This was his movie' (1993: 52), 'He still had work to do tonight. Masterpiece Theatre continued' (1993: 54), 'Gary lied, and he knew it was a pretty good one. Extremely well told, well acted' (1993: 145), 'He was another De Niro – no doubt about that – only he was an even better actor' (1993: 183), 'A special performance for all the kiddies and mommies' (1993: 183), 'He had another big part to act out' (1993: 370), and so on.

Similarly, such metaphors are evident throughout *Cat and Mouse*; 'What a handsome couple they made, and what a tragedy this was going to be, what a damn shame' (1997: 19), 'he knew every single move from this point until the end' (1997: 19), 'The scene of the crime-to-be, the scene of the masterpiece theatre' (1997: 20), 'they would be safely on board on their little commuter trains by the time the "light and sound" show began in just a few minutes' (1997: 27), and so on. As can be seen from these examples, the narrator appears to adopt and elaborate on the CRIMINAL BEHAVIOUR IS PLAY-ACTING megametaphor. The criminals and victims are viewed as actors, the crime scene is viewed as the stage for play acting, the crime a tragedy, and the passers-by or people who learn of and are terrified by the crimes as the audience to be amused/entertained.

Once again, this megametaphor appears to be closely connected to yet another metaphor in the series, that of CRIMES ARE GAMES. Examples of this metaphor, evident in *Along Came A Spider*, include 'Let's Play Make Believe' (1993: 1), 'It's time for more fun, more games' (1993: 171), 'This was the most daring part of the whole adventure' (1993: 180), and 'He was playing policeman and it was kind of neat' (1993: 394), and examples from *Cat and Mouse* include 'You, Derek, are a piece of the puzzle' (1997: 8), ' He had outdone the leg-endary Charles Whitman, and this was only the beginning' (1997: 48), '*Victory belongs to the player who makes the next-to-last mistake*' (1997: 48), '*Make no mistake about it. I will win*' (1997: 55), and so on. According to this metaphorical mapping, the criminals and detectives are thought of as players, the pursuit of the criminal as an adventure/game, the crimi-nal who gets away with it a winner, the completion of a crime a victory, and the criminal behaviour as plain childish fun.

One final extended metaphor to be analysed here is that of CRIMI-NALS ARE MACHINES. Patterson elaborates on this metaphor once again to bring out the inhuman undertones to the criminal course of action in the two novels. Examples from *Along Came A Spider* include 'Gary was like a programmed machine from the moment he spotted the police' (1993: 170), 'He was completely wired' (1993: 180), 'real high-wire stuff' (1993: 180), and the ones from *Cat and Mouse* include 'Just to look around, [..] to fuel his hatred, if that was possible' (1997: 4), and 'His murder would electrify the town' (1997: 7). According to this metaphorical mapping, criminals are viewed as machines that carry out their vicious intentions, the criminals' hatred is thought of as the fuel, the preplanning of the crimes as the machine's program-ming, their criminal behaviour as the electricity generated by the machine.

The overall use of such conceptual metaphors in the Patterson series establishes the criminals as a special kind of human species, one that is driven to criminality because they felt it was *necessary* for them to do so. Just like animals hunting to be fed, criminals are 'justified' as a species that cannot help but kill in order to survive. At the same time, criminal behaviour is presented as 'viewed' by an audience of common people who seek entertainment; in this sense, criminal behaviour forms part of the social structure, and is *wanted* rather than not. Finally, criminals are players who behave like children engaged in games, and who act on 'instinct' like programmed pieces of machinery that lack common human logic and morals.

Metonymies

The novels include a few instances of *metonymy*. Unlike metaphorical models, 'metonymic models involve only one conceptual domain, in that the mapping or connection between two things is done within the same domain' (Gibbs, 1994: 13). For instance in 'Hollywood is putting out terrible movies', the movie industry is referred to by the place where movies are made, which maps a salient characteristic of one domain (its location) as representing the entire location (the movie industry).

Such a metonymic mapping is found in 'The boy ran back across the muddy fields with the precious struggling bundle in his arms and disappeared into the darkness' (1993: 5). Here, the name of the referent, 'the baby' is replaced by the name of the element that contains it – 'the bundle', therefore bringing out the impression that the baby was as insignificant to its killer as a bundle of clothes to be carried around. Another example, and one that was previously analysed, is that of 'Soneji picked up a small reindeer sweater.. He held it to his face and tried to smell the girl.' (1997: 5). The name of the referent 'the sweater' is here replaced by the name of an entity related to it, 'the girl', therefore bringing out the impression that, in his mind, the criminal attempts to smell the girl's sweat.

Literalised metaphors and unidiomatised idioms

The novels further contain many metaphors that are literalised such as the previously analysed 'He was coming back with a vengeance that would blow everybody's mind' (1993: 5), where the narrator uses the 'blowing someone's mind' metaphor as a clue; as noted, he indeed intends to literally blow people's heads off. Further metaphors are literalised in *Cat and Mouse* such as in 'This afternoon Mr Smith was operating in the wealthy, fashionable Knightsbridge district. He was there *to study the human race*' (1997: 7). Firstly, we have the use of the verb 'operate' that is part of the common police register for 'carrying out criminal actions'. What we find out later on, however, is that the criminal is indeed performing a surgical operation; he is actually carrying out an autopsy on a living victim. We therefore acknowledge that the verb 'operate' was used literally, as opposed to figuratively. Similarly, 'study' is also to be interpreted literally (to mean 'visually investigate the physical nature of') rather than figuratively (to mean 'reflect over the psychological nature of').

What the reader faces in all these examples is what Emmott (1999: 160) refers to as 'miscuing' of the signals needed in order to understand the episodic information offered. According to the same source, the reader will, later on, engage in what Emmott refers to as a *frame repair*: 'Repairs become necessary when a reader becomes aware that they have misread the text either through lack of attention or because the text itself is potentially ambiguous' (Emmott, 1999: 225). As Emmott suggests, such repairs force readers to not only replace the 'erroneous' frame when they discover the problem, but to also reread or reinterpret the text with the 'correct' frame from the point at which the switch should have taken place. This process has also been referred to as *schema refreshing* (see Semino, 1997; Cook, 1990, 1994).

According to Gibbs (1994: 91), *idioms* have traditionally been defined as 'expressions whose meanings are non-compositional or not functions of the meanings of their individual parts'. That is, people automatically comprehend the figurative meanings of idioms and therefore do not necessarily process their literal interpretations. For instance, the figurative interpretation of *kick the bucket* ('to die') cannot be determined through an analysis of the idiom's literal meaning. According to the same source, '[s]ome scholars propose that idioms are dead metaphors, expressions that have lost their essential metaphoricity over time and now exist as frozen semantic units, perhaps in a special phrasal lexicon' (Gibbs, 1994: 91).

Another pattern that is found when looking into the poetics of the criminal mind is when *idiomatic* expressions are manipulated so as to bring out cruel, inhuman and violent undertones. It is in fact the case that the apparent idioms' meanings are now to be determined through an analysis of the individual meanings of the words they consist of. In a way, the idioms are literalised, or *unidiomatised*. For instance, in the first novel in the series, we are told that 'Less than two miles from the farmhouse, he [Soneji] buried the spoiled-rotten Lindbergh baby – *buried him alive*' (1993: 5). Even though Soneji is engaged in fantasies at this point in the novel, his choice of idiomatically describing the baby as 'spoilt-rotten' brings out vicious connotations; the baby is in fact soon expected to be literally and physically spoilt rotten. Similarly, 'Michel Goldberg weighed next to nothing in his hands, which was exactly what he felt about him. Nothing' (1993: 50) is equally disturbing; the little boy weighed 'next to nothing', which matched the kidnapper's feelings about him.

Other examples include 'Is that a mindblower or what?' (1993: 184), which in itself might not sound vicious, but is in fact so, when uttered once Soneji shoots a man in his forehead. A final interesting example from the first novel is found on p. 393, where Soneji is speaking to a former agent, whilst he is currently cutting his arm with a knife; 'Cut to the chase, hmmm.' (1993: 393). Once again, an apparently innocent idiomatic expression takes on a vicious twist and is hence interpreted on a different, or rather, literal and cruel plane.

The same manipulation of idiomatic expressions is also evident in *Cat and Mouse*. For instance, in the very first chapter of the novel, Soneji is outside the Cross household and thinks to himself; *'Enjoy every moment – stop and smell the roses.* Soneji reminded himself. *Taste the roses, eat Alex Cross's roses – flowers, stems, and thorns'* (1997: 4). Here again, the apparently innocent idiomatic expression 'stop and smell the roses' that is commonly used to mean 'enjoy yourself and relax' takes on a rather different meaning. 'Smell' is replaced by 'taste' and hence we are given the impression that 'roses' may be meant to be interpreted metaphorically as the source domain for the things that Cross loves and cares for. Once the 'roses' are elaborated as *'flowers, stems, and thorns'*, we view the three elements as three aspects of Cross's life that are to be exploited so as to cause Cross pain, probably his Nana and two children.

Another good example of such an idiomatic manipulation is that found in, 'Whatever happened was meant to, and besides, he definitely wanted to go out with a bang, not a cowardly whimper' (1997: 26). Here, the readers are once again forced to interpret the idiom 'to go out with a bang' (to mean 'to die impressively') on a literal level; Soneji indeed hopes to be able to die in the sound of a gunshot. The idiom is hence unidiomatised; the readers decompose and analyse the meanings of the individual words of the idiom in order to arrive at the criminal's intended meaning.

Linguistic connotations altered

Another pattern that is found on close examination of the stylistic nature of the extracts taken from the criminal viewpoint is that when words *acquire connotations* other than the ones that are ordinarily attached to them. According to Wales (2001: 78), in both semantics and literary criticism, *connotation* and *connotative meaning* are 'commonly used to refer to all kinds of associations words may evoke: situational, emotional, etc, particularly in certain contexts, over and above the basic *denotational* or *conceptual meaning*'. For instance, to many people 'home', defined as 'dwelling-place', also has connotations of 'domesticity' and 'warmth'. Across the two novels of the series, such connotations are manipulated and most significantly altered, especially in the context of the 'criminally-minded' extracts; we are often invited to attach additional negative meanings to words that we commonly attach positive connotations to.

In the first novel in the series, we are given noun phrases such as 'the brilliantly conceived and executed crime' (1993: 52), 'the century's most elegant crime' (1993: 52), and 'the sensational, unsolved kidnapping' (1993: 130). The adjectives 'brilliant', 'elegant' and 'sensational' usually carry such positive connotations for the nouns they are attached to as those of 'brightness', 'stylishness', and 'beauty'. Hence, they seem rather out of place when attached to the nouns 'crime' and 'kidnapping', and invite rather negative connotations – even ferocious and sadistic undertones. Similarly, the sentences 'One body at a time, he hauled the children into the barn' (1993: 49) and 'He [the victim] was propped up in the bathtub, with cold water halfway to the rim' (1993: 392) seem awkwardly structured. The verbs 'haul' and 'prop' are more often used in reference to inanimate, lifeless objects and hence their usage in these contexts seems unconventional. Even though the victims share little physical power due to the drugs the perpetrator inserted into their bodies, it seems that the verbs' connotation of 'lifelessness' need nevertheless be adjusted to that of 'lack of emotion toward them' on behalf of the criminal. The perpetrator appears to be treating his victims heartlessly and unfeelingly, as if they are lifeless objects to be handled, manipulated.

In the second novel under analysis, when addressing the inspector, Mr Smith comments 'Your life will end. May I be the first to congratulate you' (1997: 9). The contextual connotations of 'success', 'achievement' and 'praise', usually evoked by the verb 'to congratulate', are again altered. Here, 'congratulate' is used in an address to the inspector who is dying, and therefore the conventional connotations attached to the word seem out of place; death is not normally considered an achievement, and people on the verge of death are not usually to be praised. This usage instead brings out the impression that Mr Smith regards dying as 'the reaching of one's goals', 'the achievement of success', and might even regard himself as Godly since he is the one that can allocate people such a special gift. 'Congratulate' acquires vicious connotations, carries sadistic suggestions and, one can argue, ironic undertones.

Personification and the concretisation of abstract concepts

In the course of the two novels under analysis, we get various instances of *personification*, again more so within the context of the 'criminally-minded' extracts. According to Wales (2001: 294), *personification* is that 'figure of speech or trope in which an *inanimate* object, *animate* non-human, or *abstract* quality is given human attributes'. As Wales adds, sentences involving personification would be treated as strictly *deviant* in the context of transformational grammar, since 'the normal selectional rules for nouns and verbs are violated'.

One good example from *Along Came A Spider* (1993) is that found in 'He was fascinated by this condition known as *fame*. He thought a lot about it. Almost all the time. What was *fame* really like? How did it smell? How did it taste? What did *fame* look like close up?' (1993: 4). Here, Soneji *animates*, *personifies*, or rather *concretises* the condition of fame, which is, in common usage, an abstract concept. By conceptualising this abstract concept in physical terms, Soneji's fascination and obsession with the condition takes on enormous dimensions; the criminal not only craves/wants to be famous, but is more so fixated by the psychological feeling devouring/experiencing it would evoke.

Further examples from the same novel, if rather more conventional, include 'His pulse was racing' (1993: 4), 'Gary was letting his mind wander now, letting his mind fly' (1993: 129), 'So many thoughts and perceptions were crashing on him, deflecting off his brain' (1993: 183), and 'His eyes roamed from window to window' (1993: 411). In these examples, the criminal's pulse, mind, thoughts, perceptions and eyes are all personified, animated, taking on a life of their own. As previously noted (in the context of analysing the Eidolon's mind style), such personifying metaphors often project a world view that attributes a potentially threatening animacy to nature. In the context of the Patterson novels, the pulse, mind, thoughts and eyes of the criminal come to be animated; Soneji is merely a potential onlooker of the states themselves – the feelings overtake him, act on his behalf, and take responsibility for his actions away from him.

A good example of *personification* from *Cat and Mouse* (1997) is that found in 'He let the aiming post of the rifle sight gently come to rest on Christine Johnson's forehead' (1997: 19). Here, the aiming post of the rifle sight again takes on a life of its own; it is 'allowed' to 'come to rest' on a potential victim's forehead. It is presented as an animate entity, once again taking responsibility for the crime away from Soneji. Such instances of *personification* are also evident in 'The outrageous, sensational event had galvanized him back then' (1997: 30), 'A cold, hard shiver ran through his body. It was delicious, tantalising' (1997: 31), and 'The head flew apart before his eyes' (1997: 34). In the case of the first two examples, cruel, abstract criminal events of murder appear to take on the concrete form of nutrients, and are hence experienced on a physical level; the criminal 'tastes' the events, and is nourished on them. In the case of the last example, the head Soneji blows off is personified, animated, presented as a 'bird', therefore giving the impression that the event of shooting the teenager's head off was involuntary, automatic, a reflex and not the responsibility of the person who pulled the trigger.

Childishness and colloquialism evoking irony

As previously noted, with regards to register, the extracts portraying Soneji's viewpoint especially mark the criminal as a persona that is intelligent and careful, in that he has premeditated and preplanned the whole course of his criminal behaviour, takes precautions in carrying out his actions, has contingencies for every situation that may occur, and so on. Despite this fact, the narration is diffused with elements that portray a rather childlike viewpoint, in that his anticipation and excitement are more appropriate for a child rather than a serial killer: 'Cool Beans, he thought' (1993: 4). Overall, and as previously mentioned, the simplicity and informality of such passages reflect a criminal whose viewpoint blends with that of a child at play.

However, this informal, childish register is often additionally reinforced by casual conversational jargon such as 'Agent Graham obviously thought he was hot shit' (1993: 51), 'Marty's piece [of pie] was bigger than all the others. He was The Man, right?' (1993: 142), 'He thought he had a treat for everyone now' (1993: 157), 'Volpi took out his walkie-talkie' (1993: 371) and so on, all of which add a strong sense of irony to the claims made. The colloquialism employed seems somewhat unnatural in the context of a serial killer carrying out his criminal behaviour, and it is this duality of the narrator's voice that makes the extracts appear to be so ironic. Examples from *Cat And Mouse* include 'No more chitchat from Derek' (1997: 8), 'The Big Bang in miniature, no?' (1997: 34), 'He had just tripped the light fantastic, hadn't he?' (1997: 48) and 'Big unexpected surprise. Mindscrewer for the ages surprise' (1997: 54), and so on.

According to Gibbs (1994: 97), *slang* expressions are often associated with idiomatic phrases, although 'slang is usually seen as having a shorter life span within a language than idioms have and is used only by certain groups of individuals or specific communities'. Such slang metaphors, Gibbs adds, also often 'convey certain attitudes or feelings of the speaker's that idiomatic expressions do not'. For instance, the expression *He's on a trip* (meaning 'He's taking drugs') can suggest that the speaker is aware of certain social norms and attitudes about drugs and the drug culture. Nevertheless, *slang* is characteristically associated with very informal registers, and speech predominantly, and it presents an alternative lexis, of an extremely colloquial, non-standard kind, sometimes co-occurring with swearing (Wales, 2001: 361). Though many of the slang expressions noted (that is, 'hot shit', 'trip the light fantastic', 'mindscrewer', and so on) are commonly thought of as humorous, such humour being exploited in a kind of *euphemism* which softens *taboo* subjects, they are, in this context, inviting a strong sense of irony to the theme. Even though the prime motivation for such usage is obviously a desire for novelty of expression, such an expressive creativity seems unfit for the context of serial killing. Irony is found, therefore, since the words actually used appear to contradict the sense actually required in the context.

Creative metaphors

In addition to the various conventional, extended and idiomatic metaphorical mappings previously discussed, the criminally-minded excerpts contain a number of *creative metaphors*, otherwise known as *literary* ones (see Gibbs, 1994: 260), whereby the metaphors have a predominantly expressive or evocative function. Recent studies suggest that readers find such literary metaphors to be more original, less clear, and less communicatively conventional; to have a higher value; and to be less committed to moral positions than metaphors from non-literary sources do (see Steen, 1994).

Examples of such metaphors from *Along Came A Spider* include 'He felt the different textures of darkness as they blanketed the farm' (1993: 51), 'Gary just couldn't get serious about the paper blizzard of bills and invoices littering his desk' (1993: 165), and 'the FBI goons were watching the building as if it might sprout wings and fly away' (1993: 391), whereas examples from *Cat And Mouse* include 'For a while he'd been the dark star of television and newspapers all over the country' (1997: 18), 'The marble floors continued to shake as his beloved trains entered and departed the station, huge mythical beasts that came here to feed and rest' (1997: 28), and 'He watched a montage of shapes and motions and colors swim in and out of death's way' (1997: 33).

Creative metaphors of this nature, some of which involve the previously discussed process of *personification* (for example 1993: 391, 1997:

28, and 1997: 33), create a different perspective on reality than most metaphors seen in science and in mundane speech (that is, *conventional* metaphors). Making sense of such creative, literary metaphors requires that readers 'go beyond the isolated metaphor to envision better how metaphors are recognised as intentionally created by authors to make new the world we live in' (Gibbs, 1994: 261). In other words, people immediately seek authorial intention when reading such novel metaphorical expressions. In the case of the criminally-minded excerpts at hand, the creative metaphors help reconceptualise the criminals' experience of events, create new insights into their world view, and help reconstruct their frame of mind.

The study's conclusions

In this second study, I based my analysis on the argument that language is not independent of the mind but reflects our perceptual and conceptual understanding of experience. It therefore follows that when crime writers employ *deviant* linguistic structures to portray the criminal mind, they are in fact demystifying their criminal behaviour; they are justifying it, or putting readers in the position of sympathising with the criminal. By allowing readers access to the criminal's conceptualisation of reality, readers can deconstruct the criminal frame of mind, access their reasoning, even understand, if not accept, their actions.

In the next chapter, I explore the social deviance as manifested in contemporary crime fiction, and specifically explore the way in which Michael Connelly challenges the boundaries of acceptable social behaviour.

4
Social Deviance in Contemporary Crime Fiction

Defining 'abnormal behaviour': the Connelly series

'As commonly defined, abnormal behaviour is almost always regarded as undesirable and as something to be changed or modified if at all possible' (Miller and Morley, 1986: 4). According to the same source, studies published on abnormality are inversely related to the frequency with which that abnormality or condition is encountered in the general population (known as the *reverse utility law*). In fact, one important reason that has underlined recent studies in abnormal behaviour was the idea that abnormality can assist in the understanding of normal behaviour and the processes that govern it. 'Potentially, at least, the study of the abnormal can test and improve our concept of normality' (Cole, 1970: 15). It therefore seems appropriate to consider this notion under the heading of *deviation*, as the term has so far been defined as a purely statistical phenomenon.

According to Miller and Morley (1986: 8), studies of *abnormality* can be considered under three main headings which constitute the *statistical*, the *departure from cultural norms* and *subjective definitions*. Types of abnormality have also been divided into those that are *psychological* and those that are *social* in nature. In this part of the chapter, I concentrate on the social perspective of the condition, and the rule breaking that comes with it.

Price (1978: 146) suggests that *crime* is just one example of abnormal behaviour that clearly violates agreed-upon rules of any one group within a particular social environment (others being perversion, drunkenness or bad manners), while it is worth pointing out that Price regards *deviance* as the *response* of other people to the rule-breaker:

> Deviance is a quality of people's response to an act and not a characteristic of the act itself. **Primary deviance** and **secondary deviance** are distinguished from each other to refer to the fact that abnormal behaviour can arise in response to being labelled, or hospitalised (secondary), or as a response of some internal (primary) cause, such as brain damage.
>
> Price (1978: 146)

One interesting consequence of adopting the social perspective is that considerably more attention will be given to the *social context* in which the abnormal behaviour occurs, which is a claim that has interesting applications especially in the context of the genre at hand. Since an important function that may modify the reaction to norm violation is additionally the role or status of the rule-breaker, it is easy to see that the norm-violation any detective engages in would be far less damaging than that which the corresponding criminal would carry out.

For instance, in the context of Connelly's Harry Bosch series, the protagonist, though a hero maverick, is also a loner, a drinker, a smoker, and an insomniac. He has fought and killed in Vietnam, and is often motivated by vengeance. Harry is at times romantically involved with criminals, such as in *Trunk Music* (1997b), where he gets married to ex-FBI agent Eleanor Wish, who in the novel makes her living as a card cheat. He is taken to court as the chief defendant in a civil suit against the LAPD in *The Concrete Blonde* (1995), where the family of the 'Dollmaker' serial killer, a man who Bosch shot during an arrest three years earlier, takes him to court under the allegation that Bosch killed the wrong man. He even appears as the prime suspect in a complex case which Terry McCaleb, a fellow detective, investigates (*A Darkness More Than Night*, 2000). In an analysis of the same series, Bertens and D'haen (2001: 105) argue that 'Bosch is notorious for not fitting in, for disobeying rules and regulations', while later on they claim that

> [h]is essential loneliness, his resistance to authority, and his ambiguous susceptibility to alcohol, jazz, smoking, and women, make him into a 1990s reincarnation of the 1930s private eye reluctantly turned police officer and relentlessly chafing against the yoke of rules, regulations and procedures.
>
> Bertens and D'haen (2001: 107)

Despite all this, the readers of the series can be assumed to be far more tolerant of Bosch's rule-breaking than any of that of the killers he pursues, regardless of the seriousness of the crimes and rule-breaking the detective engages in, or is accused of engaging in. Readers are, therefore, somewhat forced to be in sympathy with the detective, and can thus be accused of a certain bias. This seems to be in accordance to what Holdaway (1988: 1) argues, when he claims that '[s]trangely, crime and criminals, deviants and deviance are phenomena we often feel able to define clearly, despite the equally unclear boundaries that border legality and illegality, normality and deviance'. Up until the late 1960s, criminologists were attempting to explain crime and deviance in terms of the differences between those who break the law and those who don't, whereas sociologists have criticised this narrow view of the law and the inadequate or sole dividing line between deviant and normal behaviour (Holdaway, 1988: 2–3). As Holdaway suggests, deviants are not by nature intrinsically 'different' from normal people, but 'are created by being brought within a scope of law or some other rule applied to their actions'. In other words, it would be fair to argue that judgement of abnormal behaviour indeed depends on context, biography and purpose, not to mention political convictions, and the genre does in fact expose these issues extensively.

To some other extent, and as noted in Chapter 2, the genre can be said to alter the social roles of the detective and the criminal so that the detective *becomes* the criminal's double. There are cases, in fact, where the similarity between criminal and detective – especially in the case of the Connelly series – is such that it cannot be overlooked. As Bertens and D'haen (2001: 108–9) point out, in *The Concrete Blonde* (1995), Bosch and Bremmer (the reporter who made front pages of all of Bosch's cases and who turns copy-cat serial killer in this novel) share a past featuring a broken home and a destitute mother – a prostitute in Bosch's case, an alcoholic in Bremmer's. These mothers, moreover, were killed when their sons were very young, while Bertens and D'haen also call attention to the fact that Bremmer and Bosch both have names of Dutch origin starting with the same letter.

Furthermore, Connelly's detective figure, like a psychoanalyst, often engages in transference with the criminal, since he must identify with the latter in order to trace the path back to the original trauma. As pointed out by Bertens and D'haen (2001: 109), 'in each Bosch novel the criminal affair he works on immediately and strongly affects the life of Bosch himself'. It might be for this reason that Bosch is most often presented to exude a kind of tragic aura; he appears to suffer by the association he shares with those who are criminally minded. This phenomenon can virtually be summarised in the course of a short extract from *The Black Echo* (1992), where the detective somewhat identifies his own psyche when looking at a framed print of Hopper's *Nighthawks*;

> The darkness. The stark loneliness. The man sitting alone, his face turned to the shadows. I am that man, Harry Bosch would think each time he looked.
>
> Connelly (1992: 412)

In addition to summing up the atmosphere of the Bosch series, the extract elaborates the brooding figure of the tragic protagonist. In many ways, Harry Bosch reminds us of the classic private eye of the Golden era as opposed to the maverick homicide detective he actually is. This, in fact, has been argued to contribute to Bosch coming across as 'a contemporary reincarnation of the classic private eye dropped into a contemporary police procedural' (Bertens and D'haen, 2001: 111).

In terms of the *nature* of the abnormal behaviour Connelly's criminals engage in, it seems that, as mentioned in Chapter 2, familiar motivations for murder – such as greed, ambition and jealousy – no longer prove adequate to account for the generic form. The force of unregenerate, frequently sexual obsession brings down reason to its knees; the sexual charge lying behind the murders Bosch investigates makes it no longer possible for him to rely on traditional motivations for murder leading him to the murderers. For instance, in the context of Connelly's *Angels Flight* (1999), the real murderer of a twelve-year old girl turns out to be her father who has been sexually abusing her, while Bosch's fellow police officers appear to have tortured the girl's wrongly suspected rapist and murderer when under police custody. Similarly, in *The Concrete Blonde* (1995), the 'Dollmaker' slayings are horrific, while Mora, Bosch's fellow police officer who specialises in the porn industry, turns out to be a twisted man who is in fact involved in child pornography.

The carnivalesque as social deviation in the genre

Carnivals

When modern readers think of the word 'carnival', they are likely to imagine an amusement park, a fair, or a Disney-like theme park. More specifically, in America, a 'carnival' has come to mean a fairground; in

England, a procession of street floats (Hyman, 2000: 10). Though *medieval* carnivals share the same ideas of gaiety with their contemporary counterparts, the former were in fact rather different. Burke (1994: 178) suggests that the traditional carnival was just one of those special occasions when people stopped work and ate, drank and spent whatever they had. It is often, therefore, defined as a festival of merrymaking that took place in that temporal season leading up to Lent. Hyman, however, notes that

> [w]hile Carnival is first recorded as a pre-Lenten feast only in the later Middle Ages, most anthropologists locate its origins much earlier, in pre-Christian ritual and especially in Saturnalia – the period of licence and excess, when inversion of rank was a central theme. Slaves were set free and given the right to ridicule their masters; a mock-king was elected; the lost Golden-Age of the deposed god Saturn was temporarily reinstated.
>
> Hyman (2000: 9)

This latter definition elaborates the 'organic whole' of carnival as one that encompasses both the positive and the negative; it promotes an interaction between the official and unofficial cultures of the event. According to Burke (1994: 182), in southern Europe, in particular, 'carnival was the greatest popular festival of the year, and a privileged time when what oft was thought could for once be expressed with relative impunity'. Burke adds that carnivals of this sort could even be seen as huge plays, in which 'the main streets and squares became stages, the city became a theatre without walls and the inhabitants, the actors and spectators, observing the scene from their balconies'.

This definition of the notion of carnival is the one that came to be central to the Bakhtinian project, and is often described as the 'dominant' of Bakhtin's philosophy. As Gardiner suggests,

> [u]sing a constantly recurring metaphor, Bakhtin argues that popular festivals and rituals carved out a 'second life' for the people within the womb of the old society, a world where the normal rules of social conduct were (at least temporarily) suspended and life 'was shaped according to a certain pattern of play'.
>
> Gardiner (1993: 32)

The carnival effectively broke down the formalities of hierarchy and the inherited differences between different social classes and ages, and replaced established traditions and canons with a mode of social inter-action based on principles of solidarity, cooperation, and equality. In practice, this meant that carnival engendered forms of 'free and famil-iar contact among people' by breaking down the system and all formal restraints that created distances between subjects.

> People who in life are separated by impenetrable hierarchical barri-ers enter into free familiar contact on the carnival square. The cate-gory of familiar contact is also responsible for the special way mass actions are organized and for free carnival gesticulation, and for the outspoken carnivalistic word.
>
> Bakhtin (1984a: 123)

By temporarily suspending the entire official system with all its prohi-bitions and hierarchic barriers, carnival therefore established a type of contact and communication that would be impossible in the course of non-carnival, everyday life. It, in other words, permitted the latent sides of human nature to reveal and express themselves.

Such a view of the carnival can even be characterised as an enact-ment of a transformed set of social relations, as a 'living possibility', which, in using Bakhtin's own bacteriological metaphor, Gardiner (1993: 37) refers to as an 'antibody' 'living within a pathological social body, always threatening to rupture it from within'. That is, carnival could be seen as a bacterium, in danger of corrupting the living body of the social hierarchy.

In answer to the question 'What did Carnival mean to the people who took part in it?' Burke (1994: 186) responds that in a sense the question is unnecessary; 'Carnival was a holiday, a game, an end in itself, needing no explanation or justification. It was a time of ecstasy, of liberation'. In another sense, however, he admits that the question need be multiplied, as looking for recurrent themes (real and symbol-ical) in carnival, one encounters food, sex and violence. It was meat, which put the *carne* in carnival, while in addition to being a time of particularly intense sexual activity, the festival was one of aggression, destruction and desecration. These observations allow one to draw on oppositions (a) between carnival and Lent, and (b) between carnival and the rest of the year, and hence carnival can be seen as an enact-ment of 'the world tuned upside down', or as Bakhtin (1984a: 122) puts it, 'the reverse side of the world'. As Burke exemplifies:

> There was physical reversal: people standing on their heads, cities in the sky, the sun and moon on earth [...] There was reversal of the

relation between man and beast: the horse turned farrier shoeing his master; the ox turned butcher, cutting up a man; the fish eating the fisherman [...] Also represented was the reversal of the relations between man and man, whether age reversal, sex reversal, or other inversion of status.

Burke (1994: 188)

The meaning of such a series of images could be argued to be ambiguous and ambivalent but, according to the same source, it is most easy to document the attitude of the upper classes, for which these images symbolised chaos, disorder, and misrule. Whether ordinary people saw the topsy-turvy world as a bad thing is apparently much less clear, but what is apparent is that carnival is polysemous, that is, it meant different things to different people. In short, it could be characterised as a 'time of madness' (as described by contemporaries), a time of institutional disorder, a set of rituals of reversal.

Burke (1994: 200) suggests that some functions of popular festivals of this sort seem obvious enough; they were 'entertainment, a welcome respite from the daily struggle to earn a living; they gave people something to look forward to'. In addition to the fact that these events celebrated the community itself, displaying its ability to put on a good show, carnivals may even be characterised as a dramatic expression of community solidarity.

As Hyman (2000: 16) argues, however, 'the absurdity of such a topsy-turvy image gives the Carnival game away: everything remains unchanged, all will return to the *status quo*'. That is, the whole event's abnormality can be argued to somewhat reaffirm the rules and laws of life, as opposed to challenging such rules and laws. As Burke (1994: 200) suggests, such rituals could in fact be argued to serve 'the function of *social control*' (my italics), 'in the sense that it was the means for a community [...] to express its hostility to individuals who stepped out of line and so to discourage other breaches of custom'. This argument could even help explain why it was that the upper classes permitted such re-enactments in the first place. According to the same source,

It looks as if they [the upper classes] were aware that the society they lived in, with all its irregularities of wealth, status and power, could not survive without a safety-valve, a means for the subordinates to purge their resentments and to compensate for their frustrations.

Burke (1994: 201)

That is, by allowing such 'innate foolishness' in the crowd to come out and evaporate in the course of this once-a-year event, the upper classes would be able to maintain better control of the people for the rest of the year. The dizzy carnival spirit did not undermine authority, since the release of emotions and grievances made it easier for the authorities to police the crowd in the long term. As Burke (1994: 202) puts it, a point in favour of the 'safety-valve' or 'social control' theory is 'its suggestion of a controlled escape of steam'. In other words, the argument in favour of the theory is that the state deliberately used such events to ensure that the masses have a regulated short release from the inflexibility of their lives; the state opens the safety-valve briefly to allow people to indulge in aggressive tendencies.

Finally, from the ordinary people's viewpoint, carnivals were in fact opportunities to make their views known and so to bring about change. They, in other words, could be argued to have provided forums through which to question societal norms and, in this sense, carnivals take the form of *social protest*. Many were masked, since 'wearing masks helped liberate people from their everyday selves, conferring a sense of impunity like a cloak of invisibility in folktales' (Burke, 1994: 202). Some were even armed, and 'serious violence not infrequently occurred whether because the insults went too far or because the season was too good an opportunity to miss for paying off old grudges' (Burke, 1994: 187). Burke explains that due to the heavy consumption of alcohol and the overall excitement of the occasion, 'inhibitions against expressing hostility to the authorities or private individuals would be at their weakest' (Burke, 1994: 203). Consequently, riots and rebellions would frequently take place in the course of major festivals while, on occasion, a carnival would get so violent that it turned into a massacre (such as the massacre at Shrove in 1376, known as the 'evil Carnival'; in London in 1517, known as 'evil May Day'; at Bern in 1513 and so on).

Carnivalesque

Russian theorist Mikhail Bakhtin coined the term 'Carnivalesque' in his book *Rabelais and His World* (1984b), to describe that which is created when the themes of the carnival twist and invert standard elements of societal order. That is, having described carnival culture as one that involves the 'temporary suspension of all hierarchic distinctions and barriers among men [..] and of the prohibitions of usual life' (1984b: 15), he takes carnivalesque to refer to the carnivalising of normal life.

The use of the term 'carnivalesque' in itself suggests, according to Burke (1994: 199), that major feasts of the year had rituals in common and that carnival was an especially important cluster of such rituals; '[i]t is closer to the truth to think of the religious festivals of early Modern Europe as little carnivals than to think of them as grave sedate rituals in the modern manner'. That is, there is a sense in which every festival was a miniature carnival because it was an excuse for disorder and because it did, in fact, draw from the same repertoire of traditional forms.

Bakhtin, furthermore, sees forms of the carnivalesque springing beyond the Renaissance carnival and into art, literature and even everyday life. As Stallybrass and White (1986: 7) put it, the main importance of Bakhtin's study into Rabelais's work is 'its broad development of the "carnivalesque" into a potent, populist, critical inversion of *all* official words and hierarchies in a way that has implications far beyond the specific realm of Rabelais studies'. In other words, Bakhtin informed contemporary theory with respect to popular culture in early modern Europe being involved with the flourishing traditions of carnivalesque. Literary works, in particular, continued the traditions of the Renaissance carnival, either to question dominant elements in a society or for the sake of humour. In fact, everywhere in literary and cultural studies, especially in the early 1990s, we see carnival emerging as a model.

In Castle's (1986) study of the carnivalesque in eighteenth-century English culture and fiction, for instance, he argues that masquerade is a form of carnivalesque in that 'acts of disguise and self-transfiguration include an element of wish-fulfilment', as well as betray the underlying nature of the person undertaking such disguises (the costume could be a way of acting out repressed desires) (Castle, 1986: 73). The carnival convention of inversion is still there in that one was obliged to appear, in some sense, as one's opposite, while at the deepest level the masquerade's work was that of de-institutionalisation. Finally, as with carnival, masquerade allows for one to become aware of institutional and conceptual oppositions (such as European and Oriental, masculine and feminine, human and animal, natural and supernatural, and so on), and appreciate how each institution – each cultural category – depended for its existence on an opposite. As Castle (1986: 87) puts it, 'the masquerade made hierarchies explicit by dramatically suspending them', and '[i]t offered contemporary society a negative of itself: the temporary collapse of structure intensified awareness of the structure being violated'. Masquerade could thus be argued to have highlighted structure, and demonstrated 'the fictionality of classification systems, exposing them as man-made rather than natural or divine' (Castle, 1986: 87).

According to Hall, what is original and striking about Bakhtin's 'carnivalesque' as a metaphor of symbolic and cultural transformation is that

> it is not simply a matter of inversion – setting the 'low' in the place of the 'high', while preserving the binary structure of the division between them. In Bakhtin's 'carnival', it is precisely the purity of this binary distinction which is transgressed. The low invades the high, blurring the hierarchical imposition of order; creating, not simply the triumph of one aesthetic over the other, but those impure and hybrid forms of the 'grotesque' revealing the interdependency of the low on the high and vice-versa, the inextricably mixed and ambivalent nature of all cultural life, the reversibility of cultural forms, symbols, language, and meaning; and exposing the arbitrary exercise of cultural power, simplification, and exclusion which are the mechanisms upon which the construction of every limit, tradition, and canonical formation, and the operation of every hierarchical principle of cultural closure, is founded.
>
> Hall (1993: 8)

Here, carnival is instead considered as an instance of a widespread economy of transgression that reorganises the high/low relations across the whole of the social formation.

The carnival of crime fiction

The fascination with violence and crime experienced in contemporary popular culture reveals the potential entertainment value to be realised from such acts. According to Presdee (2000: 5), the author Anthony Burgess (1990) in his own autobiography, *You've Had Your Time*, explained his own self-disgust at his emotions when creating the violence of his novel *A Clockwork Orange* (1962), when he commented, 'I was sickened by my own excitement at setting it down'. As Presdee explains,

> [h]ere he recognised how his emotions had transgressed the rules of rationality and that there was something in his cultural inheritance

that had led him to revel in and be excited by violence. Indeed, he requested that the film version of his novel, which concentrated on the violence, be withheld from the British viewing public.

Presdee (2000: 5)

Here, Presdee argues that the way we enjoy violence, crime, humiliation and hurt point clearly to the violence of human possibility and imagination, and need to be examined and thought through. It seems that there is clear evidence of humans' desire, enjoyment, and pleasure of violence and it is here that we enter the realm of challenge, control, resistance and even carnival. According to the same source, 'the quest of excitement is directly related to the breaking of boundaries, of confronting parameters and playing with the margins of social life in the challenging of controllers and their control mechanisms' (Presdee, 2000: 7). Pleasure, in other words, is sought and gained on the margins of social life, and more to the point, the illegal performance of those pleasures.

Since Bakhtin's carnivalesque 'second life of the people' is the realm of much resentment and irrationality, it is also the realm of much crime, and this second unofficial life is where everyday life resides and where the rationality of law loses its power. Presdee suggests that the expression of this second life is performed and brought to life through carnival, which for rational society is understood to be synonymous with the carnival of crime.

In this sense, the reading of a crime novel, that engages with the irrational and incomprehensible (whether it is thought of as a celebration of crime or not), can be argued to be a manifestation of the notion of carnival in itself. Devoted readers of the genre, often accused of enjoying the crimes described in such novels in a way that isn't socially acceptable (see Chapter 2 for 'crime reading as pleasure'), are in fact 'allowed' to be socially *deviant* themselves for the duration of the reading, just like carnival participants were in the course of Renaissance carnivalesque festivals. If readers of crime novels are thought of as the *spectators* of carnivals, they are enabled to consume and enjoy pain, violence, cruelty and crime in the privacy of their own homes, while in a sense 'letting others do their crimes for them'. In this sense, for them, to be involved in some way in the act of transgression as voyeurs is pleasure enough.

On the other hand, since in the course of Renaissance carnivals there was no sharp distinction between actors and spectators, readers of crime novels could be thought of as *participants* in the violence of the novels they read, while not advocating that such violence is, in the course of everyday life, acceptable. For, after all, according to Bakhtin (1984b: 7), carnival is not a spectacle seen by the people but lived by them, and 'everyone participates because its very idea embraces all the people'. In this sense, it could be argued that readers are somewhat momentarily 'criminalised', and hence even 'engage' with the crimes described. At the same time, readers are made aware of the marginalised and criminalised groups of society, while satisfying their need to know, firstly, why they are marginalised and criminalised in the first place, and secondly, to understand how the process of criminalisation works.

Furthermore, if crime is seen as the subversion of the bourgeois order, crime novels can be seen as a presentation of an alternative view of the world, reaffirming the supremacy of the dominant order, just like carnivals. Presdee (2000: 42) suggests that 'rather than offering an entire alternative structure, carnival offers a distorted reflection of the structure'. Similarly, it could be argued that crime novels offer a distorted image of reality, and function as a playful and pleasurable revolution, which may also serve as the vindication of the dominant order. Moreover, according to the same source, 'the second life of the people' is threaded through our popular culture; 'not only does contemporary mass culture make free use of the idea of carnival in the promotion of excitements, but its very nature is in part carnivalesque' (Presdee, 2000: 44). In other words, Presdee suggests that so potent are the excitements of the carnival, that the pleasure and leisure industries have utilised carnival as a form as well as a metaphor.

It is for this reason that a number of critics have found a wide variety of instances where elements of carnival have emerged in other contemporary forms of social and symbolic activities, including the reading of crime novels as one of those instances. All in all, just like carnivals, crime novels could be argued to function as both tools for oppression and as vehicles for subversive expression. They allow an escape into a restructured, distorted and criminal world challenging or mocking the ordered world, as well as reaffirming the supremacy of the ordered world over the criminal one. At the same time, since Renaissance carnivals have been argued to form part of the everyday life of the people on specific times of year, so crime and its enjoyment in crime novels can be thought of as part of the social structure to begin with; crime, like the carnivalesque, is threaded through our culture and forms part of it, in the first place.

Another way in which the carnival has so far been described is the way in which it focuses upon *inversions*. This 'reversible world' has been described as one that encodes inversions of everyday hierarchies, which links back to the previously mentioned idea (Chapters 2 and 4) of the detective often taking the form of the criminal him/herself in crime novels, and hence 'becoming the criminal's double'. When describing the structural characteristics of the carnival image, Bakhtin claims that

> it strives to encompass and unite within itself both poles of becoming or both members of an antithesis: birth-death, youth-old age, top-bottom, face-backside, praise-abuse, affirmation-repudiation, tragic-comic, and so forth, while the upper pole of the two-in-one image is reflected in the lower, after the manner of the figures on playing cards. It could be expressed this way: opposites come together, look at one another, are reflected in one another, know and understand one another.
>
> Bakhtin (1984a: 176)

According to this account, the carnival world forces opposites to switch positions, which is a claim that reinforces the image of the crime novel as carnival. As previously mentioned, detectives are often found to imitate the criminals they pursue, not to mention adopt criminal behaviour themselves for the sake of preventing such behaviour in the first place. In this sense, the crime novel's world takes the form of the carnival, encompassing the good-bad poles and yet with the property of the good pole reflecting the bad.

To go back to Connelly's Bosch novels, like much contemporary American crime fiction, there is the tendency to view America as *grotesque*, as a hellish vision of almost uncontrollable perversion, greed, and weakness. Bakhtin uses the complementary term 'grotesque body' in *Rabelais and His World* to classify the carnivalised aesthetic, which is a body that can be understood as one opposite to the Classical aesthetic. The grotesque represents degradation, and stands for the ugly, monstrous, and hideous from the point of view of 'classic' aesthetics, that is, the aesthetics of the ready-made, the cleansed, the developed and the completed (Bakhtin, 1984b: 25). The 'grotesque' here designates 'the marginal, the low and the outside from the perspective of a classical body situated as high, inside and central by virtue of its very exclusions' (Stallybrass and White, 1986: 23). Bakhtin further described the 'Unfinished' body as one 'parading its lumpy extensions, pregnant with liquids' (Hyman, 2000: 17), while it is often said to be a body that draws on oppositions between life and death. The grotesque, also represented in painting such as that by the *artist* Hieronymus Bosch (carnival is, after all, a supremely visual phenomenon), seems to be of particular interest especially in the context of Michael Connelly's *A Darkness More Than Night* (2000).

In this novel, Connelly brings together two of his previously introduced heroes: Harry (Hieronymus) Bosch and Terry McCaleb, and it is a novel in which the author's two detective series (each featuring the relevant detective) cross paths. A hero of Connelly's bestseller *Blood Work* (1998a), and former FBI agent Terry McCaleb, is invited to help the LA Sheriff's Department investigate a killing which bears similarities to certain murders he once profiled for the Bureau. When small-time criminal Edward Gunn is found dead, McCaleb becomes involved in a complex and disturbing case leading him to cross the path of Harry Bosch (though the two detectives have known and worked with each other in the past). Rather surprisingly, it appears that it is Harry Bosch, a fellow homicide detective for the LAPD, who is the suspect who fits into the profile that McCaleb develops. Bosch has always walked on the edge of darkness in order to get inside the minds of the killers he pursues, and the possibility that he has indeed stepped across that finely drawn line and entered that darkness he formerly fought against, at this point presents itself.

What is of particular interest in the novel is that McCaleb's first reading of the disturbing crime scene leads him to look for a killer who takes inspiration from the work of the Dutch late-medieval painter Hieronymus Bosch, the same real-life person from whom the detective character of Harry Bosch was named after (it was in *The Black Echo*, 1992, when we learned that his mother has named him after the painter). More specifically, the crime scene resembles the painter's religious carnivalesque visions, which dealt in particular with the torments of hell. According to the novel itself, while the artist's work is punctuated with violent scenes and depictions of torture and anguish, one need to remember that his was a time when those sorts of things were not that unusual (Connelly, 2000: 96). Moreover, the world of the artist Hieronymus Bosch appeared to have been as striking to McCaleb as it was disturbing.

> The landscapes of misery that unfolded in the pages Penelope Fitzgerald turned were not unlike some of the horrible crime scenes he had witnessed, but in these painted scenes the players were still

alive and in pain. The gnashing of teeth and the ripping of flesh were active and real. His canvases were crowded with the damned, humans being tormented for their sins by visible demons and creatures given image by the hand of a horrible imagination.

Connelly (2000: 98)

The artist and inventor of monsters, chimeras and scenes of debauchery (hence the title of the novel *A Darkness More Than Night*), described in the Connelly (2000: 94) novel as a 'tortured soul' and 'tormented genius', in the context of the same novel in particular, is paralleled by the character of detective Bosch – both by name and association. The character of Harry, previously described as a tragic hero, is one who has known a lot of demons, in the metaphorical sense of the term, and has experienced much pain – both physical and psychological – in the course of his many dire life experiences. Similarly, the artist's paintings reflect the medieval belief in the existence of demons everywhere (which is why evil lurks in all of his paintings), and depict hell as the place of payoff for humans' sins (which is also a place of myriad torments and endless pains – one of 'darkness').

What makes Bosch a likely suspect for the killings is not just the fact that his name matches that of the painter whose work inspired the slayings. He is also later on revealed to have a print of a Hieronymus Bosch painting (that called *The Garden of Earthly Delights*) at home, a print that depicts a landscape of human debauchery and torment. Even more so, Bosch, in a discussion with McCaleb over the painting, speaks of 'the big wheel', and the idea that 'nobody gets away' (Connelly, 2000: 191); what goes around, comes around, hence somehow criminals eventually pay for their sins. McCaleb learns that many scholars and critics who view artist Bosch's work see corollaries to contemporary times, and contemporary crime. He thereafter develops the theory that detective Bosch might have been influenced by his namesake to such as extent that he saw it his duty to teach contemporary criminals a lesson for their sins, and to place them in a payoff place of hell on earth, a place inspired by the disturbing paintings of torture produced by the artist.

> He [McCaleb] had come to believe that homicide detectives, a breed of cop unto themselves, called upon deep inner emotions and motivations to accept and carry out the always difficult task of their job. They were usually of two kinds, those who saw their jobs as a skill or a craft, and those who saw it as a mission in life. Ten years

ago he had put Bosch into the latter class. He was a man on a mission.

This motivation in detectives could then be broken down even further as to what gave them this sense of purpose or mission. To some the job was seen as almost a game [...] Others, [...] also saw themselves with the additional dimension of being speakers for the dead [...] McCaleb classified these cops as avenging angels. It had been his experience that these cops/angels were the best investigators he ever worked with. He also came to believe that they travelled closest to that unseen edge beneath which lies the abyss.

Ten years ago he had classified Bosch as an avenging angel. He now had to consider whether the detective had stepped too close to that edge. He had to consider that Bosch might have gone over.

Connelly (2000: 120)

It is not until later in the novel that readers, of course, find out that detective Harry Bosch was not the killer, but had indeed been set up to appear as the likely suspect.

An earlier novel in the series, *The Black Ice* (1993), a novel concerned with the wholesale smuggling of the heroin derivative 'black-ice' from Mexico into the States, and with the violent death of Cal(exico) Moore, a narcotics officer, also extends the 'saint and sinner' question to a whole range of characters. As Bertens and D'haen argue,

[n]o doubt there are echoes here of the grotesque scenes from hell typical of the world Harry's last name refers to: that of Hieronymus Bosch. Harry Bosch himself, though he repeatedly 'sins' against all rules and regulations, is obviously a 'saint' at heart, in the sense that he transcends his foibles and has the right instincts where and when it matters.

Bertens and D'haen (2001: 107)

In other words, though the correlation between 'saint' and 'sinner' is evident throughout Connelly's Harry Bosch series, especially in reference to the hero, Harry always ends up being classified as the saint. Even in novels such as *A Darkness More Than Night*, where readers themselves are forced to doubt the infamous detective, his credibility and innocence eventually gets reinstated, even if it leaves readers with a feeling of 'guilt' for having thought of him as a killer in the first place.

Overall, carnivalesque imagery (images of the grotesque often appear to be reflected in disturbing crime scenes), and notions of

Bakhtinian 'inversion' add another dimension to the reading of such contemporary crime fiction. They allow one to draw on interesting analogies, and encounter 'the second life of the people' not only in the reading of such novels as literary works, but also in the reading of the protagonists they depict.

In the next section, I introduce a theory from the discipline of psychology, the Jungian notion of *Archetypes*, and explain its manifestation in the social deviance of the genre at hand.

Jungian archetypes

> To expound the manifold and profound significance of the complex in Jung's psychology, without robbing it of its inner meaning, is itself an extremely delicate and difficult task, but any attempt to define the concept of the archetype becomes truly a hazardous undertaking.
>
> Jacobi (1959: 31)

Even though Jacobi argues that it is impossible to give an exact definition of the archetype, the author suggests its general implications by 'talking around it'. She further emphasises that no direct answer can be given to questions dealing with where the archetype comes from and whether or not it is actually acquired.

Jung (1968: 5) defines *archetypes* as archaic or primordial types, universal images that have existed since the remotest of times, myths and fairytales being well-known expressions of them. By 'primordial images' Jung then meant 'all the mythologems, all the legendary or fairytale motifs, etc., which concentrate universally human modes of behaviour into images, or perceptible patterns' (Jacobi, 1959: 33). Fordham (1953: 25) further adds that archetypes are the result of the many recurring experiences of life, like the rising and setting of the sun; it is, however, fantasies, rather than actual images of the experience that remain. Having pointed out that one must constantly bear in mind that what is meant by 'archetype' is in itself representable but it also has effects which enable us to visualise it, namely, the archetypal images, Jacobi notes that

> [c]onsequently, when we encounter the word archetype in any of Jung's writings, we shall do well to consider whether the reference is to the 'archetype as such', still latent and nonperceptible, or to an

already actualized archetype, expressed in conscious psychic
material, an archetype that has become an 'image'.

Jacobi (1959: 35)

Jung (1968: 30) argues that it is no use at all to learn a list of archetypes
by heart, since archetypes are 'complexes of experience that come
upon us like fate, and their effects are felt in our most personal life'.
Nevertheless, Fordham argues that

> it has been possible to isolate various figures, which recur in dreams
> and fantasy series, which appear to have a typical significance for
> human beings and which can be correlated with historical parallels
> and myths from all over the world; these Jung, after much careful
> research work, has described as some of the principal archetypes
> affecting human thought and behaviour, and has named the
> *persona*, the *shadow*, the *anima* and *animus*, the *old wise man*, the
> *earth mother*, and the *self*.

Fordham (1953: 28)

I do not wish to describe all these in detail, but will concentrate on the
principal archetype which has the most significance in relation to the
genre at hand: the *shadow*, the other side of ourselves, to be found in
the personal unconscious.

> The shadow is the inferior being in ourselves, the one who wants to
> do all the things that we do not allow ourselves to do, who is every-
> thing that we are not, the Mr Hyde to our Dr Jekyll. We have an
> inkling of this foreign personality when, after being possessed by an
> emotion or overcome with rage, we excuse ourselves by saying, 'I
> was not myself', or 'I really don't know what came over me'. What
> 'came over' was in fact the primitive, uncontrolled, and animal part
> of ourselves.

Fordham (1953: 49)

Since the shadow here refers to what is personal in so far as
our own weaknesses and failings are concerned, it is easily correlated with the antisocial type of behaviour we attach to criminality
and deviance. As Maitra (1967: 75) suggests, it is that part of
our personality that is continually repressed so that the *persona*
may be built up in order to face the world most profitably and
effectively.

Moreover, since the shadow is here defined as 'all those uncivilised desires and emotions that are incompatible with social standards and our ideal personality, all that we are ashamed of, all that we do not want to know about ourselves', it follows that 'the narrower and more restrictive the society in which we live in, the larger will be our shadow' (Fordham, 1953: 50). The 'shadow' archetype (often expressed as a devil or a witch) can hence, to a certain extent, be equated with what I shall refer to as the 'criminal or deviant archetype'.

In choosing the word 'shadow' to describe these aspects of the unconscious, Jung not only merely suggests 'something dark and vague in outline', but something that is unavoidable; '[i]t is in fact in the nature of things that there should be light and dark, sun and shade' (Fordham, 1953: 50). In accordance with the theory, criminal behaviour, no matter how undesirable, is also unavoidable. It is in the nature of things to have socially deviant individuals alongside law-abiding or socially non-deviant ones. Fordham (1953: 51) herself makes reference to crime as, among others, a manifestation of the *shadow* and notes that it certainly takes moral courage to realise that 'these aspects of human nature may be, and probably are, lurking within ourselves'. Fordham suggests that it is dangerous to suppress the shadow since in the unconscious it acquires strength, and hence when it eventually *does* appear (as usually happens), it is most likely to overwhelm the rest of the personality: 'This is particularly true of those collective aspects of the shadow which are displaced when a mob riots and apparently harmless people behave in the most appallingly savage and destructive manner' (Fordham, 1953: 51). This last excerpt echoes the issues raised in that section of this chapter dealing with the carnivalesque. Socially non-deviant individuals have been known to act deviantly when the environment allows them to, since according to the 'safety-valve' theory in relation to the carnivalesque, the state deliberately used such events as those of the carnival festival to ensure that the people enjoy a measured release from the rigidity of life, much like a safety-valve is opened to release tension. In other words, both theories allow for and acknowledge the 'darker side of the human nature', and see the issues that it raises as social ones and of immense importance.

In addition to being defined as psychological phenomena and as 'needs', archetypes have been described as 'patterns of behaviour', as 'innate schemata', as certain forms of 'inborn reaction to characteristic stimulus situations' (Jacobi, 1959: 42). Such characterisations remind one of the notion of *schema*, originally so used by the philosopher Kant (1963) at the end of the eighteenth century. The term 'schema' refers to skeletal organisations of conceptual know-ledge: Connected bits of general cultural information based on verbal and non-verbal experience are stored as packages or schemas or schemata, which although stereotypical, are continually 'updated' (Wales, 2001: 351). Similarly, archetypes could be described as bundles of knowledge to do with various aspects of the human nature, which is an understanding of the term 'archetypes' that is biological rather than psychological.

Developed later by Artificial Intelligence research and cognitive psy-chology in the 1970s, 'Schema theory' has come to refer to that process whereby we access and update schemata. According to Cook (1994: 9), its basic claim is that a new experience is understood by comparison with a stereotypical version of a similar experience held in memory. The new experience is then processed in terms of its deviation from the stereotypical version or conformity to it. Short (1996) uses the helpful analogy of a filing cabinet. Having described schemata as bits of infor-mation stored in the form of packages, he suggests that

> [w]hen we come across a reference to a situation we have come across before, we access the relevant 'file' in the 'filing cabinet', which consists of an organised inventory of all the sorts of things related to that situation which we have previously experienced. These schemas get updated from time to time as new information comes at hand.
>
> Short (1996: 227)

Similarly, archetypes could be defined as schemata to do with the human nature which we activate in order to make sense of situations we encounter in real life. Jung himself also draws on this type of description when he claims that

> [t]here are as many archetypes as there are typical situations in life. Endless repetition has engraved these experiences into our psychic constitution, not in the form of images filled with content but at first only as *forms without content*, representing merely the possibility of a certain type of perception and action. When a situation occurs which corresponds to a given archetype, the archetype becomes activated and a compulsiveness appears, which, like an instinctual drive, gains its way against all reason and will, or else produces a conflict of pathological dimensions, that is to say, a neurosis.
>
> Jung (1968: 48)

Having briefly pointed out some of the similarities between Schema theory and Jung's theory of archetypes, in the following section I concentrate on those archetypes which are to do with the nature of the criminal mind. According to Knapp (1986: 192), '[i]t is the artist or architect who provides shape, line, and mass to these amorphous images that have been dredged up from subliminal spheres'. Therefore, in the context of literary study, I argue that there is a limited selection of criminal archetypes which a reader of contemporary crime fiction can expect to encounter.

Criminal archetypes

When I make reference to 'criminal archetypes', I am in fact referring to those schemata that are to do with the nature of the criminal mind, and it is the skeletal organisation of conceptual knowledge to do with understanding the sources of criminality that my three-fold classification of contemporary crime fiction's criminals exemplifies. Though I do not mean to argue that all fictional criminal figures would abide to this classification, it certainly is the case that the three criminal archetypes are easily identified on close examination of the genre. In other words, the classification is more inclusive rather than exclusive, and intends to be descriptive, rather than prescriptive. Finally, though I have come across novels where criminal figures are easily slotted into one of these categories, other criminal figures have been known to switch categories midway through the novels (see Chapter 3 for the classification's repercussions for linguistic characterisation).

The first criminal archetype, referred to in the 'Linguistic Deviance' section of this book, is the 'Born Evil' criminal figure. These fictional personas are presented as having been deviant since birth, unlike those criminal figures whose actions were conditioned or justified, for instance by means of their childhood traumatic experiences. Such a criminal archetype could be described as THE MONSTER, not only because it tends to be 'abnormal' in the psychological sense of the term, but often also in the physical one. A typical exemplification of this type can be found in Patricia Cornwell's *Black Notice* (2000a), a book that forms part of Cornwell's Dr Kay Scarpetta series.

In the course of *Black Notice*, Dr Kay Scarpetta, Virginia's Chief Medical Examiner, and her colleague Captain Pete Marino discover an unidentified body in a cargo ship. Scarpetta's initial post mortem fails to reveal a cause of death or an actual identification, while the victim's personal belongings and an odd tattoo lead Scarpetta and Marino to

Interpol's headquarters in Lyon. Here, she finds herself and those she dearly cares for at deadly risk.

By the end of the novel, a number of murders have been committed, referred to as 'the Werewolf Murders' due to the large number of long fine blonde baby-like hairs recovered at each scene. Chandonne, the horrific murderer, suffers from a highly unusual condition referred to as hypertrichosis (whereby hairiness progressively increases since birth until the only areas spared are mucous membranes, palms and soles), his physical abnormality mirroring his psychological abnormality: 'I imagined him wandering like a nocturnal beast, selecting and stalking until he stuck and savaged again and again. His revenge in life was to make his victims look at him. His power was their terror' (Cornwell, 2000a: 377). It is in fact made clear in the course of the novel that Chandonne's dirty little secret of slashing, beating and biting women was known to his family, and yet he was protected so as to shield the family name. The following extract where the examiner discusses the case with a colleague elaborates on Kay's beliefs as to what it is that prompted the killing spree.

> 'I just want to stop this werewolf-freak before he kills and mutilates anybody else. I want to know what makes him tick.'
> 'Fear and avoidance,' I said. 'Suffering and rage because he was punished for something that wasn't his fault. He anguished alone. Imagine being intelligent enough to comprehend all that.'
> 'He would hate his mother most,' Talley said. 'He might even blame her.' [...]
> 'He would hate women he sees,' Talley said. 'Women he could never have. Women who would scream in horror if they saw him, saw his body.'
> 'Most of all, he would hate himself,' I said.
> 'I know I would.'
>
> Cornwell (2000a: 382)

Here, the readers are invited to believe that the anomalies the monstrous criminal figure has had were beyond the physical, if not due to the physical. Like a monster or animal, he attacks his victims with innate hatred and viciousness and, as in the previous extracts, is often described as a 'werewolf freak', as a 'nocturnal beast'. The psychological profiling taking place here could be described as a form of *potential mind style* (see Chapter 3 for my definition of 'mind style'), defined 'potential' since it represents the two colleagues' perception or understanding of the criminal's world view, rather than a view offered by an access to his actual consciousness. The two characters theorise that Chandonne feels rejected by women, if not by the whole of society, and feels to have been punished for no actual crime, but for the misfortune of his horrific condition and appearance. His fear of this constant rejection as well as his private suffering therefore are presumed to have found expression in his crimes; he finds that he can only gain power and control over his victims' terror.

At the very end of the book, Chandonne attempts to attack Scarpetta as well, but fails.

> My porch light was out, and it had never occurred to me he might be able to speak without a French accent, and I smelled that dirty, wet doglike smell as he pushed his way in and shut the door with a back-kick. I chocked on the scream on my throat as he smiled his hideous smile and reached out a hairy hand to touch my cheek, as if his feelings for me were tender.
>
> Half of his face was lower than the other and covered with a fine blonde stubble, and uneven, crazed eyes burned with rage and lust and mockery from hell. He tore off his long black coat to net it over his head and I ran and this all happened in a matter of seconds.
>
> Panic hurled me into the great room and he was on my heels making guttural sounds that didn't sound human. [...]
>
> His upper body was dense with long hair that hung from his arms and swirled over his spine. He fell to his keens, scooping up handfuls of snow and rubbing it into his face and neck again and again as he fought for breath.
>
> He was within reach of me and I imagined him springing up any moment like a monster that wasn't human.
>
> Cornwell (2000a: 402–4)

In the course of this extract, Chandonne is described through the eyes of a woman in fear, hence the breathless use of coordination of clauses ('He tore off his long black coat ... and I ran ... and all this happened in a matter of seconds'). The examiner admits that, in a form of potential mind style, his actions must have been a combination of his expression of lust, tenderness, mockery and craziness. Though a human, the criminal is correlated to a 'monster that wasn't human', as a devilish creature that came straight from hell. Such a categorisation of crime to the realm of the morally 'monstrous' is typical of the whole range of Cornwell's Dr Kay Scarpetta series, and has been noted by a number of crime fiction analysts (Messent, 1997: 3; Bertens and D'haen, 2001: 170). What is interesting however, as to this novel in particular, is the fact that someone who has a physically abnormal appearance also shares an abnormal psyche. As with *Black Notice*, in *Postmortem* (1990), the first novel in the series, not only is the criminal again psychologically presented as a monstrous psychopath, but as one who is also physically monstrous, in that he shares a strange body odour because of a rare metabolic disorder.

Other monstrous criminal figures, such as Thomas Harris's (1990) psychopathic madman in *Silence of the Lambs*, do not share such an abnormal appearance or physical condition, regardless of how abnormal they are, in the psychological sense of the term. In the latter novel, Dr Hannibal Lecter, a brilliant and evil genius (a psychiatrist), a psychotic serial killer, is referred to as 'Hannibal the Cannibal' and as 'a monster' at various points in the novel, and is presented as a criminal figure who shares psychological anomalies that lead him to commit horrific murders. Another monstrous criminal figure is James Patterson's Gary Soneji, a serial killer who was featured in two novels, *Along Came a Spider* (1993) and *Cat and Mouse* (1997). This psychopathic madman, as analysed in Chapter 3, engages in criminal actions that range from kidnapping to murder, and is again referred to as a brilliant and yet evil figure who though psychologically disturbed since birth, does not share a physical abnormality.

The second criminal archetype, referred to in the 'Linguistic Deviance' section of this book, is the 'Made Evil' criminal figure. The actions of such fictional personas are presented as conditioned or justified, for instance by means of their childhood traumatic experiences. Such criminal archetypes could be described as VAMPIRES, in that their criminal behaviour was provoked when they endured abuse (whether sexual or otherwise) at an early age. Much like the myth of vampires, they were made into the killers they now are by the abuse(s) they themselves endured as children. A typical exemplification of this type can be found in James Patterson's *Violets Are Blue* (2001), a book that forms part of Patterson's Dr Alex Cross series.

In this novel, a number of bizarre murders mystify Alex and the FBI as the victims are found dead, having been bitten and hung by their feet to drain their blood. The murder spree is considered as possibly the work of a cult, role players or even modern-day vampires. The two killers, Michael, aged twenty, and his brother William, aged seventeen, are beautiful men-children, incredibly graceful and athletic, but as the following extract suggests, much has happened in the course of their childhood, which may take credit for their current criminal behaviour in the novel.

> When he and Michael were small boys, this whole area had been a commune. Their mother and father had been hippies, experimenters, freedom lovers, massive drug-takers. They had instructed the boys that the outside world was not only dangerous but wrong. Their mother had taught William and Michael that having sex with anyone, even with her, was a good thing, as long as it was consensual. The brothers had slept with their mother, and their father, and many others in the commune. Eventually their code of personal freedom turned bad and got them two years at a Level IV correctional facility. They had been arrested for possession, but it was aggravated assault that put the brothers behind bars. They were suspected of much more serious crimes, but none could be proved.
>
> Patterson (2001: 38–9)

In the course of this extract, which comes at an early stage of the novel, some if not all responsibility for the killers' criminal behaviour is implicitly assigned to the parents of the two boys, who seem to have misdirected them at an early stage in life, and as this extract implies, sexually abused them. Since this extract is taken directly from William's viewpoint, that abuse is not referred to as such (it is described as 'their code of personal freedom'), and the boys are instead simply implied to have willingly had sex with both their parents when very young.

It is not until a later extract where the consequences of their parents' immoral teaching come to be revealed.

> He was on her in an instant and Michael took down her husband almost as easily. The brothers were incredibly fast and strong – and they knew it.
>
> They growled loudly, but that was only an element of surprise, a scare tactic.
>
> 'We have money in the house. My God, don't hurt us,' the male shrieked loudly, almost like a woman.
>
> 'We're not after your obscene money – we have no use for it. And we're not serial killers, or anything common like that.' William told them.
>
> He bit down into the struggling woman's luscious pink neck – and she stopped fighting. Just like that, she was his. She gazed into his eyes, and she swooned. A tear ran down her cheek.

> William didn't look up again until he had fed. 'We're vampires,' he finally whispered to the murdered couple.
>
> Patterson (2001: 42)

In this extract, taken from the brothers' joint viewpoint, the two appear to perceive of themselves as incredibly fast and strong, as well as special and uncommon. A sexual connotation to the killings is additionally established, in relation to the biting of the female victim's throat ('Just like that, she was his'). The killers here actually describe themselves as vampiric creatures who feed on people's blood; not only are their victims often referred to as 'prey' but, on this occasion, William is said to have only looked up at his victim once 'he had fed'. Nevertheless, it is an interesting correlation that is made in the light of their parents' teachings. Their childhood experiences could be blamed for their current behaviour; they endured abuse, somehow possibly 'turned killers' because of it, and have come to be hunters who literally drink their victims' blood so as to feed and, according to their beliefs, survive.

In the course of the same novel, the identity of the Mastermind, a serial killer from previous novels in the series, gets revealed. The readers find out that it was Kyle Craig, Alex's colleague, who has committed a number of horrific murders in the past, and the following extract, taken from Alex's viewpoint, places him in the same archetype as that of the two brothers-murderers in the novel, the 'Made Evil' Vampire archetype.

> Was his family safe – his wife and his two children? I had vacationed with them in Nags Head one summer. I'd stayed at their home in Virginia a few times over the years. His wife Louise was a dear friend. I had promised her I would try to bring Kyle in alive if I possibly could. But now I wondered – did I want to keep that promise? What would I do if I ever caught up with him?
>
> He might go after his own parents, especially since he put part of the heavy blame for his behaviour on his father. William Hyland Craig had been a general in the army, then chairman of the board of two Fortune 500 companies in and around Charlotte. Nowadays, he gave lectures at ten to twenty thousand a pop; he was on half a dozen boards. He had beaten Kyle as a boy, disciplined him ruthlessly, taught him to hate.
>
> Patterson (2001: 408–9)

Though this madman does not take pleasure from sucking people's blood, the correlation between his childhood traumas and current criminal identity is nevertheless again established. What is implied is that the killer's father had been physically abusing him as a child, ruthlessly disciplining him with hatred, teaching him to become the man he now is: one that 'hates'.

A final example from the same criminal archetype category comes from Connelly's *The Poet* (1996), where we encounter a paedophile referred to as the Eidolon, also analysed in Chapter 3. The paedophile, as previously mentioned, holds the belief that he was made into an abuser by the abuse(s) he himself endured when young. The readers are invited to believe that the Eidolon was 'made evil' and therefore it is his traumatic childhood experience that is to be blamed for his current paedophilia.

The third criminal archetype, referred to in the 'Linguistic Deviance' section of this book, is the 'Born and Made Evil' criminal figure, and *could* be classified as a combination of the first two archetypes. Such fictional personas' actions are presented as both conditioned and/or justified, for instance by means of their childhood (possibly traumatic) experiences, and as innate. Such a criminal archetype could be described as a SPOILT CHILD, since such personas often fail to take any responsibility for their actions, and are attracted to criminality solely because they are told that society forbids them to. Though it is rather early on in life that such individuals display criminal behaviour, they often claim that unlike monstrous criminal figures or abused children, they act abnormally because they like it, and because they can.

A typical exemplification of this archetype is Casanova, a criminal that features in Patterson's *Kiss the Girls* (1995). This is yet again another Alex Cross mystery, and features two killers; 'Casanova', who gathers pretty and intelligent young women on campuses on the east coast of the USA, and 'The Gentleman Caller', who is bringing havoc to LA with a number of horrifying murders. The two killers appear to be communicating and either cooperating, or competing. The following extract, taken from Casanova's viewpoint, places this madman in the third criminal archetype:

> Casanova screamed, and the loud sound coming from deep inside his throat turned into a raspy howl.
>
> He was crashing through the deep woods thinking about the girl he had abandoned there. The horror of what he had done. *Again.*
>
> Part of him wanted to go back for the girl – *save* her – an act of mercy.
>
> He was experiencing spasms of guilt now, and he began to run faster and faster. His thick neck and chest were covered with

perspiration. He felt weak, and his legs were rubbery and unde-
pendable.

He was truly conscious of what he had done. He just couldn't stop
himself.

Anyway, it was better this way. She had seen his face. It was
stupid of him to think she would ever be able to understand him.
He had seen the fear and loathing in her eyes.

If only she'd listened when he'd tried to talk to her. After all, he
was different from other mass killers – *he could feel everything* he did.
He could feel love ... and suffer loss ... and ...

He angrily swept away the death mask. It was all her fault. He
would have to change personas now. He needed to stop being
Casanova.

He needed to be *himself.* His pitiful other self.

Patterson (1995: 34–5)

In this extract, even though the madman is aware of his actions, and
even experiences guilt, he justifies his actions by claiming that 'he
could not help himself'. That is, he recognises the horror of his actions
but claims that there is indeed a merciful part to his personality.
However, he in fact takes such little responsibility for his actions, that
he ends up putting it all on his victim; 'It was all her fault' (1995: 35).
He craves for someone to 'understand him', and experiences anger here
for his female victim's inability to do so. Additionally he claims to be
different from other, possibly monstrous criminal figures, those that
lack feelings, because he does 'feel everything', and holds that he
indeed is humane in that respect. Finally, he gives way to another,
pitiful side of his persona.

The second extract is taken from a later point in the novel, where
Casanova is reminiscing over an old so-called 'best friend':

Casanova realized that he missed his 'best friend' above all else.
That was proof that he was sane, after all. He could love; he could
feel things. He had watched in disbelief as Alex Cross shot down
Will Rudolph on the streets of Chapel Hill. Rudolph had been worth
ten Alex Crosses, and now Rudolph was dead.

Rudolph had been a rare genius. Will Rudolph *was* Jekyll and
Hyde, but only Casanova had been able to appreciate both sides of
his personality. He remembered their years together, and couldn't
put them out of his thoughts anymore. They had both understood
the exquisite pleasure intensified the more it was forbidden. This

was a ruling principle behind the hunts, the collection of bright, beautiful, talented women, and eventually the long string of murders. The unbelievable, *matchless* thrill of breaking society's sacred taboos, of living out elaborate fantasies, was absolutely irresistible. These pleasures were not to be believed.

Patterson (1995: 439–40)

Here, Casanova places himself once again in the same archetype by admitting that the ruling principle behind the hunts was the pleasure intensified, as forbidden. He nevertheless thinks of himself as 'sane' due to his ability to 'feel things'. In the novel, the terms 'monster' (1995: 161, 237) and 'bogeyman' (1995: 332) are actually used to refer to the two killers that the psychologist and homicide detective Alex Cross attempts to hunt down. In a brief discussion of the same criminals, Messent (1997: 16) consigns their crimes to 'the realm of pure evil and individual moral monstrosity', as 'a way of isolating it from all social, political or economic causes, and "explaining" it as a freakish and psychopathic exception to all that we know to be normal'. However, I would disagree with such a classification on the basis of the type of justification the criminals themselves offer for their crimes in the novel. Casanova justifies his actions by claiming that the thrill of killing, the breaking of society's so-called taboos was one he found absolutely irresistible. Unlike monstrous criminals, who are born with abnormalities of various sorts, he implies that he somewhat discovered or understood the joys of killing and from then on, was unable to live without them. And that is why I would classify the character as a SPOILT CHILD, rather than a MONSTER.

Another exemplification of this same SPOILT CHILD archetype is Smoke, a criminal that is featured in Patricia Cornwell's *Southern Cross* (1998), (a novel that does not form part of the author's Dr Kay Scarpetta series), also analysed in Chapter 3. In the course of the novel, as previously noted, responsibility for the crimes Smoke carries out gets implicitly assigned not only to the juvenile himself, but also to his parents' blind trust and the system's loopholes.

A final exemplification of this archetype is that found in Jack Ketchum's *Road Kill* (1994). Though a novel that does not fit my 'crime fiction' definition (in that the novel is more concerned with what prompted the killings rather than the question of who it is that committed the killings in the first place), it features a disturbed individual who is, at the beginning of the novel, 'triggered' into committing murders he always had a craving for. The novel starts with an introduction to the character of Wayne, who keeps a record of 'offences', one that consists of anyone and everything that has ever distressed him in the least. We get access to his viewpoint, when he contemplates the acts of murder he wishes to commit.

> [S]o many of them *asked* to die. Men, women, kids, their sex didn't matter. Their age didn't matter. The Leigh kids who kept tearing up his fence at night. Roberts, the fatass next door with his goddamn dog from hell. Half – no, nearly *all* – his regular customers over at the Black Locust Tavern. [..] He kept a notepad and jotted down offences. [...]
> Just so he wouldn't forget just who and when.
>
> Ketchum (1994: 20–1)

Even though at this early point in the narrative Wayne does not carry out his vicious intentions, he is nevertheless wondering why he has not yet dared to do so. He feels that these potential victims in fact 'ask to die', no matter how small or insignificant their so-called offence actually is.

At the same time, we are introduced to the character of Carole, who has been reaching the end of her tether with her ex, Howard, who has attacked and raped her, turning her life into a living hell. She finally decides to take the law into her own hands and, along with her lover Lee, fatally attacks Howard on a mountainside. The two stories become intertwined when Wayne witnesses the murder, which points the way down the killing road for him.

> He almost felt like shouting, like whooping up there in sheer delight. My God! At first he hadn't been sure what he was seeing, it had looked like maybe nothing more than a fight down there, maybe over a woman. One of the men had a baseball bat but he'd seen worse in the parking-lots of bars at night with jacks and tire irons so that it was only at the end of it when the woman picked up the rock and brought it down on the taller, bigger man that Wayne knew what he was seeing.
> Murder.
> He felt like calling down to them. *Hey guys! Hey! Include me in!* He felt like going down there. See things up close. Hell – maybe even help out a little. Who the hell *were* these people? Where the hell did they come from? He couldn't *remember* being this excited. Not by

anything! He was aware of his heart racing and a pounding in his ears.

They dared!

Ketchum (1994: 26–7)

In this extract, we again get access to Wayne's viewpoint, who is here amazed and thrilled at this unexpected view of murder. He wants to participate in the criminal event, to share the excitement, and feels admiration for the couple that dared do what he could only fantasise doing.

Wayne eventually kidnaps Lee and Carole and sets off on a murder spree in the streets of America, killing innocents for the sake of killing, and taking the couple along for the ride. He claims that he wants them along as 'witnesses', as 'company', and is under the mistaken belief that not only do they know what he is going through, but that they also share his thrill for killing, a thrill he feels is unmatchable by any other in life. In a discussion over the thrill with the couple, he argues

> 'I think it's a secret', he said. 'I think it's just a great big secret they keep from us. That they don't want us to know about unless maybe there's a war on or something and then, sure, they want you to know so you'll line up and do it and go on doing it and enjoy yourself all to hell. But otherwise they keep it from you. It's *their* secret. About how fucking good it feels. Y'know?'

Ketchum (1994: 118)

Here, Wayne, much like the character of Patterson's Casanova, commits the crimes because he enjoys the thrill, and because he finds himself able to. He holds the belief that society holds the thrill of murder a great big secret, that people need only experience in the case of war, where murder becomes necessary. Once Wayne draws the courage to act out his vicious intentions, he admits that from then on there is no turning back. Having experienced the thrill of killing, and having allowed himself everything that society has forbidden, he classifies himself as a SPOILT CHILD who kills because he *wants* to, unlike other criminal individuals who do so because they *need* to.

Overall, these archetypes, or criminal schemata, have been repeated so much in the course of the specific genre at hand, that they marginalise old-fashioned criminal archetypes, such as those motivated by revenge, greed, ambition, jealousy, and rage. A reader of a contemporary crime novel (in accordance with my definition of what constitutes such a novel) is more likely to expect a criminal to be monstrous, an adult that endured abuse as a child, or one who murders because they enjoy the thrill. Additional dimensions to these archetypes are also (a) the *seriality* of the killings, which has become inseparable from the excitement of the new form and (b) the sexual charge that lies behind much such recent detective writing. In other words, though the old-fashioned justifications for murder would indeed be more realistic for the genre at hand, they seem to be no longer adequate.

It is also my argument that the author's choice over the different modern criminal archetypes may even have an effect over the way real-life people view criminality overall, and the way they react to it, in the context of fiction. For instance, when one encounters a criminal that had been abused as a child, one is more likely to be sympathetic compared to one's reaction to a criminal who has had an easy life. Similarly, by choosing to place a murderer in the category of pure evil, the persona is effectively removed from the world of social cause and effect, and the readers are no longer likely to be sympathetic. However, in as far as monstrous criminal figures are concerned, though the readers' sympathy is lacking, it would be more likely to be evident if physical abnormalities are also at hand. Such representations, in addition to the extent to which the readers will have access to the criminal's consciousness (with internal narration, or access to one's mind style), overall influence and determine the readers' sympathetic tendencies.

In the next Chapter, I explore the ways in which contemporary crime writers challenge the boundaries of the crime fiction genre itself, and specifically focus on the Patricia Cornwell series featuring Dr Kay Scarpetta. In the second section of this chapter, I integrate Wittgenstein's Family Resemblance theory, as well as the notions of *prototype* and *defamiliarisation*.

5
Generic Deviance in Contemporary Crime Fiction

On defining genre

Genre is a fuzzy concept, a somewhat loose term of art; it is a highly attractive word, but it is also an extremely slippery one. Even though it is often defined as a distinctive type or category of literary composition, Swales (1990: 33) suggests that nowadays *genre* is quite easily used to refer to a distinctive category of discourse of any type, spoken or written, with or without literary aspirations. Such an association 'characterises genre as mere mechanism, and hence is inimical to the enlightened and enlightening concept that language is ultimately a matter of *choice*' (Swales, 1990: 33). Hence genre is here linked to the unthinking application of formulas, such an outcome being an oversimplification brought about for pedagogical convenience.

On the other hand, viewing genre as a *classificatory category* enables one to consider the term as an 'ideal type' rather than as an actual entity. Besides, as Swales puts it, '[a]ctual texts will deviate from the ideal in various kinds of ways' (1990: 34). In the context of folklore studies, Swales (1990: 35) suggests that classifying narratives in generic categories is more of a matter of *function* rather than *form*. In the context of literary studies however, there is a tendency to de-emphasise stability, specifically designed to show how any author breaks the mould of convention so as to establish significance and originality. In fact, relevant features of a literary work will stand out aesthetically, but only if the reader shares background awareness of the genre's historical development.

According to Bakhtin (1984a: 106), '[a] literary genre, by its very nature, reflects the most stable, "eternal" tendencies in literature's development'. Even though, he adds, '[a]lways preserved in literature

are undying elements of the *archaic*', 'these archaic elements are preserved in it only thanks to their constant *renewal*, which is to say, their
contemporisation' (Bakhtin, 1984a: 106).

> A genre is always the same and yet not the same, always old and
> new simultaneously. Genre is reborn and renewed at every new
> stage in the development of literature and in every individual work
> of a given genre. This constitutes the life of the genre. Therefore
> even the archaic elements preserved in a genre are not dead but
> eternally alive; that is, archaic elements are capable of renewing
> themselves. A genre lives in the present, but always *remembers* its
> past, its beginning. Genre is a representative of creative memory in
> the process of literary development. Precisely for this reason genre is
> capable of guaranteeing the *unity* and *uninterrupted continuity* of this
> development.
>
> Bakhtin (1984a: 106)

In other words, Bakhtin argues that there is such a thing as the 'life' of
a genre. Though there is a set of what he refers to as 'archaic' elements
within any given genre, these are capable of renewing themselves,
perhaps evolving, and adjusting to the times. He claims that genre is
thus capable of 'unity' and hence its development is characterised by
'uninterrupted continuity'.

The *evolution* of the genres themselves is a necessary response to a
changing world. However, transgression, in order to exist, requires regulations to be transgressed, and it is these regulations that I need to
draw on so as to define the genre at hand. The set of presuppositions
on which the discourse of literature depends may be referred to as
generic conventions (Chapman and Routledge, 1999: 241). Bex (1996:
176) suggests that there is such conformity in the writing within particular genres that governs interaction between readers and writers,
though not to say that, within the context of literary discourse especially, such conventions are *not* liable to violation. I shall draw on
Wittgenstein's Family Resemblance theory, the theory of Prototypes,
and that of Defamiliarisation so as to arrive at these conventions (for
the genre's previously suggested rules, regularities and constraints, see
Chapter 2).

Wittgenstein's family resemblance theory

'[O]ne of the most important features of human thinking – and one
that plays a big part in producing philosophical puzzlement – is our

craving for unity' (Pitcher, 1964: 215). According to Pitcher (1964: 216), we tend to assume that there is something common to all horses, to all tables, to all men, to all games, to all religions and so on; and this is a natural assumption. He suggests that there can be no gainsaying the powerful influence this idea has exerted on man's thought from the time of Plato down to the present, and further adds that one form of the craving for unity is, therefore, a craving for essences; we have the tendency to assume that everything actually has an essence.

Wittgenstein (1953) set out to show that, though widespread and entirely natural, the belief in essences is in fact mistaken. To the idea of constant essences, Wittgenstein opposed the notion of Family Resemblance, to satisfy his craving for difference and multiplicity, in contrast to others who were in search of sameness and unity. One has to examine, for instance, the various individuals to which a given general term applies, to see that there is in fact nothing which they all have in common; as a plain matter of fact, they do not share a common essence (Pitcher, 1964: 217).

Instead of producing something common to all we refer to by the same term, Wittgenstein claims that these phenomena have no one thing in common which makes them the same word for all, but that they are *related* to one another in many different ways (Wittgenstein, 1953: 31). It is important to see the rhetorical force of the examples that Wittgenstein uses in discussing family resemblance. He begins, innocuously enough, with games.

> Consider for example the proceedings that we call 'games'. I mean board-games, card-games, ball-games, Olympic games, and so on. What is common to them all? – Don't say 'There *must* be something common, or they would not be called "games"' but *look and see* whether there is anything common to all – For if you look at them you will not see something that is common to *all*, but similarities, relationships, and a whole series of them at that. To repeat: don't think, but look! – Look for example at board-games, with their multifarious relationships. Now pass to card-games; here you find many correspondences with the first group, but many common features drop out, and others appear. When we pass to ball-games, much that is common is retained, but much is lost – Are they all 'amusing'? Compare chess with noughts and crosses. Or is there always winning and losing, or competition between players? Think of patience. In ball games there is winning and losing; but when a child throws a ball at the wall and catches

it again, this feature has disappeared. Look at the parts played by skill and luck; and at the difference between skill in chess and skill in tennis. Think now of games like ring-a-ring-a-roses; here is the element of amusement, but how many other characteristic features have disappeared! And we can go through many, many other groups of games in the same way; can see how similarities crop up and disappear.

Wittgenstein (1953: 31)

Wittgenstein's detailed investigation overall shows that games lack any common feature running through them by virtue of which they are called games. The assumption that things called by a general term have something in common has therefore, in this example, been revealed and destroyed. As Pitcher points out, however,

> we must not infer from the fact that there is no essence of games or religions, that each is nothing more than a motley, disconnected group of things which are arbitrarily called by the same name. There is no warrant for thinking that the denial of essences leaves no reason whatever why a range of different things are all named by a single term. Although they have no common sense, they have certain 'family resemblances'.

Pitcher (1964: 219)

What an examination of the actual use of the term 'games' has hence revealed is in fact 'a complicated network of similarities overlapping and criss-crossing: sometimes overall similarities, sometimes similarities of detail' (Wittgenstein, 1953: 31). Wittgenstein (1953: 32) further adds that he can think of no better expression to characterise these similarities than 'family resemblances'; 'for the various resemblances between members of a family: build, features, colour of eyes, gait, temperament, etc. etc. overlap and criss-cross in the same way'.

He further claims that kinds of number form a family in the same way. In answer to the question 'Why do we call something a "number"?', he replies that we do so because it has a direct relationship with several things that have hitherto been called a number, and this can be said to give it an indirect relationship to other things we call the same name:

> And we extend our concept of number as in spinning a thread we twist fibre on fibre. And the strength of the thread does not reside in

the fact that some one fibre runs through its whole length, but in the overlapping of many fibres.

Wittgenstein (1953: 32)

In other words, Wittgenstein suggests that the application of a word is not everywhere bounded or circumscribed by rules, and hence convinces us that numbers, like games, form a family, in that they share a family likeness which enables us to regard them as variations of the same ungiven theme.

Pitcher (1964: 219) argues that Wittgenstein's point can be generalised if we look at the matter not – as we have been doing – from the side of things to which words apply, but rather from the side of the words. Pitcher distinguishes the notion of having a *unitary* meaning from that of having a *single* meaning, and claims that most, perhaps all general terms have no unitary meaning.

In setting out various characteristics which games typically have, Pitcher indicates that not all games have all of them, but that what is required for something to be a game is that it has some of the cluster of game-characteristics, though not every combination of game-characteristics will do. A thing can lack all, or even very many, of the typical game properties, and still be a game; but there is no one property, or group of two or three properties, which one theme must have to be properly called a game; games have no essence, and no unitary meaning.

Pitcher (1964: 221) finally points out an important distinction between those terms that do and those that do not fall under Wittgenstein's thesis; Wittgenstein's thesis, although highly plausible for words such as 'game', is not at all plausible for terms like 'brother' and 'vixen'; for to be a brother, it is essential that one is male, and to be a vixen, it is essential that a fox is female. As Pitcher (1964: 223) puts it, 'it is clear that he held that all words which are involved in philosophical puzzlement, all words which are philosophically interesting, have no unitary, fixed meaning'.

The prototype approach to sense

Sense, the mental representation of a lexical expression independent of the context of its use, can be characterised as either (1) a relation between a language expression and certain characteristics of the referents (denotata) of that language expression or (2) as a relation between language expressions in a system, that is, within a single language, independent of the referents of the language expressions.

In the context of the first characterisation of 'sense', the term corresponds to the essential characteristics of the referents of a language expression. This is the characterisation of the term that has been revealed and destroyed by Wittgenstein's line of argumentation in the previous subsection. That is, as mentioned, not all potential referents of X can be argued to share a set of common features and properties, which people know and are aware of.

In the context of the same characterisation of 'sense', the term can also be defined in terms of *necessary* and *sufficient* conditions (see Saeed, 1998: 35). Necessary are those conditions that must be met in order for the entity to qualify as a potential referent (denotatum) of X. For instance, in order for one to qualify as a 'mother', she needs to be 'female'. Sufficient are those conditions which, if met, are enough in themselves to guarantee that a given entity is a potential referent (denotatum) of X. For instance, for one to qualify as 'mother', she needs to have given birth to offspring. However, both these types of conditions prove inadequate, especially when one considers the vast variety of other lexical items which share these conditions (for example, 'female' is also a necessary condition for 'woman', 'grandmother' and 'girl'), or those uses of the lexical item which don't share the conditions (for example, one needn't have given birth to an offspring for her to be called a 'mother'; she can be a stepmother, an adopting mother, a godmother and so on).

Rather than looking at all possible denotata, others have looked at the perceived salient characteristics of the prototypical ones. According to Allan (1986: 107), William Labov's *Denotational Structure* (1978) reports various kinds of labelling tasks involving the application of such labels as *cup, mug, bowl, glass, goblet,* and *vase* to line drawings of containers of different shapes and configurations. In the experiment, subjects were asked to label the drawings with and without a particular context being mentioned. In the results of the experiment, the evaluation of the potential referents proved to have been depended on and affected by both context and use. To make their decision, subjects were claimed to have considered the characteristics of each of the drawings in conjunction with the characteristics of the relevant *prototypical* object, this being defined as 'an abstraction, a concept, with all the perceived characteristics of the typical denotatum which we refer in spelling out the sense of the denoting expression' (Allan, 1986: 109). In other words, the subjects drew on the prototypical approach to sense, whereby the sense of X is taken to be a reflection of the perceived salient characteristics of the prototypical denotata of X. Taking perception to be a mental act in which sensory cues set up expectations which project the fundamental defining properties of the prototype of the perceived phenomenon, Allan (1986: 137) claims that '[i]t is these characteristic properties of the prototype which are referred to in giving the sense of the language expression used to label (i.e. denote) the phenomenon'.

According to this approach, in the context of human categorisation, not all members of a category are equally representative of the category; some members are more representative than others. One need only consider the categories of 'birds', 'vehicles' and 'furniture' to arrive at this conclusion. That is, there is a continuum of category membership, based on perceived characteristics, stretching from the most representative to less representative to least representative to non-member, while one need keep in mind that the categories of the mind do not always have clear-cut boundaries. What this implies is that the members of a category need not all share a common set of characteristics, while not all the characteristics of the prototypical members of a given category are equally important; some are perceived to be more salient than others.

A prototype can hence be defined as the best example of a particular entity, a salient example of a particular entity or as a 'run of the mill' instance of a particular entity. It could also be defined as a mental representation of a particular entity, as a cognitive reference point, as something which is innately available to the human mind. Prototypes are additionally culture specific, and can vary according to age, gender and personal background, since for different people there are different ways of categorising a set of references.

The prototype approach to sense is not, however, without its problems. What is not explained is firstly how one can determine the prototypical instances of the denotata of X, and secondly, how it is that one can determine the most salient features of the prototypical instances of the denotata of X.

In the next section, I consider the notion of defamiliarisation in the context of literary genres, and then proceed to apply the various notions introduced in the whole of Chapter 2 onto contemporary crime fiction.

Defamiliarisation and genre

As Lemon and Reis (1965: 4) put it, Victor Shklovsky's concept of defamiliarisation functioned as a critical formula that defined the difference between literature and non-literature, and also stated the purpose of literature. *Defamiliarisation* is the usual English translation of *ostranenie* (literally, 'making strange'), another of those invaluable critical terms coined by the Russian Formalists. According to Lodge (1992: 53), in a famous essay first published in 1917, Shklovsky argued that 'the essential purpose of art is to overcome the deadening effects of habit by representing familiar things in unfamiliar ways'; presenting the known in terms of the unknown.

> Shklovsky's argument, briefly stated, is that the habitual way of thinking is to make the unfamiliar as easily digestible as possible. Normally our perceptions are 'automatic', which is another way of saying that they are minimal. From this standpoint, learning is largely a matter of learning to ignore [...] When reading ordinary prose, we are likely to feel that something is wrong if we find ourselves noticing the individual words as words. The purpose of art, according to Shklovsky, is to force us to notice. Since perception is usually too automatic, art develops a variety of techniques to impede perception, or at least, to call attention to themselves [...] According to Shklovsky, the chief technique of promoting such perception is 'defamiliarisation'. It is not so much a device as a result obtainable by any number of devices.
>
> Lemon and Reis (1965: 4–5)

In other words, Shklovsky viewed defamiliarisation as a technique that is designed especially for perception, for attracting and holding attention, therefore bearing meaning, and forcing an awareness of its meaning upon the reader. Besides, as Shklovsky (1965: 13) himself argues, '[t]he technique of art is to make objects "unfamiliar", to make forms difficult, to increase the difficulty and length of perception because the process of perception is an aesthetic end in itself and must be prolonged'. Thompson (1971: 67) similarly argues that '[t]he aim of art is to make us see things instead of merely recognising them'. She claims that, in accordance with Shklovsky's theory, in the course of living, we cease to see objects, we only recognise them. Thompson suggests that defamiliarisation is part and parcel of artistic presentation, and it is only when an object or idea looks strange, unknown and difficult, that we attend to it, enter into direct contact with it, really 'see it'. At the same time, Lodge claims, it is this effect of *defamiliarisation* that makes books 'original':

> What do we mean – it is a common term of praise – when we say that a book is 'original'? Not, usually, that the writer has invented

something without precedent, but that she has made us 'perceive' what we already, in a conceptual sense, 'know', by deviating from the conventional, habitual ways of representing reality.

Lodge (1992: 55)

Lodge here offers *defamiliarisation* as another word for *originality*, and presents the notion as a form of deviation from conventional ways of viewing the world.

The device of defamiliarisation or 'making strange' has been much discussed since it was first identified, but Birnbaum (1985: 149) suggested that the notion of literary technique or device in the narrow sense, as a way of shaping and reshaping the semiotic structure of a given text to achieve a higher artistic quality, has primarily been applied to prose, notably narrative prose. Trying to determine the approximate limits of defamiliarisation's application is difficult since, as Shklovsky (1965: 18) himself puts it, 'defamiliarisation is found almost everywhere form is found'. In the context of the novel, applications of the term range from use of wordplay, figurative language and riddles, to disorder (that is, plot being distorted in the process of telling; events not being bound each-to-each in a cause-and-effect relationship) and the adaptation of novel viewpoints, all of which can make the reader *perceive* by making the familiar seem strange.

By violating forms, authors force readers to attend to them, this awareness of the forms through their violation often constituting the content or subject matter of the novels themselves. This claim has interesting applications in the context of genre. Authors working against the background of specific generic forms often use defamiliarisation to bring awareness of the genre at hand. Since often the work of art is perceived against the background of and through associations with other works of art, its form is also determined by its relation to the forms that existed before it. As Steiner (1984: 56) argues, new works come about to change our perception of the artistic form itself, which has become automatised through our acquaintance with older works.

According to Steiner (1984: 59), Shklovsky's conception of historical process states that 'the development of a literary genre is not an uninterrupted continuum, a chain of works successively defamiliarising each other, but instead a qualitative leap, an abrupt ascent to a higher level of literary consciousness'. This conception states that the 'naïve' novelist creates characters and events without realising that in fact he is complying with the historical demand for defamiliarising artistic form, whereas the 'cunning' modernist, conscious of his historical role, analyses the present state of literature and designs his writings in such a way so as to achieve maximal effect. Steiner finally suggests that sophisticated modern writers defamiliarise the genre they are writing within itself and therefore reaffirm the existence of the generic conventions that govern its literary past.

The crime fiction genre

As pointed out in Chapter 2, there have been many attempts to define the nature of the genre at hand. I defined *crime* or *detective* fiction (as previously stated, the two terms are used interchangeably) as those stories which involve the detection of (most usually) a murderer, regardless of whether the detecting is being done by a police officer, a private detective, or someone else. The sort of definition I adopted for contemporary crime fiction is: a past event of murder gets to be resolved, and yet a present action of events is followed. In the context of the same section, I outlined various suggestions as to sets of 'rules' on how detective stories are supposed to be written, and then suggested that these rules, some being inclusive and others exclusive, have almost all certainly been violated.

In the light of Wittgenstein's theory, however, it seems that crime fiction could be defined as a Family Resemblance type of genre instead (in fact most, if not all, literary genres can be understood in terms of Wittgenstein's theory, including science fiction, romance, self-help books and so on). One need, that is, examine the various novels to which the term crime fiction applies (for example, in the context of the 'crime fiction' section of a bookstore), to see that there is in fact nothing which all crime novels have in common, but that the novels are instead *related* to one another in many different ways. For instance, whereas a number of such novels feature significant murder cases, every clue discovered by the detective is readily available to the reader (that is, *fair-play* rule), the number of suspects is known from the start and the murderer is among them and so on, not all crime novels share these characteristics. As the genre evolves and changes, perhaps adjusts to the times, some characteristics crop up and others disappear; in accordance to Wittgenstein's theory, a complicated network of similarities overlap and criss-cross, sometimes these being overall similarities, but at other times these being similarities of detail. The application of the term *crime novel* need therefore not be circumscribed by rules, since the novels could be said to have formed a family, enabling us to regard each of them as variations of the same theme.

In other words, all that is required for something to be regarded as a crime novel is for it to have some of the cluster of the 'crime novel' characteristics, though not every combination of these will do. A novel can lack a great number of the typical relevant properties and still be a crime novel, but there is no one property which all novels share: crime novels, like games, have no unitary meaning.

However, 'family resemblance' has not been without its critics. One should be wary of any one theorist's choice of examples for illustrative purposes and as Swales (1990: 50) points out, 'games' may particularly favour Wittgenstein's observations (Swales argues that nearly all games offer a contest or a challenge, and admits to be solely left with an unaccounted for residue as represented by such children's games as ring-a-ring-a-roses). Rather more seriously, he also claims that it can be objected that a family resemblance theory can make anything resemble anything (1990: 51). Turning to the analysis of the genre at hand, therefore, one could claim that distinct crime novels such as A and B might have nothing in common other than the fact that they both share a feature with crime novel C. In any case, one need remember that Wittgenstein was concerned with *family* resemblances and that families cohere with a whole range of features (for example, physical characteristics, blood types, shared experiences), so there are bound to be a whole range of such links with novels from the genre that would additionally enable the two novels, A and B, to be classified as crime ones.

In light of the prototype approach to sense, rather than looking at all possible denotata (potential referents for *crime fiction*), we can look at the perceived salient characteristics of the prototypical ones. That is, we can draw on the prototypical approach to sense, whereby the sense of *crime fiction* is taken to be a reflection of the perceived salient characteristics of the prototypical denotata of *crime fiction*. The most typical 'crime novel' category members are *prototypes*. According to Swales (1990: 52, 58), properties such as communicative purpose, form, structure and audience expectations operate to identify the extent to which an exemplar is *prototypical* of a particular genre.

In the case of the genre at hand, the prototypical detective novel would probably need to be a *'golden age'* novel, one from the 1920s and 1930s when the traditional English whodunit included practitioners such as Agatha Christie. We then need to account for there being a continuum of category membership, based on perceived characteristics, stretching from the most representative (approximate to the prototype) to the least representative of the crime fiction category. What this implies is that not all perceived characteristics of the prototypical crime novel are equally important, while there are bound to be difficulties in such a characterisation since, as previously mentioned, for different people there are different ways of categorising a set of references (varying, in this case, according to cultural background, age, and so on). Also, as Swales (1990: 54) put it, knowledge of the conventions of a genre is likely to be much greater in those who professionally or routinely operate within that genre rather than in those who do so occasionally. That is, in accordance with this claim, a certain novel's prototypicality will depend on the knowledge that one has of the genre at hand, and therefore of the type of generic conventions that (s)he has come to be aware of.

However, since crime fiction, in its present form, no longer adheres to the rules or generic features of the prototypical crime novel that started it all, the prototype approach to sense seems inadequate. That is, even though antecedent prototypical genres operate as powerful constraining models, equally powerful are those novels written as a revolt against the prototypical novels of the genre.

In Chapter 2, the crime novel, whether English or American, has been identified as an essentially conservative form, and yet it was noted that the detective writing school has given rise to a number of parodies and pastiches. The genre has also been the object of literary experiments, such as Paul Auster's *The New York Trilogy* (1988), where one encounters three brilliant variations upon the classic detective story.

As previously mentioned, authors working against the background of specific generic forms often use defamiliarisation to bring awareness of the genre at hand. Old works have automatised the artistic form, and new works come about to change our perception of it.

In the opening entry from Auster's trilogy, 'City of Glass', a detective writer, Daniel Quinn, is drawn into a curious investigation. The novelist is hired by a man named Peter Stillman to follow his father upon his release from prison. The elder Stillman, a former linguistics academic, kept young Peter locked in a dark room for nine years of his childhood in an experiment to study his son's communicative skills (The father was hoping that in the absence of any human communication, the boy would forget his native English and recreate 'God's language'). At the start of the novel, Peter contacts Quinn to look for a detective called Paul Auster (note the naming of the character after the author) and, on the third phone call, Quinn assumes the name of the person Stillman is seeking while, for the purposes of the investigation for which he is hired by the Stillmans, he also takes on the identity of the detective. In the early part of the novel we also learn that Quinn writes under the pseudonym William Wilson (a reference to Edgar Allan Poe's story of that name regarding identity and doppelgangers), and that he identifies with the hero of his series, detective Max Work. Quinn becomes absorbed in the case and the clues regarding elder Stillman's motives, and eventually he himself loses track of his own identity in the process.

In their analysis of the same story, Chapman and Routledge (1999: 244) argue that '[t]he difficulties experienced by the reader of Auster's novel are compounded by the extent to which it appropriates and subsequently dismembers the conventions of the detective fiction genre'. In other words, though they recognise that the genre has been identified as being particularly reliant on its formal structures, this particular story dismembers the conventions, makes readers aware of the conventions and simultaneously defamiliarises the genre itself. In 'The Typology of Detective Fiction', Todorov (1977: 43) emphasises the importance of generic conformity to the extent that, for him, to disobey the rules of the genre is to depart from it: 'The masterpiece of popular literature is precisely the book which best fits its genre [...] The whodunit par excellence is not the one which transgresses the rules of the genre, but the one which conforms to them.' In other words, Todorov viewed the genre as rather stable, much like the character of Quinn in the story who, as a reader of detective stories himself, relishes their 'plenitude and economy';

> In the good mystery there is nothing wasted, no sentence, no word that is not significant. And even if it is not significant, it has the potential to be so – which amounts to the same thing. The world of the book comes to life, seething with possibilities, with secrets and contradictions. Since everything seen or said, even the slightest, most trivial thing, can bear a connection to the outcome of the story, nothing must be overlooked. Everything becomes essence; the centre of the book shifts with each event that propels it forward. The centre, then, is everywhere, and no circumference can be drawn until the book has come to its end.
>
> Auster (1988: 8)

In the context of this extract, Quinn also appears to bring to his reading those presuppositions about genre which necessarily need to be fulfilled, namely that the text will have been constructed with perceived generic conventions in mind.

Chapman and Routledge (1999: 245) argue that it is possible to express these formulaic requirements as a series of presuppositions (using 'presupposed' as that which is synonymous with that which is given or agreed) shared by writer and reader, and argue that '[t]he idea of the genre of detective fiction itself provides a pool of presuppositions with which both writer and reader approach the text, and which are therefore readily available for inspection'. This seems to be in accordance with Swales (1990: 62–3), when he argues that there is a reciprocity of semantic effort to be engaged by both the reader and the author in the writing within a specific genre, a contract binding the two together in reaction and counter-reaction.

Chapman and Routledge argue, for instance, that in engaging with a typical detective story, the reader presupposes that it will contain such things as a detective, a mystery, a perpetrator, and a solution. They further describe these presuppositions as 'obligations' of the detective story writer to the reader, alongside Chandler (1976: 38), who refers not to 'rules' of the genre, but to a set of 'implied guarantee[s]', that the reader's expectations will be fulfilled. However, Chapman and Routledge (1999: 245) disagree with Todorov that to violate the rules of the genre is to go outside of it since, as they argue, shared presuppositions have no epistemological security. In other words, they claim that while the reader may have expectations that certain presuppositions will not be disappointed, there is no guarantee that those expectations will be fulfilled.

To go back to the story at hand, Chapman and Routledge claim that

> [w]hile recognizably a work that might fall within the genre of detective fiction, *City of Glass* is striking in its abandonment of many of the conventions on which the genre might be considered to depend, such as the viability of the deductive method, the competence of the detective and, crucially, the prior existence of the crime.
>
> Chapman and Routledge (1999: 245)

For instance, Peter Stillman fails in the role of detective's client, Quinn fails in 'solving' the case, while it appears that there really is no mystery, no case at all. As a matter of fact, Quinn is unable to contact his clients, the supposed suspect appears to merely be a retired professor, and finally Quinn discovers that he was never actually paid for the job; the cheque he was given bounces.

In addition to Auster's disregard of presuppositions concerning the genre of detective fiction, Chapman and Routledge add Auster's exploration of the failure of presuppositions in the linguistic interactions of the characters in the novel itself. For instance (and as noted in Chapter 1), Peter fails to comply with the apparent purpose of his first exchange with Quinn in the narrative; 'This is what is called speaking' (Auster, 1988: 16). Here, Peter is not conveying anything beyond the literal, making explicit that which is presupposed in normal conversation; he is stating the obvious.

Chapman and Routledge (1999: 249) also add the shedding of a number of other presuppositions to do with general questions of truth, fiction, subjectivity and identity. For instance, despite the challenges to Quinn's and the reader's expectations as to the novel as a detective story, both Quinn and the reader continue to maintain the central presupposition that Quinn is working on a case. Once the character of Paul Auster explicitly tells Quinn that there really is no mystery and no case, Quinn's dissolution takes the form of an attempt to return to his life as it was before he adopted the detective persona, a return that ends in disappointment (he returns to his apartment after a considerable period of absence to find that it has been let to another tenant). Ultimately, Quinn disappears and all that remains are his words in a red notebook.

Despite the loss of generic security (Chapman and Routledge (1999: 251) argue that 'generic presuppositions are never secure, but are normative and relative rather than absolute'), readers nevertheless are not disabused of the belief that they have indeed read the novel as such, since the discourse between reader and text continues to operate. As Chapman and Routledge (1999: 252) claim, any presupposition can fail, any generic convention can be abandoned, as well as any 'requirement for the reader to attempt to maximise relevance', without revealing the text to be meaningless, irrelevant or incoherent. Chapman and Routledge (1999: 252) suggest that once the generic presupposition of the story as detective fiction has failed, readers can still 'approach the text with its lack of coherence in mind and, like Stillman and Quinn, simply observe objects and events as they are described with no requirement to construct meaning or seek relevance'. That is, readers are invited to approach the novel with no regard for contextual meaning, much like Quinn's strategy of observing and noting events toward the end of the story itself.

Another novelist that uses similar *defamiliarisation* to force readers to attend to the generic conventions of crime fiction is Philip Kerr. In his novel *A Philosophical Investigation* (1992), Kerr seems to work on the background of the detective genre since the novel is concerned with the pursuit of a serial killer. Yet the novel changes our perception of the genre since it questions some of its conventions, as well as incorporates a number of aspects that accord to the science fiction genre, not to mention the large number of dashes of philosophical speculation and social criticism that are thrown in. It can, in other words, be said to be a refreshing and *original* (defamiliarising) new take on the detective fiction or noir crime genre, which takes much from criminology to computer hackery to philosophy, and may even require some knowledge of Wittgenstein's work on behalf of the reader (if only for them to get a few of the many references of the novel, such as that made to Wittgenstein's philosophy in the novel's namesake title).

The novel is futuristic, set in twenty-first century London, the year of 2013 to be more precise, where serial killing and violence has reached tremendous proportions. Chief Inspector Jakowich is in charge of tracing and stopping a murderer whose victim selection comes to threaten government security. DNA profiling is so advanced, that it is possible to identify those men who are actually genetically predisposed to become serial killers, 'those males whose brains lack a Ventro Medial Nucleus (VMN) which acts as an inhibitor to the Sexually Dimorphic Nucleus (SDN), a preoptic area of the male human brain which is the repository of male aggressive response' (Kerr, 1992: 42). The details of those identified males, known as VMN-negative, are securely held on a computer system, but when dead bodies of these individuals are found, Jakowich suspects that the system's security has been breached. As a result, she gets on a hunt for the potential serial-killers' serial killer.

The potential killers on the list are given pseudonyms after authors from the Penguin Classics catalogue. The actual serial killer, presented to have routinely taken the test and found himself to be VMN-negative as well, is given the pseudonym Wittgenstein by the VMN-negatives computer program. The unstated question lingering throughout the course of the book is whether his reaction to the results was what caused him to be murderous (that is, it could be put down to the stress of the news) or whether his reaction was simply to show that the diagnosis was right all along.

The villain, also a computer expert and hacker, could alternatively be viewed as one who is trying to protect the rest of society by killing off those on the list. In this sense, he could be taken to be a hero who, having removed his real name from the records, begins to systematically assassinate those posing a criminal threat to the world. Our sympathy toward the character could also be assigned to the fact that Kerr interpolates passages from the murderer's journal into the third-person narrative (along with citations from the work of Ludwig Wittgenstein and other philosophers); we get access to his viewpoint, which manipulates readers' empathy with the villain/hero. In other words, one could argue that what we have here is a violation of that generic convention/presupposition whereby in the context of the crime fiction genre, the villain is a threat to the world; Kerr's villain is, in some ways, a saviour to the world instead.

Another violation to the conventions of the genre is Kerr's view of the potential killers in the novel. In the context of the crime fiction genre, criminals are referred to as such once they have acted criminally, and usually retain that position or classification throughout the book. As mentioned, the potential killers in Kerr's novel are treated as sufferers by the novel's society, which provides them with appropriate counselling. In the course of the novel, they are also victimised by the killer code-named Wittgenstein. Therefore, the men in Kerr's *Philosophical Investigation* are not only criminalised by being set on the list as potential murderers when they have not yet committed any criminal acts, but also switch from the position of sufferers/potential victimisers to that of victims in the course of the novel.

In fact it seems to be the case that it is science which is the real 'criminal' in the novel. Science forms part of the ideology of the novel, which makes implications that it is the kind of abuse of the scientific processes that the character of Wittgenstein engages in that is the cause of criminal behaviour in the first place. Had it not been for science's developments as presented in the book, and for the maltreatment of the discoveries it led to, none of the murders would have taken place. Finally, what needs to be pointed out here is that the generic fuzziness of the novel could also be a result of the *fusion* of two genres: crime fiction and science fiction; the science-fiction characteristics which this crime novel exhibits do in fact contribute to the difficulty in the novel's classification in a genre category.

In addition to the violation of these generic presuppositions, the novel breaches presuppositions as to the state of the world, especially ones that are set up by the novel itself. The detective hero of the book, the heroine Jake Jakowich, is a Scotland Yard detective specialising in male serial killers of women (and apparently there are a lot of them in this near future time). Even though the novel appears to be rather sexist in its presentation of women as victims and men as victimisers (the book itself revolves around the scientific discovery that it is only men who have the brain function to be violent and murderous), in the case of the murderer Wittgenstein, he actually sets out to kill other men. So the classification of men as non-victims is invalidated within the course of the novel itself; the victims in the novel as well as all being potential death dealers, are also all men.

A further presupposition, which the novel both sets and breaches, is that crimes happen for biological, as opposed to social reasons. That is, even though the Lombroso program screens and identifies potentially dangerous individuals on the basis of their biological structure, the murderer code-named Wittgenstein appears to kill for philosophical reasons; the novel succeeds in bringing the philosopher Wittgenstein's system into a genuine connection with the murder cases at hand. In other words, the parallels between the novel and philosophical enquiry are extraordinary, and the killer raises a number of philosophical arguments in celebration and justification of the act of murder itself, all of which however somewhat falsify the initial presupposition that criminals are genetically pre-determined.

The heroine Jake, finally, though presented as a man-hater – much like contemporary detectives from the genre – develops deep feelings and strong connections with the male serial killer, who is eventually captured and put down in 'punitive coma'. That is, though she initially appears to hate mostly all men, her later connection with the killer falsifies that presentation.

Cornwell's generic form: a subgenre or a new genre?

In Chapter 2, I argued that there has been a critical mass of commentary that relished the cultural inferiority of detective fiction; it was said to be abjectly repetitive in that it consisted of the same few stories written over and over again. In this sense, the genre is believed to adhere to the same regularities, or constitutes mere variations of the same given pattern: someone is murdered, an investigation takes place in pursuit of the murderer, and eventually the killer is captured and brought to justice. Porter (1981: 99) specifically argued that if reading detective novels is always a rereading, it is one in which a limited number of structural constants are combined with an indefinite number of decorative variables in order to make the familiar view. In other words, he argued that the pleasure of reading such a genre depends both on being familiar with the structure of the whole and on not knowing the specific outcome. He was also noted to have pointed out that the genre of detective fiction, like that of jokes, shares the feature of surprise at the very end, a so-called 'predictable formal term' (Porter, 1981: 99), the nature of which we are not to have access to until the story's very end.

Patricia Cornwell's work can certainly be used to pull these ideas together, as it in fact exhibits a set of formulaic regularities. Her work *can* be classified under the *police-procedural* genre where major investigations tend to be on the go con-currently, a team of professionals – with a number of personal problems of their own – work together on the solutions of crime, and the adopted formula welcomes realism since not all crimes investigated are actually solved. At the same time, however, the series features forensic science at its very heart, and hence could also be classified as a *forensic crime* series as well.

The protagonist of the Patricia Cornwell series is Dr Kay Scarpetta, the chief Medical Examiner of the Commonwealth of Richmond, Virginia. She is single, has no children and at the beginning of the series appears to be in her early forties. In spite her official status, she operates not unlike a private investigator. As Bertens and D'haen (2001: 170) put it, Scarpetta is 'an extraordinarily competent, high-ranking professional who values her independent state and is easily equal to the males that surround her'. The novels could be read in terms of feminism (that is, the criminal element and Medical Examiner's co-workers are almost exclusively male), while Cornwell makes use of recent advances in forensic science so that we have an exciting mixture of private investigation, police procedural and medical clue-hunting to add to the nature of the investigations she undertakes. Across the whole range of the series, we expect the medical examiner to go on a hunt for information, enabled by her status, which would eventually lead her to the killer. We also expect her post-mortem to reveal both the cause of death and identification, if not at an early stage of each novel, then certainly by the end of it. As Messent (1997: 13) puts it, 'she becomes, like Poe's Dupin, the one with the superior understanding necessary to solve the puzzles challenging her, though, in her case, this comes predominantly from her forensic abilities'.

At first, the information she gathers would seem rather disjointed, only to eventually fall into place, and readers may also be expecting to find the examiner herself and those she holds most dear directly in harm's way, if not at mortal risk. That is, she succeeds in solving the puzzles she faces but with a price to pay; not only do the criminals she pursues often attempt to attack the examiner herself – either in an attempt to stop her from revealing their identity or out of sheer revenge for her having managed to do so – but also try assaulting her close family members and friends.

The author additionally favours THE MONSTER criminal archetype (see Chapter 4), in that she consigns crime to the realm of the morally 'monstrous'. As Messent (1997: 16) puts it, Cornwell 'consign[s] crime to the category of pure evil and individual moral monstrosity as a way of "explaining" it as a freakish and psychopathic exception to all we know to be normal'.

Readers also expect that primary suspects are unlikely to turn out to be the killers, and it is most likely to be the case that it is someone close to the doctor herself that would be the perpetrator (such as a colleague or a lover). In other words, readers are often mislead into believing that an innocent character is in fact a murderer, only to later have the real murderer revealed as one who is much closer to Scarpetta's home than Cornwell would have readers initially believe.

Another evident regularity is that of the *seriality of the killings* which, as previously noted, has come to be inseparable from the excitement of the police procedural series; it not only brings an urgency to the chasing of the murderer at hand (he must be captured fast, before he kills again), but it also allows the sense of there being a pattern, the justification of which remains withheld up until the end.

Finally, regardless of the vast number of structural constants evident in the Cornwell series, it is the combination of these constants with an indefinite number of variables that make the series so popular. Like the genre of jokes, the series features surprise at the very end, a definitive aspect of the genre of crime fiction as a whole.

In the context of the first book in the series, *Postmortem* (1990), a serial killer appears to be on the loose in Richmond. Three women have been found brutalised and strangled in their own bedrooms, and though the killer appears to strike at random, he always does so early on Saturday mornings. Scarpetta is invited to dig up forensic evidence so as to help the police, and do so fast, before the killer strikes again. However, her being a woman in such a powerful job does become a problem, and her reputation and career appear to be at risk.

At one point in the novel, she even suspects that the man she is seeing romantically, Bill Boltz – the Commonwealth's attorney for Richmond – may have committed one of the murders out of revenge. For Boltz, it is discovered, has previously sexually assaulted the journalist Abby Turnbull, after spiking her drink, and both this and his general attitude toward Scarpetta carry echoes of the murderer's responses to his victims. At the same time, the extent of Boltz's responsibility for his wife's suicide is also subject to the Examiner's speculation. Commissioner Amburgey also tampers with criminal evidence because of hatred for the Examiner who, through no fault of her own, has publicly humiliated him during an earlier case. Though Amburgey, however, is pressurised by the journalist Abby into resigning his job, Boltz remains untouchable.

Later on, the actual killer attempts to attack Scarpetta but fails, for her eventual success at solving the murders is ensured even before the criminal's move against her; her discoveries lead her colleague, police officer Marino, to recognise her being in danger and, in keeping her under surveillance, shoots the killer dead. Eventually it is revealed that the killer has worked as a Communications officer for Richmond, and as a dispatcher. All victims have dialled 911 in the past, and the killer was the one that answered the phone in all cases, this being what prompted him to choose the relevant women for the subsequent killings; he has chosen his victims when hearing their voices on the emergency calls he has processed. And it is at this point in the narrative that a connection between the murder victims and their killer is finally established, this being the faint and only link of the 911 calls.

The social cause of the crimes is here stifled by its consignment to the category of the monstrous moral exception to the general rule. In an analysis of the same novel, Messent argues that

> [t]he serial killer is 'the monster' (p. 23). Scarpetta explains to Lucy [her ten-year old niece] that he is one of those 'people who are evil … Like dogs … Some dogs bite for no reason. There's something wrong with them. They're bad and will always be bad', and when Lucy replies 'Like Hitler' (p. 39), the simile is allowed to stand unchallenged. This kind of discourse runs through the text ('He is *sick* … He's antisocial, he's evil …' p. 92) and returns the reader to a black-and-white world where evil stands as pure 'other', finally abolished with the return to social 'normality' brought about by the (mostly) rational, analytic, and commanding figure of the female detective.
>
> Messent (1997: 16)

That is, the image of monstrosity, which has become prevalent in the recent period, is here preferred, as with a number of other novels in the series. In addition to being a murderous psychopath, the serial killer here described also has a strange body odour because of a rare metabolic disorder; as with many monstrous criminals, his physical deficiency mirrors his psychological abnormality.

The novel overall draws on almost all elements typical of what came to be known as a 'Scarpetta novel'; the seriality of the killings, Scarpetta's initial inability to put the clues together and her later success in doing so, the mortal danger she herself encounters, the revelation of her lover as a dangerous rapist and – perhaps indirectly – a type of murderer, the monstrosity of the serial killer's murders, the realism in that not all crimes are appropriately resolved (Boltz remains publicly unrevealed and unpunished), and the eventual predictable and yet surprise ending.

Even though the novel, as its title suggests, takes the reader directly into the autopsy room, it does not reveal nearly as much detail as the later novels do. In fact, later on in the series, Scarpetta's scientific knowledge is revealed to be extreme, including that of the processes of death and decay; as she herself mentions in the second novel in the series, *Body of Evidence* (1991: 5), Scarpetta literally knows every inch of the dead body. Not only is such knowledge excessive, however, but it also additionally contradicts the kind of qualities associated with her gender. As Vanacker puts it,

> indeed, as a pathologist, Scarpetta functions in the reader's emotional field like Frankenstein in reverse, unpicking what used to be a living body into its component parts. Not only does she assume the unselfquestioning activity of the male detective's unified subject position – her actions are indeed determined, confident and incisive – but she also departs considerably from the traditional constraints and qualities associated with her gender. Rather than being culturally associated (as female) with life and life giving, this woman hero is a dealer in death, who aggressively 'manhandles' the corpses of victims and gruesomely thrives off decaying and decomposing bodies.
>
> Vanacker (1997: 66)

In other words, the macabre nature of her profession is frequently and deliberately highlighted, while often contrasted to her rather 'housewify' activity of cooking, which is presented, in the first novel in the series, as Scarpetta's strategy for coping with apparently insoluble problems; 'When everything fails, I cook.' (1990: 150). Similarly, in *Cruel and Unusual* (1993), the fourth novel in the series, Scarpetta's autopsy assistant is pregnant, further transgressing gender expectations. The author overall uses the Medical Examiner so as 'to subvert traditional gender roles which associate femininity both with the giving of life and preparing of food' (Vanacker, 1997: 66), just like much feminist crime fiction of this period often does.

However, Cornwell remodels the genre by rejecting the concept of the detective who remains unaffected by her work. As Vanacker (1997: 66) argues, the masculine ideal of objectified knowledge is exposed in Cornwell's novels as a 'dangerous illusion'; she remembers the faces of the victims' parents and is influenced by her work to the extent that she is prone to bad dreams. In addition to drawing information from a detailed pathological examination and systematic documentation which requires professional impartiality, she uses imaginative and empathic reconstruction of the emotional processes undercutting the procedures and motivations of the murders at hand.

In addition, later novels in the series often emphasise the acts of sabotage on the part of male rivals. In the course of *All That Remains* (1992), the third novel in the series, the bodies of young couples turn up in remote forests. The latest girl to go missing is the daughter of one of the most powerful women politicians in America, a woman whom Scarpetta deeply admires. Once the FBI feels threatened by this woman's questions, she is thrown to the 'media wolves' (1992: 15), while Scarpetta watches her fate in dismay and yet is unable to help her. As Vanacker (1997: 66) puts it, Scarpetta 'is in such a vulnerable position herself with regard to the secretive intrigues of the male hierarchy which surrounds her that she does not get involved'; she too is 'a woman outsider, pitched against a patriarchical organisation that has its own unspoken and unshared rules'.

Later novels in the series also emphasise the killer who targets Scarpetta herself. In the context of *Black Notice* (2000a) (a novel also analysed in Chapter 4), the tenth novel in the series, a physically and psychologically monstrous criminal (due to a genetic defect, his body is entirely covered with long fine hair) attempts to murderously attack the Examiner. Similarly, in *The Last Precinct* (2000b), the eleventh novel in the series, she is held at gun point by a murderer, only to be saved later on by her niece.

Finally, the theme of her being involved romantically with suspicious individuals is recurrent in the later novels. In both *Body of Evidence* (1991) and *All That Remains* (1992), her lover, FBI agent Mark James seems to be conspiring and spying against her. Similarly, in the course of *The Last Precinct* (2000b), French Special Agent Talley, a lover of Kay's from the previous novel in the series, *Black Notice* (2000a), again is subject to the Examiner's suspicions. He is later revealed to be a murderer and the blood relative of the same monstrous criminal who attempted to kill her in *Black Notice.*

Having analysed the major themes recurrent in the novels from Cornwell's Scarpetta series, I shall next draw parallels between this and a crime series developed by Kathy Reichs. Though Reichs has written a much smaller range of crime novels, and has started doing so a few years after the first Scarpetta novel, the similarities between the two series are extraordinary. I outline the major themes of Reichs's series so as to illustrate the evolution of the medical examiner's crime genre. That is, I demonstrate how the Cornwellian subgenre of crime fiction has currently evolved into a separate medical examiner's crime fiction or forensic genre altogether. I also argue that the extent to which a subgenre evolves into a separate genre depends upon the way the readers receive the subgenre in the first place, and the extent to which other writers take on board the subgenre's conventions and themes in their own work. Contemporary TV series such as *C.S.I.* (Crime Scene Investigation) and *Crossing Jordan* similarly help establish the forensic crime genre as separate crime writing altogether, whereby the dissecting of bodies is seen as an alternative metaphor of looking at crime.

The American Kathy Reichs, like her protagonist, is a forensic scientist. Her knowledge of forensic anthropology is evident in her Temperance Brennan series, while her actual real-life experience generated her best selling novels. Reichs's first novel, *Déjà Dead* (1998) introduced her heroine, Dr Brennan (also known as Tempe) as a separated woman in her late forties, who spends most of her days in the autopsy suite, the courtroom and the crime lab, having taken on the challenging assignment of forensic anthropology director for the Quebec province. She faces a murder mystery that shows parallels with a case from the past (hence the title of the novel), and is invited to call upon her forensic skills, including bone, tooth, and bite mark analysis to prove that the cases are related and to stop the killer before he strikes again. In addition to featuring a seriality to the killings, the novel incorporates modern technological advances in medical examining, and reconstructions of biological profiles (determining the age, sex, race, and height of the victims whilst also identifying indicators of medical history).

The novel was justifiably compared with Cornwell's Scarpetta novels. Both feature adult women with a string of failed relationships, though admittedly Scarpetta bears no competition to Brennan in the romance department. Brennan has a grown child from a previous marriage, Katy, and a nephew she is very close to, Kit, similarly to Scarpetta looking after her niece Lucy, who features in the corresponding series as more of a surrogate child. Since neither of the two heroines are in long-term relationships, they both have various close female friends at different points in their series, which function as companions and confidantes. Men to whom the heroines are, at times, romantically or sexually attracted to, also surround them.

Like Scarpetta, Brennan is stubborn and astute when it comes to her work. Both medical examiners are independent in their personal lives, incredibly knowledgeable in their field, committed and highly competent. They take an emotional and personal approach to their work (attending the victims' funerals, dreaming of them, getting close to their families, and reconstructing their emotional state at the time of their attack). They deal with the 'how' rather than the 'why' of the deaths; they consider the physical evidence so as to figure what happened, how it happened and in what way to the victims, leaving the 'why' to the law enforcement.

Much like Cornwell, Reichs does not offer the criminal viewpoint in the way that Patterson's Alex Cross series does, and additionally portrays the scientific as opposed to the police procedural aspect of the crime investigation. Brennan and Scarpetta work backwards from the physical evidence recovered from human remains and purely speculate as to the human nature. Starting from hard evidence, the facts and theories are formed, as opposed to starting with a theory and trying to make it fit. The forensic crime genre further concentrates on the process of identifying the unknown victims, unlike police procedurals that try to capture the personality of the attackers. In other words, whereas police procedurals deal with the criminals of murder investigations, the medical examiner's genre concentrates on the victims. Therefore, the two opposing genres could be said to approach murder from two ends of the same spectrum; different members of the same team generate different genres, since the behavioural viewpoint of the police procedurals is here juxtaposed to the forensic viewpoint.

Both Scarpetta and Brennan are marginalised as women in a male-dominated world. In the latter series, the criminal element and Brennan's co-workers are primarily (but not exclusively) male, while the examiner is often unappreciated and encounters sexism in her work environment. In particular, the police officer Claudel who recurrently figures in the series appears to dislike Brennan who has to fight for his approval since she is forced to admit that his opinion and acceptance matters to her. In the first novel in the series, Claudel even intends to file a complaint against her since he believes that she is overstepping her bounds, interfering with police business and putting the murder cases in jeopardy. It is not until the end of the novel that the officer acknowledges Brennan's expertise and offers his acceptance in the form of a handwritten letter to her. The same process is later repeated in the third novel in the series, *Deadly Decisions* (2001), where after constant lack of appreciation for Brennan's skills throughout the novel, Claudel again comes around to acknowledge her value both as a colleague, and as a member of the same investigative team. Similarly, in the fourth novel in the series, *Fatal Voyage* (2002), male colleagues wrongly accuse Brennan of being obsessive with the cases she investigates and of tampering with police evidence, while her interest is argued to have gone beyond what is professional or ethical. It is again not until later in the novel that the charges are dropped and she is reinstated.

Another evident similarity between the Scarpetta and Brennan series is the fact that both characters' investigations put themselves and those they hold most dear at mortal risk. In *Déjà Dead*, Brennan is stalked and attacked twice, while a human head is planted in her backyard. She also blames herself for the death of her closest and long-time friend Gabby, murdered by the killer the examiner pursues at a time that Gabby seeks refuge in Brennan's house, while Tempe also fears for the safety of her college-age daughter Katy. In *Deadly Decisions*, someone leaves an envelope containing a jar with a human eyeball on the examiner's windshield, she again fears for her daughter's safety, throws herself into jeopardy by seeking out potential biker-killers, and blames herself for getting her nephew Kit shot. Finally, in *Fatal Voyage*, someone attempts to run her over, breaks into her flat, and tampers with her engine. She also blames herself for the death of her friend and colleague Primrose, and is again attacked by the killer she pursues.

Unlike the Scarpetta series, however, the Brennan one fails to exclusively assign crime to the category of pure evil. In opposition to Cornwell's recurrent choice of the MONSTROUS criminal archetype, Brennan uses all three criminal archetypes; THE MONSTER, THE VAMPIRE and THE SPOILT CHILD. In *Déjà Dead*, though the criminal in pursuit is referred to as a 'madman', 'monster' (1998: 119) and 'terrified animal' (1998: 126), Brennan seeks help from a psychological profiler who describes the sexual sadist as one with a personality disorder. The criminal is referred to as one that seeks control in the humiliation of his victims (1998: 338), engages in fantasies that involve excessive cruelty, and is sexually aroused from the victim's fear and pain (1998: 340–1). It does, however, turn out that the sadistic killer himself blames his grandmother, a domineering and fanatically religious woman, for the person he has become and is thus assigned onto the VAMPIRE criminal archetype. His childhood traumatic experiences (he endured abuse both from his grandmother and his priest uncle) are, in other words, said to be the reasons lying behind his criminal behaviour in the novel.

In *Deadly Decisions*, the examiner is propelled on a harrowing journey into the world of outlaw motorcycle gangs, when a nine-year old is cut down in a biker crossfire, and the parts of the skeleton of a North Carolina teenager – last seen hitching a ride with a transient biker – are found scattered around the country. The biker-killers are de-glamorised in the novel, and described as 'degenerates' and 'subhumans' (2001: 379):

> I'd never seen Claudel so animated.
> 'And who are these degenerates who make their living off the weak? Most have neither the moral nor the intellectual ability to complete a traditional educational process or function in an open market. They use women because, deep down, they fear them. They are uneducated, self-deluded, and, in many cases, sexually inadequate, so they have themselves tattooed, create nicknames, and band together to reinforce their shared nihilism.'
>
> Reichs (1998: 379)

Here, the killers, who may initially seem very dramatic and powerful, are actually revealed to be deeply inadequate people, maybe even sexually inadequate ones. Such killers are presented as withdrawn, resentful, suffering from both low self-esteem and a sense of superiority. Much like SPOILT CHILDREN, they kill because it is a choice they made themselves, and though mentally ill, are not – by and large – categorised as insane. Such repeat offenders plainly act out their fantasies because they enjoy doing so and because it gives them satisfaction.

Finally, in *Fatal Voyage*, whilst assisting in the process of body recovery and identification following an airplane crash, the examiner stumbles across a disembodied foot found near the debris field. Having established that the foot could not have belonged to any of the airplane's passengers, she uncovers a shocking story of killings and cannibalism; a group of power brokers have engaged in a series of disturbing killings when gathering for years in a nearby cabin. The killers are described as 'crazy' (2002: 380), and as suffering from 'egomaniacal delusion[s]' (2002: 407). They are under the belief that they can increase their IQs by consuming the flesh of their victims, and that the weaker the victims the stronger they get. They attack and devour the old since they hold the greatest reservoirs of wisdom and yet are weak and vulnerable (which additionally makes them easier targets to pursue). As one of the madmen himself proclaims in the novel, 'As flesh wastes away, so does strength. But mind, spirit, intellect, those elements are transferable through the very cells of our bodies' (2002: 408). The madmen, the 'society of sickos' (2002: 407), are here hence classified under the MONSTER criminal archetype, and are seeking revenge over the medical examiner whose intrusiveness has uncovered their devious doings. They are eventually captured and brought to justice.

Having drawn on a number of parallels and some differences between the two forensic series, I have illustrated the ways in which a subgenre of crime fiction has managed to break free from the genre to such an extent that it has established another of its own. Writers such as Reichs have adopted and elaborated on some of the Cornwellian conventions and identified the medical examiner's type of crime fiction as a different genre altogether. It is a genre that is focused on the scientific as opposed to the police procedural aspect of crime investigation, and concentrates on the victim rather than the perpetrator. It is more concerned with establishing the identity of victims and their physical and emotional state at the time of death as opposed to the identity and state of mind of the killer. It does go a certain way into identifying the killer and the criminal archetype under which (s)he is classified, but is restricted to speculations. As previously stated, it is a genre that focuses on the 'how' and the 'what' of the death rather than the 'why'.

What constitutes generic deviance?

In the previous section, I argued that the extent to which a subgenre breaks free to establish a genre of its own is strictly a matter of reception. If other writers adopt the conventions of a deviant novel within a given genre, that novel has the potential of developing into a genre in itself.

Finally, what need to be pointed out, is that this aspect of 'readerly knowledge' necessary for the classification of novels into generic categories is also handled theoretically within 'Schema theory'. This theory suggests that, in any novel's categorisation, the readers' generic mental representations, knowledge, memories and expectations ought to be taken into account.

6
Conclusion

Book review

In investigating the poetics of deviance in contemporary crime fiction, I started by offering some background to studies surrounding the notion of 'genre', and a few that particularly investigate the linguistic aspects of various types of fiction. I outlined the aims of my study, defined the term 'deviance' in the context of stylistics, sociology and genre theory, and explained the ways in which my study provides new research in the disciplines surrounding the field. I then introduced my methodology and material, and explained why each author was used as a case study in the three different forms of deviance.

Chapter 1 was devoted to the fields of narratology and deviance. I discussed the structure of stories and briefly analysed the genre of crime fiction using frameworks by Brémond and Labov. I explained the reasons underlying crime fiction's definition as 'genre' and as 'popular literature', but questioned the latter classification on the basis that it is an issue of reader approach. I also introduced the models necessary for investigating deviance under the guise of the different disciplines, and established a number of connections among them.

Chapter 2 formed a literary review of various studies that surround the genre at hand, and particularly concentrated on establishing its origins and tracking its generic evolution. I offered various definitions of 'crime fiction', as well as some rules and constraints, before finally narrowing down some of the genre's formulaic regularities. I discussed some attempts at explaining the attraction of the genre, and established that such reading is treated as 'pleasure' and as 'addiction'. Since crime fiction has also been discussed alongside the notion of 'realism', I argued that many developments of the genre have been attempts to mirror contemporary society. I finally raised issues pertaining to the characters of the genre, and focused on the investment that contemporary writers have come to make upon the serial killer.

Chapter 3 explored the stylistics of criminal justification. I focused on the portrayal of the criminal mind and the way it becomes morally situated, through an exploration of the notion of 'mind style' and a development of 'criminal mind style'. Contrary to the traditional view, I concluded that the term mind style, unlike that of ideological viewpoint, needs to refer to the way in which a character's particular reality is perceived and conceptualised in cognitive terms. Hence the range of linguistic phenomena portraying such a distinctive presentation of a mental self needs to include metaphorical patterns, transitivity, lexical choices, as well as certain instances of thought presentation, the process of nominalisation, the deletion of agency, metonymy and the type and tone of narration.

I additionally undertook a further investigation into the portrayal of the criminal mind by Patterson, and specifically concentrated on the deviant figurative language employed. I concluded that by employing deviant language to portray the criminal mind, novelists allow access to criminals' reasoning and conceptualisation of reality. Such deviant linguistic choices included the use of megametaphors, unidiomatised idioms and literalised metaphors, metonymies, various types of personification, the concretisation of abstract concepts and the altering of linguistic connotations.

Chapter 4 investigated the social deviance of the genre, and explained that the genre uses labelling to define what is socially normal and what is abnormal. Once the character roles of detective and perpetrator are recognised, the socially established normality is taken to be that which correlates with the detective's behaviour, while abnormality is attached to the criminal, regardless of either of the two characters' actual behavioural patterns. In the context of the same section, I discussed the genre as carnival and thereafter introduced the criminal archetypes that are evident with a number of examples.

Chapter 5 investigated the generic deviance of contemporary crime fiction. In an attempt to redefine the genre, I drew on *family resemblance* theory, the *prototype* approach to sense, and *defamiliarisation*, and argued that novelists such as Paul Auster and Philip Kerr dismember the conventions of crime fiction, changing our perception of it, defamiliarising the novelistic form. I finally concentrated on the Cornwellian generic form and held that it has evolved into a subgenre of its own on which writers such as Reichs have based their own forensic series. Therefore, the subgenre has taken on generic dimensions of its own and has broken free from the originating genre.

Metafunctions of deviance

This study explored the poetics of deviance in contemporary crime fiction. In other words, I investigated the stylistic, socially-situated and generic nature of the genre at hand through an exploration of the notion of *deviance*. These three aspects of deviance are in fact roughly analogous to the Hallidayan model as to the metafunctions of language (1973, 1985), a tripartite system that forms the theoretical base of his Systemic Functional Grammar.

According to Halliday (1973: 42–4), '[t]he internal organization of language, is not accidental; it embodies the functions that language has evolved to serve in the life of social man'. He argues that three principal components can be recognised under the headings 'ideational', 'interpersonal' and 'textual':

> The ideational component is that part of the grammar concerned with the expression of experience, including both the processes within and beyond the self – the phenomena of the external world and those of consciousness – and the logical relations deducible from them. The ideational component thus has two sub-components, the experiential and the logical. The interpersonal component is the grammar of personal participation; it expresses the speaker's role in the speech situation, his personal commitment and his interaction with others. The textual component is concerned with the creation of text; it expresses the structure of information, and the relation of each part of the discourse to the whole and to the setting.
>
> Halliday (1973: 99)

In other words, these 'macro-functions' of language serve as the expression for content and representation of the world (ideational function), establish relationships between interactants (interpersonal function), and organise the message through the linking of ideas (textual function). These macro-functions or *metafunctions* in fact operate simultaneously; to be able to attend to a text effectively and with understanding, one has to be able to interpret it in terms of all three. One can even argue that all aspects of life can be explained on the basis of these three functions. In extension, in order to be able to interpret the crime novel, we need to explain it on the basis of these three dimensions of meaning which coexist and interact in all discourse, and which correspond to the three aspects of deviance here considered.

Since the ideational function is the one expressive of experience, it correlates to those *generic* aspects of novels; besides, genre is expressive of the world around us, and forms a representation of that experience. Included in the Hallidayan ideational metafunction is the representation of both physical and internal (thoughts, feelings) experience. Similarly, different subgenres are expressed in the context of any genre, on the basis of the adaptation of novel viewpoints (for example, the detective's experience is expressed in the police procedural, much like the forensic scientist's experience is expressed in the medical examiner's form, both of these being crime fiction subgenres). The logical sub-function of the Hallidayan ideational aspect is also of relevance to the genre at hand; the expression of fundamental logical relations lies at the heart of any genre that purports to represent a naturalistic or realistic world.

Since the interpersonal aspect is that function expressive of relations between and attitudes of people, it correlates with those aspects of my framework that are *social* in nature. How the relationships between participants are enacted and negotiated is expressed in the social roles that characters occupy in the genre. And the choices that characters make in this social context enable them to occupy certain social positions and identities.

Finally, since the textual metafunction deals with text building and creation, it correlates with the *linguistic* nature of any one text. The extent to which certain bits of information are foregrounded or backgrounded, both in relation to the text itself (the preceeding and following parts of the text) and those that exist outside it (including the situation surrounding the text), comes down to certain linguistic choices.

In order to get a holistic view of any novel, one needs to investigate the text in relation to these three issues, and particularly the deviancy in all these aspects. That is, there is indeed a scale of value of crime fiction that is structured around these three aspects; a crime novel needs to be structured around defamiliarising or new uses of language, needs to challenge social positionings and deviate from its genre to some extent, in order for it to be appreciated fully.

In the context of the genre at hand, however, one needs to take into account that certain forms of deviance in fact form part of the norm or represent formulaic regularities in this context. When socially deviant characters feature in crime novels, it is indeed acceptable and often required that deviant language will be employed (perhaps in portraying the criminal mind), and that a certain departure from generic features will be evident. In other words, within the frame of contemporary crime fiction, deviance *is* often the norm. The formulaic nature of such fiction additionally presupposes that a lot of its readership does not *want* any type of deviance or departure from the formula, and may in fact react against any such departures from the form's own deviance.

Investigating deviance

At the beginning of my research into the genre, I intended to undertake an exploration of the language of crime novels and, in doing so, established that the definition of such novels is not at all clear. By narrowing down my research to three novelists from a bestsellers list, I instead undertook a number of case studies that would help me develop a model for investigating any one genre and, in turn, any one novel. I found that what is needed to get a full picture of a novel is a *triangular* approach. Basing my analysis on an exploration of *deviance* in three disciplines, I argued that the three approaches are (a) the linguistic, (b) the social, and (c) the generic. I expect the kind of research undertaken in this book to be representative of the genre, as it seems to me that the manipulation of all three types of deviance is the key to any novel's success.

In the case of the Patterson novels, I demonstrated that the access to criminals' conceptualisation of reality allows readers to not only understand (and even accept) their actions, but also access their reasoning. By employing deviant linguistic structuring when allowing access to the criminal consciousness, Patterson established his portrayed criminals as a unique type of human species, one which – much like animals – kills to survive (that is, feed). Metaphorically presented as actors, the criminals entertain the human species through their criminal behaviour; as children, they play games with the world; as machines, they are programmed to kill disregarding normal morals of conduct. In addition, Patterson's manipulation of fixed lexical units enabled him to bring out vicious undertones and describe the criminal behaviour engaged in with ironic undercurrents. Overall, Patterson has proven to be an expert in psychological thriller writing. His skill in putting the readers right into the killers' minds as well as into his detective's consciousness as he tries to understand and predict their next moves, definitely feature as important ingredients to his success.

Michael Connelly's series featured in the study as a generic form that can be classified as both a private eye series and a police procedural. His choice of naming his detective after a real historical figure, the 15th century painter Hieronymus Bosch, contributes to this generic fusion (though, admittedly, Connelly was to a small extent continuing literary tradition; many writers, including Raymond Chandler, have drawn their characters' names from literature and the visual arts). Not only does the character act independently, deviantly, and relentlessly against authority, but he is also, in one of the novels in the series, accused of stepping across the line between order and disorder: he is the suspect who fills the profile of a wanted and unknown serial killer. Much like the notion of carnival itself, Connelly's *A Darkness More Than Night* (2000), encompasses both the good (that is, detective) and the bad poles (that is, criminal), and yet with the property of the good pole reflecting the bad. Overall, I feel that Connelly's crime writing success lies in the depiction of his protagonist. Connelly portrays Bosch as a dramatic persona who is fuelled by his need to prove himself not just by breaking the cases he engages with but also by surviving them, and it is his deviancy as a character that makes him to be so prone to danger and death. And as if a soldier of God himself, Bosch endures his private suffering whilst fulfilling his mission of bringing criminals to justice.

I showed that linguistic deviance is particularly manifested in the construction of the mind style of the criminal consciousness, which additionally places such minds on the 'justification of crimes' continuum or, as shown in Chapter 4, into the well-established and schematic criminal character slots referred to as archetypes. I named THE MONSTER, THE VAMPIRE, and THE SPOILT CHILD as contemporary criminal archetypes that feature in the genre, and additionally dealt with the implications that such a classification brings. In addition to marginalising those old-fashioned criminal archetypes that are motivated by greed, jealousy, rage and so on, the three archetypes suggested here would in fact function as restrictive to the view and reaction that real-life people have with respect to criminality, in the course of their everyday lives.

I investigated the Patricia Cornwell series featuring Dr Kay Scarpetta who, in using recent advances in forensic science to unravel the events leading up to killings, allows insight into the evolution of the forensic crime novel. In her series, one that is similar to Kathy Reich's

Temperance Brennan series, criminals are de-glamorised, whilst the dissection of bodies is used as a metaphor for looking at crime. I finally argued that the extent to which such subgenres break free of the genre they originated from is a matter of reception; such subgenres have the potential to create new genres of their own if other writers adopt those deviant conventions that set them apart from the original form in the first place. Overall, Cornwell proves to be a wonderfully evocative writer who, in transcribing the details of autopsies in a very technical and yet accessible manner, explores the depths of the forensic crime fiction subgenre she herself made famous.

On the basis of claims I made in Chapter 2, the development of the genre of crime fiction can now be delineated. Crime novels from different periods feature different generic cores, and are always surrounded by a number of peripheral novels. Contemporary core crime novels have, for instance, differed so much from the 1920s–1940s core generic form that none of the features they once maintained are nowadays evident. In fact, it is typical of contemporary crime novels or films that feature 'Golden Age' (see Chapter 2) generic conventions (for example, Robert Crais's (2001) Elvis Cole novelistic series, and director Carl Reiner's film *Dead Men Don't Wear Plaid*, 1990), to be treated as parodies.

Overall, I found that the three different case studies offered three different poles to criminal investigation. The Cornwellian generic form views the investigation from the scientific or victim pole as opposed to those series by Patterson and Connelly that take on the detective's pole. It was even argued that since Patterson allows access to his criminals' viewpoint, he could be said to additionally adopt the criminal pole. In a way, different members of the murder investigative team and actual murder event come to generate different genres.

I further found that deviance is a term that remains difficult to define in the context of any one discipline, in addition to meaning different things for different disciplines. In fiction, the language of the criminal mind often deviates from the language portraying the detective's consciousness. The criminally-minded extracts, however, also *become* deviant due to the fact that these are attached to individuals who readers *take* to be abnormal. The detective's social abnormalities are only tolerated as the readers consider detectives to be *normal*. Since character roles are part and parcel of the genre's conventions, social deviance goes hand in hand with generic deviance. By and large however, I found that deviating from societal norms and normal language usage can be a lot more objective than deviating from generic norms.

It has also been my argument that social deviance is nowadays manifested as an issue of space and/or place. Carnivalesque practices are no longer a holiday, and contemporary reincarnations of carnival are evident in the reading of certain genres, in the visiting of certain art galleries and so on. Manifestations of the notion hence nowadays take different forms, not to mention the fact that they are much more accessible than carnivalesque practices had been in medieval times. This study has mainly referred to the reader's experience and interaction with carnivalesque material. Though issues to do with function have indeed been raised early on, the issue as to whether carnivalesque is ultimately subversive has not been resolved one way or another.

Another issue that is worth discussing here is the nature of contemporary America, as depicted in my data. Overall, crime fiction of this era has proven a critique of contemporary America, where innocence and youth are lost to drugs, alcohol and corruption, where nothing is genuine nor anyone honest. Even members of the police force easily succumb to criminality's charms, which has – in the course of the 20th century – become glamorised, much like an increasingly fashionable form of social art. Violent crime features as an act for profit and empowerment, while the obsession with personality disorders, sexual deviancy, and serial killing, no matter how unrealistic to real life, takes a central position in contemporary American crime solving. Perpetrators and detectives are often interchangeable, criminals are monster-like, and America itself features as grotesque.

It is also worth touching on the social context in which these novels are produced and consumed. Crime fiction appeals to a cross-section of the population, from ordinary travellers in need of escapism, to scholars and general seekers of intellectual stimulation. It is often treated as an expendable product whose appeal extends no further than replication and critique, but its function goes a lot further than that. Contemporary crime fiction changes one's perspectives and challenges one's perceptions, necessitates questioning of one's attitude towards murder, capital punishment and the state of our culture, while finally reminding us that anyone, given cause, might be a potential killer.

The linguistic work I undertook in researching this book was qualitative rather than quantitative. The length of novels does not allow for extensive linguistic analysis, so I limited myself to the analysis of selected extracts. I also did not attempt a corpus linguistic analysis (computational linguistics) of the data due to the nature of the linguistic aspects I aimed to analyse. It would have been difficult, if not impossible, to program a computer in identifying, for instance, all manifestations of certain megametaphors; the wording involved in any one metaphorical mapping is limitless. Furthermore, I did not attempt a reader-response analysis (such as an interview-based or questionnaire-based research), on the basis that there are too many reader variables to consider and therefore control (age, nationality, familiarity with and interest in the genre, and therefore their 'crime fiction' schemata, and so on) in a research of that kind. As a consequence, the results would not have been testable. Besides, my aim was not to analyse specific texts, but to analyse *specific readings* of them. As noted in Chapter 1, discourse stylistics is a method of analysis that takes fully into account the reader as an actively mediating presence, and it is hence that reader's responses that can be described with some precision. Finally, I did not focus much on the puzzle-solving element of crime fiction since, as noted in Chapter 2, such fiction is more of a game with loaded dice and therefore a game that the reader need not win; had the reader of a crime novel been able to discover the identity of the perpetrator too early, the remaining part of the novel would have become redundant. The enjoyment of reading crime novels lies instead in the engagement with an intellectual game that the reader secretly wishes to lose.

Further research could extend the analysis of deviance in all three aspects: the linguistic, the generic and the social. One could consider the linguistic deviance expressed in real-life killers' autobiographies, and compare the relevant linguistic choices to those of fiction. In other words, this newly emerging genre would be interesting to consider, since it not only allows a criminal viewpoint into murder cases, but one that extends to the whole of the narrative. Since this research investigated the nature of the detecting and criminal mind in fiction, further research could explore the linguistic portrayal of the victim's mind (in determining, for instance, the responsibility the author assigns to the victim). Investigating the portrayal of criminals and detectives in film could also extend the enquiry into the nature of social deviance, and finally an analysis of generic deviance could cover European contemporary crime fiction as well.

As mentioned in the introductory section of this book, this research would be of value to a number of scholars who share interest in the field. Literary theorists, stylisticians, crime fiction specialists and other genre analysts – not to mention criminologists – could use information about this dynamic subgenre of popular narratives to develop techniques for analysis, investigate further the generic form and explore the ways in which devoted viewers are affected by its depictions not only of the criminal mind but also of the present state of the world.

Writers on their work

> Write what you know. That is the adage every writer hears often and then contemplates while staring at the blank screen. It is probably good and valuable advice. But when it comes to the mystery novel the writer must be inclined to write what he or she does not know and never wants to. For the art of the mystery is the art of turning chaos into calm. And it is that chaos that you must write about and still not ever want to fully know.
>
> I write about the deeds of the fallen. The killers. The chaos. The disorder. With one good man – the investigator – I then restore order. I take the box of jumbled pieces and make the picture whole. That is what the mystery is all about. Not the solution to the puzzle but the act of putting the pieces together. There is a difference. It may be subtle but it is there. And in that difference is the reason we love mystery novels. They reassure us. They tell us that indeed the puzzle can be carefully constructed and put back together, that order can always be restored, that chaos does not win the day.
>
> Connelly (1998b)

The above extract, taken from the Michael Connelly official website, expresses what the author believes to be 'The Mystery of Mystery Writing'. According to this source, the writing of a crime novel is governed by the principle of restoring order, reassembling puzzle pieces, and yet the 'writing about what one truly does not want to know'. This concept reasserts my idea of crime fiction as carnival. Being involved in the act of transgression through the reading of crime novels is pleasure enough for readers as well as for writers. Such an involvement with the abnormal acts described in the course of such novels does not render such acts acceptable. Instead, the involvement can be seen as a pleasurable and playful revolution, whilst the supremacy of the ordered world over the criminal world is reaffirmed and accepted.

Kathy Reichs (2000) touches on the same topic, in an interview by the book critic Jocelyn McClurg:

> I think that murder mystery readers are definitely voyeurs. Why they're intrigued with murder and death is a tougher question. But I think you read murder mysteries going all the way back to Sherlock Holmes or whoever it might be because you're able to vicariously participate or observe without really putting yourself into danger. You're able to work your way through the entire situation.
>
> I think the other thing that's satisfying about the murder mystery is that usually it does resolve itself. And good wins over evil and the bad guy ends up in jail or removed from a position where he or she can do that kind of violence again. So I think there's that satisfaction in reading the murder mystery.
>
> Reichs (2000)

Here Reichs, much like Connelly, reaffirms the idea of crime fiction as carnival in arguing that readers of the mystery, whether referred to as 'participants' or 'observers', are indeed voyeurs in that 'they allow others do their crimes for them'. The readers are additionally being reassured in the belief that, like carnival, order will be eventually restored and all will return to the 'status quo' by the time they reach the end of the story. As Reichs (2000) herself adds in the interview later on, such a vicarious living protects the readers in that they need not experience the trauma of murder themselves, in getting 'to those primal elements that we're all interested in, in a very raw manner'. Reichs additionally explains that readers are fascinated with violence only because it is out of their range of possibilities; it is something that they could not possibly imagine doing themselves.

In the same interview, Reichs touches on the criminal archetypes I introduced in my book. She refers to the SPOILT CHILD murderer type, who kills strangers 'for no apparent reason other than it gave him satisfaction to do so'. John Douglas, another author that is interviewed alongside Reichs in this same context also discusses the same archetype:

> I think the thing that most people find very difficult to understand and what we try to explicate is that the kind of killer we are talking about – the sexually motivated repeat offenders, serial killers, rapists, and sexual predators – they do it because they enjoy it. Because it gives them satisfaction. Because it makes them feel alive in a way that nothing else in life does. And it's difficult for people to

understand that they do it because they want to. At least, that's
been my experience.

Douglas, see Reichs (2000)

Douglas, later on, also discusses personality traits that I attached to the
MONSTER criminal archetype:

> You've got these people who are withdrawn. They are socially resent-
> ful. They have this very dangerous combination of very low self-
> esteem and a sense of personal aggrandizement and superiority at the
> same time. And that's a very dangerous combination, particularly
> when they say, 'Yeah, I'm gonna get back at everybody.'
>
> Douglas, see Reichs (2000)

Douglas also further talks about wanting to de-glamorise serial killers,
and revealing them as deeply inadequate people, no matter how dramatic and powerful they appear to be; he, in other words, stresses 'the
banality of evil':

> There's nothing grandiose here. These are small-minded, very inade-
> quate, pathetic people. And the only way that they can rise above
> that [...] is by manipulating, dominating and controlling others.
> And having the power of life and death over them.
>
> Douglas, see Reichs (2000)

Another issue that Reichs touches on in the same interview with
McClurg is the fascination of the forensic genre with the 'how' as
opposed to the 'why' of the event of murder. Since she is a forensic scientist in real life, she claims that in dealing with the victims and the
physical evidence rather than the perpetrators themselves, she comes
to concentrate on the 'what happened', 'how it happened', and 'in
what way' to the victim. Even though Reichs admits that she is
inevitably led to speculate as to 'why they did this', she allows serious
consideration of the latter issue to the law enforcement end of the
investigative team.

  In another extract taken from the Michael Connelly official website
(Connelly, 2002), the author pretends to interview his protagonist,
Harry Bosch.

> MC: What are your thoughts on evil? Where do you stand on the
> age old debate about whether it exists in the world or is it some-

thing that is fostered and cultivated. Grown, if you will, inside a person, just the same as maybe love and joy are.

HB: I guess it's an age old question because there is no sure answer. At times I think I've felt both ways about it. Certainly, I have been in contact with people who are flat out evil. And with some of them I could look back across their lives and see where different gateways opened that led to other gateways and eventually a path of evil intent was arrived at. But for every person like that there is also the case where you see the evil behind their eyes and in their deeds and you have no earthy idea where it came from and how it got there. It's a mystery that can never be solved. It's just part of their nature to be evil. It's like evil just existed out there and somehow they walked in on it. Like somebody hitting a cobwed walking through an attic. But I have to tell you I don't spend a lot of time contemplating on this question. For me, I know it is out there, no matter what its source. And I don't worry about where it came from. Because to think about it might be a dangerous distraction. That might get me killed. My bottom line take on the human existence is that each one of us comes with an unlimited capacity to love and hate, to be afraid, to be lonely, and so on. Most often you get a good blend of all of that in everybody's milkshake. But why somebody's cup gets filled up with only hatred and evil intent might make for a good intellectual question and discussion, but ultimately it doesn't matter. What matters is going out there and taking that evil out of the world.

Connelly (2002)

As this extract suggests, even though the age old question as to where evil comes from is evident in the genre at hand, it is ultimately the capturing of the criminals that it focuses on. Regardless of whether the crimes are consigned to the category of 'pure evil' or to the world of 'social cause and effect', crime novels are concerned with bringing the criminal to justice. What matters is dealing with the problem criminals pose, as opposed to investigating why criminality arose in the first place.

Finally, another issue that I have come across in the course of my research is the extent to which some authors find themselves able to access criminal minds. The following extract, also from the Michael Connelly official website (Connelly, 1997a), deals with the issue:

I was at a book signing not unlike the many before it and the many that would come after. In fact, I don't remember what bookstore

I was at or even which city I was visiting. But the man who approached my table asked a question I had never been asked by a reader.

'You don't have children, do you?'

I looked at him and smiled politely, the tired smile you see when you've just been thrown a curve ball and all you really want to do is quietly sell a pile of books and then get on to the next bookstore in the next city.

'What makes you say that?' I asked.

'Because of your book,' he said. 'A father wouldn't have written it.'

'He, of course, had been right.'

Connelly (1997a)

What this extract refers to is Michael Connelly's *The Poet* (1996), the story of the hunt of a serial killer who travelled across the country kidnapping and murdering children, before uploading photos of his so-called 'work' on an internet bulletin board accessed by fellow paedophiles. The author admits: 'I felt as if though he were accusing me of a crime [...] His advice was to stay clear of children – in the literary sense, I assumed'. *The Poet* is the only novel Connelly ever wrote which contains chapters that allowed access to the criminal consciousness, and that, he felt, was held against him. Having since become a father, Connelly went back to reading *The Poet* and saw the point the man was trying to make; 'He was right. A father would not have written it. It cut too close to the bone'. Therefore, another aspect to be taken into account in an investigation of those authors' work that accesses the criminal mind, is their biographical background. As Douglas (see Reichs, 2000) argues in the previously mentioned interview with McClurg, to 'get inside the criminal's mind and actually think as he does' is something certain novelists are, as he puts it, 'guilty of'.

I asked James Patterson (in attending the 5th *Dead on Deansgate* festival in Manchester, UK, on 9 October 2002) whether he faces a similar problem when portraying the criminal mind in his own novels; he said that he does not. He added that though he takes many liberties, and people indeed react to his books as very accurate emotionally, they are *not* realism, they do not claim to be real. Perhaps it would be fair to say that Patterson's novels purport to verisimilitude instead; by giving his readers an air or impression of life, he places some distance between fiction and reality that allows him to access the criminal mind without being affected by it. As Douglas (see Reichs, 2000) puts it, both writers and forensic scientists 'have to be able to think like a criminal' so that, particularly in the case of the latter, they are able 'to work backwards from the physical evidence'. However, to think that this is a particular gift that some people have is 'simplifying the whole thing':

> One of the great fallacies of fiction and of crime fiction [...] is that there seems to be this mystical idea that the best detective or the best profiler is somebody who has this incredible double-edged-sword ability to think like the criminal.
>
> Douglas (in Reichs, 2000)

And perhaps it is fair to argue that this 'special gift' or 'skill' that Douglas refers to here is yet another one of those myths that crime fiction has helped reinforce in the world.

References

Allan, K. (1986) *Linguistic Meaning*. London: Routledge and Kegan Paul.

Aristotle (1996) *Poetics*. (trans. M. Heath) London: Penguin.

Auden, W.H. (1974) 'The Guilty Vicarage', in D. Allen and D. Chako (eds), *Detective Fiction/Crime and Compromise*. New York: Harcourt Brace Jovanovich, pp. 400–10.

Auster, P. (1988) 'City of Glass', in *The New York Trilogy*. London: Faber and Faber, pp. 3–132.

Austin, J.L. (1962) *How to do Things with Words*. Oxford: Oxford University Press.

Bakhtin, M. (1981) *The Dialogic Imagination* (trans. C. Emerson and M. Holquist). Austin: University of Texas Press.

Bakhtin, M. (1984a) *Problems of Dostoevsky's Poetics* (trans. E. Caryl). Minneapolis: University of Minnesota Press.

Bakhtin, M. (1984b) *Rabelais and His World* (trans. H. Iswolsky). Bloomington: Indiana University Press.

Bal, M. (1985) *Narratology: Introduction to the Theory of Narrative*. Toronto: Toronto University Press.

Ball, J. (ed.) (1976) *The Mystery Story*. San Diego: University of California Press.

Bartlett, F.C. (1932) *Remembering: A Study in Experimental and Social Psychology*. Cambridge: Cambridge University Press.

Benveniste, E. (1966) *Problèmes de Linguistique Générale*. Paris: Gallimard. (*Problems in General Linguistics*. Coral Gables: University of Miami Press, 1971.)

Bertens, H. and D'haen, T. (2001) *Contemporary American Crime Fiction*. New York: Palgrave.

Bex, T. (1996) *Variety in Written English*. London: Routledge.

Birnbaum, H. (1985) 'Familiarization and its Semiotic Matrix', in R.L. Jackson and S. Rudy (eds) *Russian Formalism: A Retrospective Glance*. New Haven: Yale Centre for International and Area Studies, pp. 148–61.

Black, J. (1991) *The Aesthetics of Murder: A Study in Romantic Literature and Contemporary Culture*. Baltimore: Johns Hopkins University Press.

Blake, N. (1946) 'The Detective Story – Why?' in H. Haycraft (ed.) *The Art of the Mystery Story: A Collection of Critical Essays*. New York: Simon and Schuster, pp. 398–405.

Bloom, C. (1996) *Cult Fiction: Popular Reading and Pulp Theory*. London: Macmillan.

Bloom, C. (2002) *Bestsellers: Popular Fiction since 1900*. Basingstoke: Palgrave Macmillan.

Bockting, I. (1994) 'Mind Style as an Interdisciplinary Approach to Characterisation in Faulkner', *Language and Literature* 3 (3): 157–74.

Boëthius, U. (1995) 'Populärlitteratur – finns den?', in D. Hedman (ed.) *Brott, kärlek, äventyr. Texter om Populärlitteratur*. Lund: Stydentlitteratur, pp. 17–34.

Bönnemark, M. (1997) *The Mimetic Mystery*, unpublished PhD thesis, Stockholm University, Stockholm.

Booth, W. (1961) *The Rhetoric of Fiction*. Chicago: University of Chicago Press.

Brémond, C. (1966) 'La Logique des Possibles Narratifs', *Communications* 8: 60–76.

Burgess, A. (1962) *A Clockwork Orange*. New York: W.W. Inc.

Burgess, A. (1990) *You've Had Your Time*. London: Heinemann.

Burke, P. (1994) *Popular Culture of Early Modern Europe*. Aldershot: Scholar Press.

Cameron, D. and Frazer, E. (1992) 'On the Question of Pornography and Sexual Violence: Moving Beyond Cause and Effect', in C. Itzin (ed.) *Pornography: Women, Violence, and Civil Liberties*. Oxford: Oxford University Press, pp. 359–83.

Capote, T. (1966) *In Cold Blood: A True Account of a Multiple Murder and its Consequences*. London: H. Hamilton.

Carter, R. (ed.) (1991) *Language and Literature: An Introductory Reader in Stylistics*. London: Routledge.

Carter, R. and Nash, W. (1990) *Seeing Through Language: A Guide to Style of English Writing*. Oxford: Basil Blackwell.

Castle, T. (1986) *Masquerade and Civilisation: the Carnivalesque in 18ᵗʰ Century English Fiction and Culture*. London: Methuen.

Cawelti, J.G. (1976) *Adventure, Mystery and Romance: Formula Stories as Art and Popular Culture*. Chicago: University of Chicago Press.

Chandler, R. (1976) 'Twelve Notes on the Mystery Story', in F. MacShane (ed.) *The Notebooks of Raymond Chandler and English Summer, A Gothic Romance*. New York: Ecco Press, pp. 35–40.

Chapman, S. and Routledge, C. (1999) 'The Pragmatics of Detection: Paul Auster's City of glass', *Language and Literature* 8 (3): 241–53.

Christie, A. (1924) *The Murder of Roger Ackroyd*. Glasgow: Fontana.

Clark, K. and Holquist, M. (1984) *Mikhail Bakhtin*. Cambridge: Harvard University Press.

Cole, L.E. (1970) *Understanding Abnormal Behaviour*. Pennsylvania: Chandler Publishing Company.

Connelly, M. (1992) *The Black Echo*. London: Orion.

Connelly, M. (1993) *The Black Ice*. London: Orion.

Connelly, M. (1995) *The Concrete Blonde*. London: Orion.

Connelly, M. (1996) *The Poet*. London: Orion.

Connelly, M. (1997a) *First Person*. url: http://www.michaelconnelly.com/Other_Words/First_Person/first_person.html (Date last accessed: April 2006)

Connelly, M. (1997b) *Trunk Music*. London: Orion.

Connelly, M. (1998a) *Blood Work*. London: Orion.

Connelly, M. (1998b) *The Mystery of Mystery Writing*. url: http://michaelconnelly.com/Other_Words/the_mystery_of_mystery_writing.htm (Date last accessed: 10 September 2003)

Connelly, M. (1999) *Angels Flight*. London: Orion.

Connelly, M. (2000) *A Darkness More than Night*. London: Orion.

Connelly, M. (2002) *Michael Connelly Interviews Harry Bosch*. url: http://www.michaelconnelly.com/BoschQA/boschqa.html (Date last accessed: April 2006)

Cook, G. (1990) *A Theory of Discourse Deviation: the Application of Schema Theory to the Analysis of Literary Discourse*, unpublished PhD thesis, University of Leeds, Leeds.

Cook, G. (1994) *Discourse and Literature*. Oxford: Oxford University Press.

Cooper, N. (2000) 'Inside the Mind of a Crime Writer', *The Times Sep 30th 2000*, p. 9.

Cornwell, P. (1990) *Postmortem*. London: Warner Books.

Cornwell, P. (1991) *Body of Evidence*. London: Warner Books.

Cornwell, P. (1992) *All That Remains*. London: Warner Books.

Cornwell, P. (1993) *Cruel and Unusual*. London: Warner Books.

Cornwell, P. (1998) *Southern Cross*. London: Warner Books.

Cornwell, P. (2000a) *Black Notice*. London: Warner Books.

Cornwell, P. (2000b) *The Last Precinct*. Kent: BCA.

Couture, B. (1986) 'Effective Ideation in Written Text: a Functional Approach to Clarity and Exigence', in B. Couture (ed.) *Functional Approaches to Writing Research Perspectives*. Norwood: Ablex, pp. 69–92.

Crais, R. (2001) *Robert Crais: Three Great Novels: The Monkey's Raincoat, Stalking the Angel, Lullaby Town*. London: Orion Books.

Culler, J. (1975) *Structuralist Poetics: Structuralism, Linguistics and the Study of Literature*. London: Routledge and Kegan Paul.

Culpeper, J. (2001) *Language and Characterisation*. London: Longman.

Dibdin, M. (1989) *The Last Sherlock Holmes Story*. London: Penguin.

Dine, S.S. van. (1946) 'Twenty Rules for Writing Detective Stories', in H. Haycraft (ed.) *The Art of the Mystery Story: A Collection of Critical Essays*. New York: Simon and Schuster, pp. 189–93.

Dworkin, A. (1981) *Pornography: Men Possessing Women*. London: Women's Press.

Eagleton, T. (1996) *Literary Theory: An Introduction* (2nd edn). Oxford: Blackwell.

Eco, U. (1966) 'The Narrative Structure in Fleming', in O. Del Buono and U. Eco (eds), *The Bond Affair*. London: McDonald, pp. 35–75.

Emmott, C. (1999) *Narrative Comprehension: A Discourse Perspective*. Oxford: Oxford University Press.

ffrench, P. (2000) 'Open Letter to Detectives and Psychoanalysis: Analysis and Reading', in W. Chernaik, M. Swales and R. Vilain (eds) *The Art of Detective Fiction*. New York: Snt Martin's Press, Inc., pp. 222–32.

Fillmore, C. (1985) 'Frames and the Semantics of Understanding', *Quaderni de Semantica* 6: 222–54.

Fish, S. (1980) *Is There a Text in This Class? The Authority of Interpretive Communities*. Cambridge, Mass: Harvard University Press.

Fiske, J. (1987) *Television Culture*. London: Routledge.

Fiske, J. (1989a) *Reading the Popular*. London: Unwin Hyman.

Fiske, J. (1989b) *Understanding the Popular*. London: Unwin and Hyman.

Fordham, F. (1953) *An Introduction to Jung's Psychology*. Harmondsworth, Middlesex: Penguin.

Foucault, M. (1979) *Discipline and Punish* (trans. A. Sheridan). Harmondsworth: Penguin.

Fowler, R. (1977) *Linguistics and the Novel*. London: Methuen.

Fowler, R. (1986) *Linguistic Criticism*. Oxford: Oxford University Press.

Freeman, R.A. (1946) 'The Art of the Detective Story', in H. Haycraft (ed.) *The Art of the Mystery Story: A Collection of Critical Essays*. New York: Simon and Schuster, pp. 7–17.

Frye, N. (1957) *Anatomy of Criticism*. Princeton, New Jersey: Princeton University Press.

Furst, L.R. (ed.) (1992) *Realism*. London: Longman.

Gardiner, M. (1993) 'Bakhtin's Carnival: Utopia as Critique', in D. Shepherd (ed.) *Bakhtin Carnival and Other Subjects*. Amsterdam, Atlanta: Rodopi, pp. 20–47.

Genette, G. (1980) *Narrative Discourse*. Oxford: Basil Blackwell. (Figues III. Seuil: Paris, 1972).

Gibbs, R.W. (1994) *The Poetics of Mind: Figurative Thought, Language, and Understanding*. Cambridge: Cambridge University Press.

Gregoriou, C. (2002a) 'Samarakis in Search of Hope: A Labovian Analysis of Antonis Samarakis's "Hope Wanted" with a Focus on "Evaluation"', in S. Csábi, and J. Zerkowitz (eds) *Textual Secrets: the Message of the Medium. (Proceedings of the 21st PALA Conference)*, Budapest: Akadémiai Nyonda, Martonvásár, pp. 302–7.

Gregoriou, C. (2002b) 'Behaving Badly: A Cognitive Stylistics of the Criminal Mind', *Nottingham Linguistic Circular* 17: 61–74. (also at http://www.nottingham.ac.uk/english/nlc/gregoriou.pdf)

Gregoriou, C. (2003a) 'Criminally Minded: the Stylistics of Justification in Contemporary American Crime Fiction', *Style* 37(2): 144–59.

Gregoriou, C. (2003b) 'Demystifying the Criminal Mind: Linguistic, Social and Generic Deviance in Contemporary American Crime Fiction', *Working with English 1*: 1–15. (also at http://www.nottingham.ac.uk/english/working_with_english/Gregoriou)

Grice, H.P. (1975) 'Logic and Conversation', in P. Cole and J. Morgan (eds) *Syntax and Semantics III: Speech Acts*. New York: Academic Press, pp. 41–58.

Hall, S. (1993) 'Metaphors of Transformation', in A. White (ed.), *Carnival, Hysteria and Writing*. Oxford: Clarendon Press, pp. 1–25.

Halliday, M.A.K. (1973) *Explorations in the Functions of Language*. London: Edward Arnold.

Halliday, M.A.K. (1985) *An Introduction to Functional Grammar*. London: Edward Arnold.

Harris, T. (1990) *Silence of the Lambs*. London: Mandarin.

Haut, W. (1999) *Neon Noir: Contemporary American Crime Fiction*. London: Serpent's Tail.

Haycraft, H. (1972) *Murder for Pleasure: The Life and Time of the Detective Story*. New York: Biblo and Tannen.

Holdaway, S. (1988) *Crime and Deviance*. London: Macmillan.

Horsley, L. (2005) *Twentieth-century Crime Fiction*. Oxford: Oxford University Press.

Humphrey, C. (2000) 'Bakhtin and the Study of Popular Culture: Re-thinking Carnival as a Historical and Analytical Concept', in C. Brandist and G. Tihanov (eds) *Materialising Bakhtin*. London: Macmillan, pp. 164–72.

Hyman, T. (2000) 'A Carnival Sense of the World', in T. Hyman and R. Malbert (eds) *Carnivalesque*. London: Hayward Publishing, pp. 8–73.

Ingarden, R. (1973a) *The Literary Work of Art: An Investigation on the Borderlines of Ontology, Logic, and Theory of Literature* (trans. G. Grabowics, from the 3rd edition of *Das literarische Kunstwerk*, 1965; after a Polish revised translation, 1960; from the original German, 1931), Evanston, Ill: Northwestern University Press.

Ingarden, R. (1973b) *The Cognition of the Literary Work of Art* (trans. R.A. Crowley and K. Olson, from the German *Vom Erkennen des literarischen Kunstwerks*,

1968; original Polish *O poznawaniu dziela literackiego*, 1937). Evanston, Ill: Northwestern University Press.

Iser, W. (1974) *The Implied Reader: Patterns of Communication in Prose Fiction from Bunyan to Beckett*. Baltimore: John Hopkins University Press.

Iser, W. (1978) *The Act of Reading: A Theory of Aesthetic Response*. Baltimore: John Hopkins University Press.

Jacobi, J. (1959) *Complex – Archetype – Symbol in the Psychology of C. G. Jung*. London: Routledge and Kegan Paul.

Jakobson, R. (1956) 'Two Aspects of Language and Two Types of Aphasic Disturbances', in R. Jakobson and M. Halle (eds) *Fundamentals of Language*. The Hague: Mouton, pp. 55–82.

Jakobson, R. (1960) 'Linguistics and Poetics', in T.A. Sebeok (ed.) *Style in Language*. Cambridge, Mass: MIT Press, pp. 350–77.

Jameson, F. (1970) 'On Raymond Chandler', *Southern Review* 6 (July): 624–50.

Jauss, H.R. (1985) in J. Demougin (ed.) *Dictionnaire Historique, Thématique et Technique des Littératures*. Paris: Larousse.

Jung, C.G. (1968) *The Archetypes and the Collective Unconscious* (2nd edn). London: Routledge.

Kant, E. (1963) *Critique of Pure Reason*. London: Macmillan.

Kerr, P. (1992) *A Philosophical Investigation*. London: Chatto and Windus.

Ketchum, J. (1994) *Road Kill*. London: Headline Book Publishing.

King, L.R. (1996) *The Beekeeper's Apprentice. or On the Segregation of the Queen*. New York: Bantam.

Knapp, B.L. (1986) *Archetype, Architecture and the Writer*. Bloomington: Indiana University Press.

Knight, S. (1980) *Form and Ideology in Crime Fiction*. London: Macmillan.

Knight, S. (2004) *Crime Fiction 1800–2000: Detection, Death and Diversity*. Basingstoke: Palgrave Macmillan.

Knox, R.A. (1929) 'Ten Rules for a Good Detective Story', *Publishers' Weekly* Oct 5, p. 1739.

Labov, W. (1972) *Language in the Inner City: Studies in the Black English Vernacular*. London: Basil Blackwell.

Labov, W. (1978) 'Denotational Structure', in D. Farkas et al (eds) *Papers from the Parasession on the Lexicon*. Chicago: Chicago Linguistic Society, pp. 220–60.

Labov, W. and Waletzky, J. (1967) 'Narrative Analysis: Oral Versions of Personal Experience', in J. Helms (ed.) *Essays on the Verbal and Visual Arts*. London: University of Washington Press, pp. 12–44.

Lakoff, G. and Johnson, M. (1980) *Metaphors We Live By*. Chicago: University of Chicago Press.

Leech, G. (1969) *A Linguistic Guide to English Poetry*. London: Longman.

Leech, G.N. and Short, M. (1981) *Style in Fiction*. London: Longman.

Lemon, L.T. and Reis, M.J. (eds) (1965) *Russian Formalist Criticism: Four Essays*. Lincoln, Nebraska: University of Nebraska Press.

Lodge, D. (1992) *The Art of Fiction*. London: Secker and Warburg.

Maitra, S. (1967) *Psychological Realism and Archetypes: The Trickster in Shakespeare*. Calcutta: Bookland Private Ltd.

Mandel, E. (1984) *Delightful Murder: A Social History of the Crime Story*. London: Pluto Press.

McCarthy, M. and Carter, R. (eds) (1994) *Language as Discourse: Perspectives for Language Teaching*. London: Longman.

McCracken, S. (1998) *Pulp: Reading Popular Fiction*. Manchester: Manchester University Press.

Messent, P. (ed.) (1997) *Criminal Proceedings: The Contemporary American Crime Novel*, London: Pluto Press.

Messent, P. (2000) 'Authority, Social Anxiety and the Body in Crime Fiction: Patricia Cornwell's *Unnatural Exposure*', in W. Chernaik, M. Swales and R. Vilain (eds) *The Art of Detective Fiction*. New York: Snt Martin's Press, pp. 124–37.

Miller, E. and Morley, S. (1986) *Investigating Abnormal Behaviour*. London: Weidenfeld and Nicolson Ltd.

Minsky, M. (1975) 'A Framework for Representing Knowledge', in P.E. Wilson (ed.) *The Psychology of Computer Vision*. New York: McGraw-Hill, pp. 221–77.

Minsky, M. (1986) *The Society of Mind*. London: Heinemann.

Moretti, F. (1983) *Signs Taken for Wonders: Essays in the Sociology of Literary Forms*. London: Thetford Press Ltd.

Morson, G.S. (1991) 'Bakhtin, Genres and Temporality', *New Literary History* 22: 1071–92.

Mukařovský, J. (1970) 'Standard Language and Poetic Language', in D.C. Freeman, *Linguistics and Literary Style*. New York: Holt, Rinehart and Winston, pp. 40–56.

Munt, S.R. (1994) *Murder by the Book? Feminism and the Crime Novel*. London: Routledge.

Nash, O. (1954) *The Face is Familiar*. London: J.M. Dent.

Nash, W. (1990) *Language in Popular Fiction*. London: Routledge.

Neale, S. (1981) 'Genre and Cinema', in T. Bennett, S. Boyd-Bowman, C. Mercer and J. Woollacott (eds) *Popular Television and Film*. London: Open University Press, pp. 6–25.

Nickerson, C. (1997) 'Murder as Social Criticism', *American Literary History* 9(4): 744–57.

Nowottny, W. (1962) *The Language Poets use*. London: Athlone Press.

Oates, J.C. (1995) 'The Simple Art of Murder', *The New York Review of Books* Dec 21st 42 (20): 32–40.

O'Faolain, S. (1935) 'Give us Back Bill Sikes', *Spectator* Feb 15th: 242–3.

Patterson, J. (1993) *Along Came a Spider*. London: HarperCollins Publishers.

Patterson, J. (1995) *Kiss the Girls*. London: HarperCollins Publishers.

Patterson, J. (1996) *Jack and Jill*. London: HarperCollins Publishers.

Patterson, J. (1997) *Cat and Mouse*. London: Headline Book Publishing.

Patterson, J. (1999) *Pop Goes the Weasel*. London: Headline Book Publishing.

Patterson, J. (2001) *Violets Are Blue*. London: Headline Book Publishing.

Pepper, A. (2000) *The Contemporary American Crime Novel; Race, Ethnicity Gender and Class*. Edinburgh: Edinburgh University Press.

Pitcher, G. (1964) *The Philosophy of Wittgenstein*. Englewood Cliffs: Prentice Hall.

Polanyi, L. (1985) *Telling the American Story: A Structural and Cultural Analysis of Conversational Storytelling*. Norwood: Ablex Publishers Corporation.

Porter, D. (1981) *The Pursuit of Crime: Art and Ideology in Detective Fiction*. New Haven: Yale University Press.

Pratt, M.L. (1977) *Toward a Speech-Act Theory of Literary Discourse*. London: Indiana University Press.

Presdee, M. (2000) *Cultural Criminology and the Carnival of Crime*. London: Routledge.

Price, R.H. (1978) *Abnormal Behaviour: Perspectives in Conflict* (2nd edn). New York: Holt, Rinehart and Winston.

Priestman, M. (1990) *Detective Fiction and Literature: The Figure on the Carpet*. London: Macmillan.

Priestman, M. (1998) *Crime Fiction: from Poe to the Present*. Plymouth: Northcote House Publishers Ltd.

Radway, J.A. (1987) *Reading the Romance: Women, Patriarchy and Popular Culture*. London: University of North Carolina Press.

Rankin, I. (2000) *Criminal Minded*. Edinburgh: Canongate Books Ltd.

Reichs, K. (1998) *Déjà Dead*. London: Random House.

Reichs, K. (2000) *Kathy and John Douglas Discuss Their Work*. url: http://www.kathyreichs.com/mybooks.htm. (Date last accessed: 30 May 2003)

Reichs, K. (2001) *Deadly Decisions*. London: Random House.

Reichs, K. (2002) *Fatal Voyage*. London: Random House.

Richards, I.A. (1936) *The Philosophy of Rhetoric*. London: Oxford University Press.

Rosch, E. (1973) 'Natural Categories', *Cognitive Psychology*, 4: 328–50.

Rosch, E. (1975) 'Cognitive Reference Points', *Cognitive Psychology*, 7: 532–47.

Rosch, E. and Mervis, C. (1975) 'Family Resemblances: Studies in the Internal Structure of Categories', *Cognitive Psychology*, 7: 573–605.

Rosch, E., Mervis, C., Gray, W., Johnson, D. and Boyes-Braem, P. (1976) 'Basic Objects in Natural Categories', *Cognitive Psychology* 8: 382–439.

Roth, M. (1995) *Foul and Fair Play: Reading Genre in Classic Detective Fiction*. London: University of Georgia Press.

Rumelhart, D.E. (1975) 'Notes on a Schema for Stories', in D.G. Bobrow and A. Collins (eds) *Representation and Understanding: Studies in Cognitive Science*, London: Academic Press, pp. 211–36.

Rumelhart, D.E. (1980) 'Schemata: The Building Blocks of Cognition', in R.J. Spiro, B. Bruce and W. Brewer (eds) *Theoretical Issues in Reading Comprehension: Perspectives from Cognitive Psychology, Linguistics, Artificial Intelligence and Education*. Hillsdale: Lawrence Erlbaum Associates, pp. 33–58.

Rumelhart, D.E. (1984) 'Schemata and the Cognitive System', in R.S. Wyer and T.K. Srull (eds) *Handbook of Social Cognition, Vol. 1*. Hillsdale: Lawrence Erlbaum Associates, pp. 161–88.

Rumelhart, D.E. and Norman, D.A. (1978) 'Accretion, Tuning and Restructuring: Three Modes of Learning', in J.W. Cotton and R.L. Klatzky (eds) *Semantic Factors in Cognition*. Hillsdale: Lawrence Erlbaum Associates, pp. 37–53.

Rzhevsky, N. (1994) 'Kozhinov on Bakhtin', *New Literary History*, 25: 429–44.

Saeed, J.I. (1998) *Semantics*. Oxford: Blackwell.

Sanford, A.J. and Garrod, S.C. (1981) *Understanding Written Language*. New York: Wiley.

Sayers, D.L. (1947a) *Unpopular Opinions*. New York: Harcourt, Brace.

Sayers, D.L (1947b) ' "... and Telling You a Story": A Note on the Divine Comedy', in *Essays Presented to Charles Williams*. London: Oxford University Press, pp. 1–37.

Scaggs, J. (2005) *Crime Fiction*. London: Routledge.

Schank, R.C. (1982a) *Dynamic Memory: A Theory of Reminding and Learning in Computers and People*. Cambridge: Cambridge University Press.

Schank, R.C. (1982b) *Reading and Understanding: Teaching from the Perspective of Artificial Intelligence*. Hillsdale: Lawrence Erlbaum Associates.

Schank, R.C. (1984) *The Cognitive Computer*. Reading: Addison-Wesley.
Schank, R.C. (1986) *Explanation Patterns*. Hillsdale: Lawrence Erlbaum Associates.
Schank, R.C. and Abelson, R. (1977) *Scripts, Plans, Goals and Understanding*. Hillsdale: Lawrence Erlbaum Associates.
Semino, E. (1997) *Language and World Creation in Poems and Other Texts*. London: Longman.
Semino, E. and Swindlehurst, K. (1996) 'Metaphor and Mind Style in Ken Kesey's "One Flew Over the Cuckoo's Nest"', *Style* 30 (1): 143–65.
Shklovsky, V. (1925) *O Teorii Prozy*. Moscow: Federatsiya.
Shklovsky, V. (1965) 'Art as Technique' (trans. L. Lemon and M.J. Reis, eds), in *Russian Formalism Criticism*. Lincoln: University of Lebraska Press.
Short, M. (1982) ' "Prelude 1" to a Literary Linguistic Stylistics', in R. Carter (ed.) *Language and Literature: An Introductory Reader in Stylistics*. London: Allen and Unwin, pp. 55–61.
Short, M. (1994) 'Understanding Texts: Point of View', in G. Brown, K. Malmkjaer, A. Pollitt and J. Williams (eds) *Language and Understanding*. Oxford: Oxford University Press, pp. 170–90.
Short, M. (1996) *Exploring the Language of Poems, Plays and Prose*. London: Longman.
Simpson, P. (1988) 'Access Through Application', *Parlance* 1 (2): 5–28.
Simpson, P. (1993) *Language, Ideology and Point of View*. London: Longman.
Simpson, P. and Montgomery, M. (1995) 'Language, Literature and Film', in P. Verdonk and J.J. Weber (eds) *Twentieth Century Fiction: from Text to Context*. London: Routledge, pp. 138–64.
Stallybrass, P. and White, A. (1986) *The Politics and Poetics of Transgression*. London: Methuen.
Steen, G. (1994) *Understanding Metaphor in Literature*. London: Longman.
Steeves, H.R. (1946) 'A Sober Word on the Detective Story', in H. Haycraft (ed.) *The Art of the Mystery Story: A Collection of Critical Essays*. New York: Simon and Schuster, pp. 513–26.
Steiner, P. (1984) *Russian Formalism: A Metapoetics*. London: Cornwell University Press.
Stern, P.V.D. (1974) 'The Case of the Corpse in the Blind Alley', in H. Haycraft (ed.) *The Art of the Mystery Story: A Collection of Critical Essays*. New York: Carroll and Graf, pp. 527–35.
Steward, D.M. (1997) 'Cultural Work, City Crime, Reading Pleasure', *American Literary History* 9 (4): 676–701.
Stockwell, P. (2002) *Cognitive Poetics: An Introduction*. London: Routledge.
Stockwell, P. (2003) 'Schema Poetics and Speculative Cosmology', *Language and Literature* 12 (3): 252–71.
Swales, J.M. (1990) *Genre Analysis: English in Academic and Research Settings*. Cambridge: Cambridge University Press.
Swales, M. (2000) 'Introduction', in W. Chernaik, M. Swales and R. Vilain (eds) *The Art of Detective Fiction*. New York: Saint Martin's Press Inc, pp. xi–xv.
Symons, J. (1973) *Mortal Consequences*. New York: Schocken.
Symons, J. (1981) *Critical Observations*. London: Faber and Faber.
Symons, J. (1994) *Bloody Murder. From the Detective Story to the Crime Novel: A History* (rev. 3rd edn). London: Pan.

Talbot, M.M. (1995) *Fictions at Work: Language and Social Practice in Fiction*. London: Longman.

Tannen, D. (1984) 'What's in a Frame? Surface Evidence for Underlying Expectations', in R.O. Freedle (ed.) *New Directions in Discourse Processing*. Norwood: Ablex, pp. 137–81.

Taylor, B. (1995) *Bakhtin, Carnival and Comic Theory*, unpublished PhD thesis, University of Nottingham, Nottingham.

Taylor, B. (1997) 'Criminal Suits: Style and Surveillance, Strategy and Tactics in Elmore Leonard', in P. Messent (ed.) (1997) *Criminal Proceedings: The Contemporary American Crime Novel*. London: Pluto Press, pp. 22–41.

Thompson, E. (1971) *Russian Formalism and Anglo-American New Criticism: A Comparative Study*. Amsterdam: Mouton.

Thorndyke, P.W. (1977) 'Cognitive Structure in Comprehension and Memory of Narrative Discourse', *Cognitive Psychology* 9: 77–110.

Thorndyke, P.W. and Yekovich, F.R. (1980) 'A Critique of Schema-Based Theories of Human Story Memory', *Poetics* 9: 23–49.

Todorov, T. (1973) *The Fantastic: A Structural Approach to a Literary Genre*. London: The Press of Case Western Reserve University.

Todorov, T. (1977) 'The Typology of Detective Fiction', in *The Poetics of Prose* (trans. R. Howard). New York: University Press, pp. 42–52.

Todorov, T. (1984) *Mikhail Bakhtin: The Dialogical Principle* (trans. W. Bodzich). Manchester: Manchester University Press.

Todorov, T. (1990) *Genres in Discourse*. Cambridge: Cambridge University Press.

Toolan, M. (2001) *Narrative: A Critical Linguistic Introduction* (2nd edn). London: Routledge.

Turner, G.W. (1973) *Stylistics*. Harmondsworth: Penguin.

Turner, M. and Fauconnier, G. (1995) 'Conceptual Integration and Formal Expression', *Metaphor and Symbolic Activity* 10: 183–203.

Vanacker, S. (1997) 'V.I. Warshawski, Kinsey Millhone and Kay Scarpetta: Creating a Feminist Detective Hero', in P. Messent (ed.) (1997) *Criminal Proceedings: The Contemporary American Crime Novel*. London: Pluto Press, pp. 62–86.

Wales, K. (2001) *A Dictionary of Stylistics* (rev. 2nd edn). London: Pearson Education Ltd.

Werth, P. (1999) *Text Worlds: Representing Conceptual Space in Discourse*. Harlow: Longman.

Winks, R.W. (ed.) (1980) *Detective Fiction*. Englewood Cliffs: Prentice-Hall.

Wittgenstein, L. [1953] (1967) *Philosophical Investigations* (3rd edn). (trans. G.E.M. Anscombe) Oxford: Blackwell.

Wright, W.H. (1946) 'The Great Detective Stories', in H. Haycraft (ed.) *The Art of the Mystery Story: A Collection of Critical Essays*. New York: Simon and Schuster, pp. 33–70.

Index

19634379R00107

Printed in Great Britain
by Amazon